FLI(

Tales of spi...
challenges of life on the rea p....

The three parts set on Mars in the twenty-third Earth century… if Earth had survived.

Book One
THE EDEN SOLDIERS

Book Two
SATURN'S VANGUARD

Book Three
THE SOL REUNION

A thought-provoking story of the habitation of the planets, the artificial atmosphere, trees and forest, with grass and streams built from the wind-blown, rock-filled deserts.

Colonies are established on Mars, food is grown and a sophisticated economy is established.

As man adjusts so do the animals and other terrestrial creatures with breathtaking results. Some of the new life came not from Earth and now war and peace have new meanings…

The Flight of Man… first to Mars, then Saturn…

ABOUT THE AUTHOR

Canadian writer and author, Andrew Bell was born and bred in the shadows of the Rocky Mountains. His strong and active imagination has resulted in the trilogy – The Flight of Man – a novel of life and its challenges on Mars. Eden Guard, the first book in the series, is set in the year 2251.

Back on Earth, Andrew studied commerce, majoring in accounting. A strange combination – an imaginative accountant! After a variety of jobs, writing now occupies his life. He continues to live in Alberta with wife Kristine.

Copyright © 2012-15 Andrew Bell
Published by

Noveletta IMPRINT
CUSTOM BOOK PUBLICATIONS

All the characters are fictitious and any resemblance to real persons, living or dead, is purely coincidental.

COVER PHOTOGRAPH Mars ...NASA 2011-12
Vehicle image ©Christian Pearce

FLIGHT OF MAN

Book Two
SATURN'S VANGUARD

by **Andrew Bell**

The sun, Sol, protected mankind for thousands of years and the solar system for millions before that. It was prophesied the Earth would end in 2191. Who knew thirty five years later that prophecy would come true! On that day, Sol reached out to save what planets it could from an attack beyond our imagination.

A star, Bane, tore into our backyard bent on snuffing out all traces of our people. We all knew Bane's henchmen planets would ultimately destroy our Earth but it was Sol that held Bane, pulling it from the murderous rampage, to spare Mars. Still the two giants battle in the sky above and now we give thanks to our protective star. Sol, the marvelous ball of gas did what no God has done, actually saved our tiny butts!

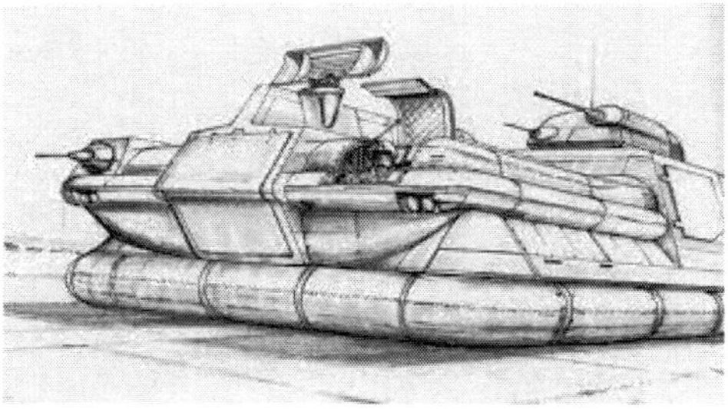

CHAPTER XX
Tuesday, 10 April, 2251

The Tuesday morning in the port city of New Terra was as wondrous as so many mornings before. A shower of sparkling yellow streaks split the greenish-grey haze and greyer clouds to dazzle the dock workers and morning strollers on the lush green walkway inside the city's dome. During the construction of the city, engineers had managed to keep the ocean level views crystal clear while warping the sky view portion of the dome. The effect was a magnified sun, larger to look at and bringing in more heat. Since Bane was a smaller star to begin with the magnification had little impact on its perceived size.

The air was still, fragrant and warm, same as every day of the year within the protective glass and steel ringing the city. Some of the walkers on the path system were clearly tourists in town to absorb the Earth-like conditions. Residents of the city could easily identify them as the ones marveling at the peace on this side of the dome while a moderate breeze buffeted the dock workers. They were also the only ones sunbathing on the beach, a beach with water but without waves thanks to the glass dome cutting into the ocean a dozen feet off shore.

Dr. Shirley Masters had little time to enjoy the spectacle on this morning. She moved quickly around her spacious apartment picking up various articles of clothes and putting an overload of dishes into the recycler. She had no idea how this place became this messy so quickly. She was sure she had run the same course yesterday, maybe she did, a truly frightening thought.

'Hey mom,' a young boy called from a lounging position on the couch. His perch was acting as the epicenter of Dr. Master's cleaning cyclone. At least he pressed pause on this video game when he talked this time. The picture on the screen looked as if some amount of the bad guy's blood had splashed on the television at the particular moment of stoppage.

'Yes dear?' she stopped in mid-stride with an arm load of crumpled clothes.

'My friends wanted to watch the army drills in the central courtyard. Can I go?'

'Yes you may but you have school tomorrow, just remember that. Be home by D7,' she resumed her flurry of cleaning.

'But it's D2 already. That's not fair,' he leaned back in a pout-filled protest.

Shirley kept picking up some bits of clothing, lots of dishes and a few things even she could not identify. The mystery things were easily dealt with by use of the garbage recycler. The dishes were handled in much the same way, she would have to fabricate more for supper time. Mangled clumps of clothing would be a different matter. Those things would have to be washed since her son, Jason, seemed to wear the faded stains like medals or something. She would have to clean them, allowing them to pass all but the strictest of inspection while trying to not look new.

The knock at the door was merely a speed bump in her cleaning anti-tornado. Shirley struggled to maintain her grasp on the dozen articles of clothes in her arms as she punched in the access code to unlock the door. The fact she did the maneuver without dropping so much as one of her son's very off-white athletic socks made her happy and sad. To think a trauma surgeon would have to do the laundry dance in the first place amplified her strained situation. If her ex would pay his legally required support payments she might be able to afford a maid.

'Come in, it's open,' she yelled at the door even as she turned away.

A moment later the door opened admitting a tall man in a well-tailored navy-blue suit. She did not pay too much attention to the visitor since he was likely some bureaucrat wanting to talk policy. Her immediate situation prevented interaction since she still had to deal with an armload of unfortunately fragrant clothes.

'I'll be right back. Have a seat,' she said while walking to the laundry around the corner. She was curious about her visitor but running the house came first.

'Daddy!' the small voice from the couch called out followed by the sounds of pattering feet. Seems the question of *who* got answered.

'Oh no,' she muttered and started the cleaning cycle. She did not need this today.

'Hey buddy!' came the overly cheerful reply.

Stepping from the laundry she got to see her son hugging the deadbeat David Randall. The city's Interior Secretary was all smiles and jokes in his interactions with the boy. That was not bad, but he never took anything except his job seriously and that was a problem for a marriage.

'Hi, David,' Shirley said with little energy. She could not spare it.

'Good morning, sweetheart,' he smiled.

'Don't call me that. What do you want, David?'

'Always so serious. Fine, we need you to come in early today,' he smoothed the dusty-blonde hair of his son, still all smiles.

'I can't come in early. The sitter doesn't get here for another hour,' she walked into the living room for more space in case she wanted to take a swing at her ex.

'I'll watch Jason. Look, we got an odd walk-in and the resident wants a second look before calling Idmod.'

'Idmod? He's psyche though. They think the patient is unbalanced?' Now she was interested.

David held out his hand, signaling Jason he was

3

released with a jerk of the head, 'I don't know, just the messenger here.'

'Fine, I'll go in. You,' she pointed at David, 'You, stay here and watch Jason.'

'Yes, ma'am,' he playfully saluted.

She was not going to be drawn in by his games, instead went to the closet and grabbed her lab coat. A psyche case requiring a second consult from a trauma doctor, this was shaping up to be an interesting day. Fortunately, the hospital was in the building on the next block allowing her to walk instead of needing to flag down a taxi cart. Location was one of the major reasons for choosing her apartment.

It only took a couple minutes to descend the five floors to the pedestrian level and a couple more to get to the ER entrance. The internal dome temperature was warm, as always, so she had not had the need to put on her white coat until she was walking into the hospital. It was a nice treat to enjoy the sunshine, even if it was through the dome. Today was a particularly clear day too.

'Dr. Masters, room eight please,' the charge nurse pointed down the hall for clarity.

Shirley turned left and walked toward the last room on the right side of this hall. She slipped her arms into the coat and clipped her light brown hair out over the collar. No need to hurry on this case, her shift did not start until D300, she paced herself accordingly. The patient had already been seen by at least one doctor, she assumed, there was no further danger to the patient.

'Okay, what do we…' she stopped short inside the door.

Standing in the middle of the room was a militia trooper judging by the markings and badging still visible. This trooper differed from others she had seen, primarily due to the addition of the power armour. Two nurses and the resident were scanning the suit's bio readouts at the side workstation, as far away from the trooper as possible. By the looks of the armour, the occupant still required further medical care but did not seem too concerned.

One of the nurses handed Shirley the chart pad while keeping an eye on the torn up suit in the middle of the room. Identity tags from the suit named the trooper as Lieutenant Ladore from Fort Grey. Her vital signs were low but stable at the moment.

'Lieutenant...' Shirley started.

'Captain!' Ladore yelled at Dr. Masters.

'Your ID shows your rank as Lieutenant,' Shirley tapped the pad and looked into the trooper's open visor. 'Why don't you take off your suit and let us patch you up while we have a talk about ranks?'

'I can wait for treatment. We need to get this city's defenses strengthened before they get here,' Ladore pointed roughly south and east in the direction of Fort Grey.

'Who would that be Lieutenant?'

'Captain!'

'Fine, Captain. Who is coming and why are they so dangerous that you don't think the military can defend this city?'

'The military is probably in on the conspiracy. The militia in the outer territories has a secret weapon, some bio-engineered creature that can rip through the sides of an outpost without slowing down! They even tested those things against Fort Grey and now it's gone!' she was yelling and pacing adding thunderous booms to her rants in the small yellowish room.

'Calm down please, Captain,' Dr. Masters said while dancing away from the metal-wrapped trooper gesturing wildly.

'We don't have time. They tried to blame me for everything that went wrong. Their Commander Martel court martialed me when I tried to stand up for what was

5

right! He sent me into the grasslands without any supplies to shut me up!'

'Not the worst idea,' one of the nurses muttered.

Shirley smiled slightly before addressing the anxious officer. 'Okay, if you will just get out of the armour and have a seat I will call in a few favors and get the city council to send someone down here to get things rolling.'

'Really?' Ladore stopped her dramatic show, spinning to stare at Shirley. 'You can do that? You would do that for me... us?'

'Yes I would, after all it sounds quite serious. First off we need to have a look at your injuries.'

Ladore slowly began the process of unhooking the various components of her armour letting them crash to the floor with no attempt to place them in a neat pile or even soften their impact on the floor. The medical staff stayed well back to give the trooper plenty of space to shred the metal skin. Since the Captain was still armed, they were perfectly fine letting her take whatever time she needed. A full ten minutes later the clanging, debris-filled strip was finished and Ladore finally sat on the edge of the bed while still holding her non-energized blade.

The closest nurse cautiously approached the patient to ease her back onto the bed. Ladore was tense and slow to move, eventually allowing herself to be lowered to the bed so Dr. Masters could examine and treat her wounds. Long bleeding lines were cut across her chest and abdomen while her arms and legs had several clotted gashes. Without the armour Shirley was sure the trooper would not have survived half these injuries.

'Now Captain, some of these cuts look like a blade did them and some of these look like plasma burns. Were these bio-creatures using torches or blades or claws?'

'Those things had plasma-like beams on their arms but those blade cuts came from the militia boys under Martel.' Ladore had a slight smile on her lips now.

Shirley was not sure how to read the look on the trooper's face since a happy expression did not match up with the Captain's current situation. She would have to figure that out later. For now there was a patient to attend to and a different issue to figure out. 'And what about these other burn marks. They look like beam cannon marks but much more confined.'

Ladore lifted her head to see what the doctor was referring to and fell back into the pillow before replying, 'Those are from the dragons in the woods.'

'Uh, dragons?'

'Yeah, there's some kind of wingless dragon in the Sky Trees that runs around firing plasma bolts from its mouth. Its ten feet tall and has eyes like Bane itself!'

Shirley was stunned by the scope of the stories being told by this woman. How much could be believed... none of it sounded real? Maybe some, maybe none, or worst, maybe all. This was not the kind of thing she was trained for. It was time to call in someone who will know about lying and falsehoods.

'Nurse,' Shirley put the data pad down signaling the end of her involvement in patient care, 'Close up these smaller cuts and get the resident over here to see about these bigger cuts. They're not too deep, he should be able to handle them. I have to make a call to a professional to help with Captain Ladore's other concerns.' The trooper sighed with relief once she heard that last part.

That this trooper was crazy, was without question but she now needed a second opinion. Calling Dr. Idmod would be her second call, this first one would be to David. She punched in the number for her apartment and waited three rings before the answer came, it was David on the other end and it bothered her that he was in her place unsupervised.

'Hello?' he said cheerfully.

'David, its Shirley, I need you to come to the medi-centre to talk with this patient you sent me to see. Her story needs more ears I think.'

'I'm sorry darling, I have meetings all day. It will have to wait.'

'No, David. You have to come down here now! I am calling the sitter to get her there faster. As soon as she gets there to watch Jason you get your ass over here.' The memories of why they broke up came rushing back and threatened to boil her blood in an instant.

'Okay, okay. I'll be over as soon as I can,' he said before closing the connection.

That was the first time he had hung up on her. Probably for the best, if she had clicked the off switch it would have been smashed. She spun back around to look at the trooper laid out on the white sheets with the blade hilt still in-hand. Shirley wondered what happened to her out beyond the walls, bringing her almost three hundred miles from where she started and wrecked the armour carrying her. Shirley turned again to the communication panel to make her next two calls.

Fifteen minutes later the Interior Secretary strolled into the exam room as cheery as the sun. He looked around at the medical staff finishing up on the lounging soldier before looking at Shirley at the side counter. He walked over to her with no display of urgency but definitely an air of irritation.

'Hello.' The sunny disposition was gone. 'What's the trouble.'

'Go talk to her and see for yourself,' Shirley was equally unimpressed.

'Fine,' he walked to the far side of the table and began talking to the excitable militia trooper. This retell of the story was as grandiose as the first go around. When David tried to reassure her that the military was better equipped and trained than the militia and that they were all fine, the trooper went off the deep end, screaming about how the militia was trying to take over the peninsula. The blade came to life in a flash and began its arc toward David but faltered and fell with its blade digging into the floor.

Everyone in the room took a jump back when events started to unfold except for the nurse at the trooper's bedside. He had stayed calmly in one place as the deadly weapon began its journey, continuing his calm as he injected the trooper with a sedative. Now he finished cleaning up his work area before walking out of the room with his own smile.

'Thank you nurse,' Shirley said, still slightly shocked.

'Well, Lieutenant Ladore seems convinced of her story,' David said as he peeled himself off the wall. 'I'll make a couple calls to see if anything she's saying is true. I'll give you a shout in an hour or so.'

'Sounds good, thanks,' Shirley moved to the trooper's side to check her vitals.

Dr. Masters waited an hour and a half before she finally heard from David Randall and the news was not good. He had tried to contact both Fort Grey and Fort Saturn but was not able to punch through some kind of odd interference. While the Fort Grey channel was completely dead, a powerful screech coming through the Fort Saturn line had the foul odour of bad news approaching. Nothing about this problem had ever been seen before.

David had talked with other members of the council and decided until they were able to determine what was going on they would put the military guard on alert. They were not going to let some militia coup destroy their homes too. Messengers were dispatched to Port Mars to get some answers from the Eden Council since communication with that city was also being blocked.

Shirley was not going to wait for the bureaucrats to figure things out. She quickly ordered the staff to begin lock-down procedures before she left the medi-centre to collect her son. The sun was setting as she walked out, casting a pale yellow glow across the dome. The glow of the sun was no match for the evil blue light coming from the other star in the Sol System, Bane.

*****

CHAPTER XXI
Thursday, 12 April, 2251

The mighty city of Fort Saturn was a marvel of twenty-third century technology and design. The centre of the city was the original stone grey fortress, towering five levels above the ground and one level above the city's dome. The view from the unobstructed fifth level was a treat reserved for the Militia Command. The fort was larger and similar to the design of the four point star of the former Fort Grey. To provide better protection for the residents of Fort Saturn and to accommodate the growing population, the fort had added Arrow Head extensions to each of the four points in the year 10 NEC.

When the city started to grow around the fortress, the problems with atmosphere control still existed. Civil defence decided to construct walls around the fledgling city to provide a safe, easy living environment for the residents. Since the military had no say in the construction, the walls were not armoured to the same degree as the fortress but they did add their beam cannons to the walls to discourage rioters. The military also moved their wind deflection barriers to the new city limits since the heavy winds could no longer press on those walls which were once a fortress.

To replace the defensive benefit of these sloped walls, the military dug a trench around the arrow heads to a depth of fifteen feet. They left the ground level intact to the approach points to the fort for easy movement. Four large doors decorated the octagonal perimeter – one in line with each of the gaps in front of the fort arrow heads. Military engineers imposed a building limit on the new city of three stories for all future projects, allowing the fortress' turrets to continue to operate on the fourth.

The dome for the city was fixed at forty feet in height at the city wall, five feet below the top of the barrier, then again at fifty feet at the fortress wall, ten feet below the top. This configuration allowed the turrets of Fort Saturn to defend the city walls as well as preventing potential attackers from scaling the dome to get on top of the fort.

The buildings within the walls of the city were aligned in a starburst pattern, angling away from the fort. This allowed the fort militia a ninety percent field of vision under the dome. The unique pattern gave the city a star-like appearance.

Once the difficulties with the atmosphere were starting to come into a more favourable light, the city grew beyond its bounds again. Because the walls could not be moved easily, the new population built self-contained structures. Although life was noticeably more inconvenient outside the walls, the city continued to grow.

Again, the military stepped in and imposed building restrictions on any construction outside the protective walls. The structures could be no higher than two stories and had to run parallel to the city wall with nothing blocking the exit avenues. This would allow the defenders of the city the best view of any attackers when they approached the city.

The city had grown to the size of eighteen thousand residents before the catastrophe occurred. The rash of looting and destruction convinced city officials to build a second wall around the newer sections of the city. The dome was extended in the same fashion as the first expansion, for maximum firepower. Three gateways in this new wall were positioned to prevent vehicles from making a mad dash straight for the fort.

Today the city had more than twenty thousand residents within its walls and more establishing themselves outside. Many of the people living in Fort Saturn expected to see a third ring added in their lifetime.

Despite the city's reputation and provision of security,

TJ still felt nervous. For the first time in days the fear of attack did not strike him when morning came, today's fear was of the ceremony he was going to attend. Today, he and three of his squad were to be promoted for their actions in the siege of Saturn, four days ago. Other members of the former First and Second Recons from Fort Grey were to be decorated and honoured as well, though several had been laid to rest the day before, including Major Amanda Harte who had succumbed to her injuries hours after the battle.

The loss of the Major had been hard on the Second Recon, especially on TJ and Daniella. The last four original squad members held a private ceremony to honour her and the other members who had violently left their ranks. Now was the time to honour the living.

TJ stood at his full-length dressing mirror and fussed with his collar even though it did not need to be fussed over. His room was on the fourth floor of the officers' barracks with a view of most of the training grounds through the space between the primary ring wall and the central buildings. The two-tone chime at his door caught him off guard and irritated him since, in his mind; he was moments from getting the collar problem under control.

'Enter,' he raised his voice before starting over with his collar.

The door slid open admitting Ashley and Ken into his room. They were both dressed in their formal uniforms. The edging remained crisp even while they moved, wrinkling only slightly when an elbow or knee bent.

'What's keeping you, sir?' asked Ken smoothing a wrinkle seeming to not go away. His dress uniform was clearly not wide enough, since they only received them less than one hour before the ceremony it would have to do. Ashley's uniform on the other hand was a perfect fit, seemingly tailored to the curves of her body specifically.

The military dress uniform had not changed much in the last few centuries. The hat was the same pristine snow-white with rank insignia gold above the glossy black of the visor. The pants were black cotton with the customary blood-red stripe down the outside seam of each leg. Spit-and-polish black dress boots completed the lower half of the uniform.

Worn over a smoky-grey dress shirt, the dark grey jacket was three-quarter length with gold braid indicating rank at the sleeve cuffs and the epaulets on the padded shoulders. Black edging trimmed across the shoulder seams to the inch-high mandarin collar and around the bottom edge each sleeve cuff. A white braided lanyard circled the left shoulder through the epaulet and white gloves completed the uniform.

'This collar doesn't feel right,' TJ said impatiently.

'Take your fingers out of it,' Ken said, still trying to flatten his own persistent wrinkle.

'Here, let me do it,' Ashley offered.

TJ turned toward Ashley and let her try to fix his hopeless collar. 'You know, this doesn't feel right. We're missing something.'

'Just your marbles, sir,' Ashley patted him on the shoulder. 'Now, go get your hat before you lose whatever you've got left.'

'Hey… you fixed it.' smiled TJ, looking into the mirror before retrieving his hat off the bed.

'How'd you fix it, Ash?' Ken asked having given up on his wrinkled jacket.

'I didn't do anything. I think he's a little stressed.'

'He should take lessons from Paul,' Ken said, looking toward the west training compound.

'All set.' TJ said, coming out of the bedroom. 'What was that all about, Paul?'

The three of them walked out of TJ's room and made their way out of the barracks across simple yet stylish rust and grey coloured carpeting. To the troopers the colours reminded them of their training times in the elements of

Mars beyond the peninsula. They passed a squad on a training run on their way to the western compound which threw the trio a quick salute. Returning the salutes was an automatic action but a kind of shock slowed the lowering of their arms. Shock they were the ones being saluted, by troopers from another base. They emerged into the light of one of Fort Saturn's two compounds located at the west and east points of the *star*. The troops' barracks flanked each point, allowing for quick assembly if needed.

As chance would have it, an assembly was already there. A triple ring of troopers surrounded the sparring platform. On the platform was a young Blademaster, goading his opponent with profanities under a strained pant. TJ recognized him as Mike McMillan, a master sergeant of Fort Saturn's Fourth Encounter Team.

'Guess he got bored waiting,' Ken said, indicating the opponent.

'Oh, no,' Ashley sighed.

TJ looked to the other trooper on the sparring platform. He sighed as well when he recognized the opposing trooper was in dress uniform minus the jacket. It was the Blademaster from his own squad, Paul Nivek. TJ didn't have to watch the pre-show to know poor Mike was going to regret some of the things he was saying.

'Fighting Bregan has made you soft, old timer. Do you really think you're ready to fight against a human?' Mike mocked.

Before TJ could speak up to warn the Encounter trooper to back off and Paul to not wreck his uniform, Kain launched at the younger Blademaster with a furious assault. The blows came swiftly, all Mike could do not to be hit was a series of defensive swings. In less than ten seconds, it was over. Kain's finely tuned and battle-hardened skills put a minor flesh wound on his opponent and disabled his blade in the best five swings of the skirmish. Kain's blade was in the ceremonial scabbard before Mike hit his knees.

'Get cleaned up, trooper,' Paul said with a smile, 'we've all got a ceremony to attend. TJ, about time!' All eyes turned to follow Paul's comment and fell on TJ, or more precisely, on his rank insignia.

'Officer present!' shouted the nearest trooper. The entire gathering of troopers instantly sprang to rigid attention and somehow managed to create a path to the platform at the same time. Obviously operational protocols were stricter here than at Fort Grey. A lieutenant would not have received this treatment at the smaller fort. Possibly though, they had heard about the upcoming promotion, that or TJ's actions in the battlefield.

'Stand easy, please,' TJ announced.

Paul came trotting up the path through the crowd with his jacket slung over his shoulder. TJ gave him the spin-around signal and looked him over for any slashes that may have been recently acquired.

'Satisfied then, chief?' Paul asked with his arms out to both sides and a smirk on his face.

'Your shirt's ruffled, Mr. Nivek,' TJ pulled out one side of Paul's shirt, shaking his head, only slightly annoyed. He was relieved his friend had not suffered more injury in a sparring match with another Blademaster.

Paul smiled at Ken and Ashley as they walked off toward the central structure and he tucked in his shirt. They smiled back and shook their heads in amusement. By the time they rounded the corner of the mess hall to the immediate west of the large five-storey building; Paul had his jacket on and nicely smoothed out.

The central office tower in Fort Saturn looked like an accordion and was sixty-six feet tall, fourteen of which were above the dome. The ribs of the building were five feet deep and extended to full height of the structure. They were comprised of mirrored glass and true mirrors, designed to deflect any beam cannon shots in the event of a breach in the fortress walls. To aid this plan, the gloss and mirror sections were no doubt magnetically shielded – a technology still too new to be used to protect vehicles or even personnel.

In front of the building were the remains of the First and Second Recon Squads, in their formal best. They snapped to attention when the foursome approached. TJ had not even known privates were issued with formal dress uniforms.

'All present and accounted for, Lieutenant Marso.' Daniella saluted then winked.

TJ and Daniella had spent the past few days in each other's company, taking turns consoling each other for the losses they had sustained. Rumours circulated throughout the base there was more to their friendship, but the squads defended their two commanders when the issue came up. There was no mistaking the two were closer than before the battle in the shadow of Fort Saturn's walls.

TJ could count the Fort Grey originals on one hand and the reinforcements that had come with Commander Martel on the other – a total of eight troopers and officers besides himself and the three with him.

'That's not saying much, is it, Lieutenant?' TJ asked grimly. 'But I'm very pleased to say that we will all be working together in the future. Even if it's under a different name.'

A spontaneous cheer erupted from the gathering filling TJ's heart with the pride only a squad leader could get when he or she knew the troopers supported them.

'We have to get going now, TJ,' Paul said, when TJ did not move.

Falling out of his pride-induced trance he said, 'Yes, thanks Paul. Everyone, fall in. It's time for our entrance.'

The squad formed into a double column behind Daniella and TJ. Their steps fell into sync and they marched proudly into the building. With a series of discreet hand signals, the building parade guard lining the approach to the building's main entrance notified the ceremony chamber of the arrival of the guests of honour. Four honour guards fell in beside the formation of troopers, two on either side, while two more guards took up a rear position.

When the procession reached the chamber's main doors, two parade guards pushed open the doors and stood at attention. The chamber was two floors tall and occupied half the floor space of those floors. The approach aisle was lined on both sides with Fort Saturn staff and troopers in well-pressed uniforms, though not in dress style. The personnel were lined thirty deep toward the stage and fifty wide to either side in a crescent and a magical array of colours.

The aisle ran along the floor wide enough for six soldiers to walk abreast before a ramp angled up to the oval center stage, widening so ten could stand shoulder to shoulder. The gathering filled a third of the chamber, normally holding a thousand people if packed in tighter company. The room was mainly used for movie holograms, or on occasion, mission briefings for large operations. Until recently, these operations were mass cargo transfers or Fort-establishing tours of duty, one of which had been the establishment of Fort Grey.

Three command rank individuals were already on the stage to the left side of the dais, District Commander Shawn Norris, Commander Walter Martel and Air Captain Bill Zedluk in a black dress uniform. Buzz had received a promotion, without the usual fanfare, from the senior officers in Port Mars, which took him a giant step to his current rank. No one knew how he jumped to Captain but everyone was happy for Buzz.

When all the participants in today's ceremony were in position, the marathon of speeches commenced. The first came from Commander Norris to announce recent happenings and welcome the survivors from Fort Grey, something in his eagerness for future operations seemed wrong. Next up was Air Captain Zedluk with a eulogy for the residents of Fort Grey who did not survive and the members of the militia who did not live to see this day.

Commander Martel was next. As his last act as Base Commander of Fort Grey, he dealt out medals and commendations to the squad before he started announcing promotions for some. 'And now I've been given the privilege of promoting some of the many exceptional people who have served under my command and who I feel I could call *friends*. First of all, Private Krushell. Despite sustaining multiple injuries, Private Krushell performed well above the call of duty and has now achieved the rank of Corporal. Congratulations, young man.' The applause was quick to start and slowly died away as Erik stepped back into the formation, his pride evident in a half smile.

'Next is Corporal Ken Michelson. His dedication to service and his loyalty to his commanding officer enabled many of us, if not all, to arrive safely at these superb gates of Fort Saturn! Corporal Michelson has more than earned his new rank of Sergeant.'

Applause rang through the chamber long after Ken had stepped back into the line. Instead of the smile Erik still wore, Ken seemed to be embarrassed at the attention.

'Our third promotion is Master Sergeant Paul Nivek.' Walter started. The applause erupted into a thunderous drone which was punctuated by loud cheers and whistles. The outburst lasted for several minutes, much to the annoyance of Commander Martel.

'Apparently Master Sergeant Nivek needs no introduction, therefore I'll just announce his new rank of Warrant Officer, First Class.' Cheers rang out again, but only lasting a minute this time.

'Finally, I'd like to ask Squad Leader Trevor James Marso to approach the podium. Lieutenant Marso is like a son I would be honoured to have. His intuition and quick thinking has saved us all. He has shown all the abilities of a top-notch officer and, therefore, with the blessing of the Troop Command in Port Mars, he is hereby promoted to the rank of Captain.'

Instead of a burst of cheers when Commander Martel pinned TJ's new rank insignia on his lapel, the entire assembly snapped to attention and saluted in a deafening stomp. The group of people on the platform joined in, including the three high-ranking officials. With tears of pride and a mix of other emotions shimmering in his eyes, TJ returned the salute. Then, and only then, did the cheers begin.

After the ceremony, Buzz and Walter stopped TJ in the foyer. They took a moment to make sure no one else was within earshot.

'What's up?' asked the newly minted Captain Marso.

'Captain,' started Commander Martel, 'the Captain and I have been ordered to Port Mars for re-assignment. We wanted to tell you even though we were told not to tell anyone.'

'And we wanted to wish you luck on whatever assignment you're given,' Buzz smiled, obviously pleased with his situation.

'Thanks, my unit will appreciate that. And, sir, it has been a pleasure serving under you. With both of you, actually.'

'Now, go join your unit – we head out tonight.'

'Thank you, sir!'

*****

CHAPTER XXI
Friday, 13 April, 2251

The following day, the new Warrant Officer was polishing his new insignia for the third time. They shone almost painfully and irritated the group of armoured troopers from the squad standing around him.

'You done with that yet, sir?' Ashley asked. 'You'll do well with TJ.'

'Yeah! No doubt,' Ken laughed, 'a couple of polishers and fussy-pants.'

'I just want to look good for the new Captain,' he looked concerned at a minuscule smudge.

'Speak of the devil,' Ashley smiled.

TJ and Daniella emerged from the central building, immersed in a whispered discussion. They had been called to see the base commander early this morning and it was now noon. They looked tired. Dressed in his standard uniform, Paul approached the pair, also in their standard dress.

'Hey Paul, what's going on?' TJ asked.

'Rumour has it we're moving out today,' he smiled.

'Amazing things, those rumours,' Daniella shook her head.

'Gather the squad, Paul. We might as well tell everyone at once.'

WO Nivek walked back and barked the order light-heartedly, returning with the squad in tow a moment later. The first thing they did was form a semi-circle around the two officers and salute.

'Okay, we can stop that right now,' TJ said

'You twelve are no longer to salute either TJ or myself, unless there are other senior officers around. We're still the same people you trained and lived with two weeks ago,' Daniella said behind a mild smile.

The troop laughed lightly, lowering their arms and relaxing noticeably even in their armour. The group consisted of entirely Fort Grey personnel. Except for Commander Martel and Buzz, these were all that remained of the disaster.

'That's much better. Now, we have a few items to go over,' TJ said. 'But not here, let's move to a more secure location.'

Three stories up, they were clustered into a service way spanning the gap between the mess hall and the central tower. They made a powerful, if not intimidating sight to anyone attempting to cross – so much so most people opted for crossing on a lower level. Even though they were in plain sight, they were alone.

'First item on the list is the whereabouts of Commander Martel and Buzz. They've been reassigned to Port Mars for the time being,' TJ announced.

A murmur ran through the group. Daniella nudged TJ, which was her signal to indicate Ann Huston had not reacted in a similar fashion. TJ still was not sure about Ann and had encouraged Daniella to maintain a watch on her. While the Fort Saturn investigation into the pre-battle disappearance of a Fort Grey trooper had not pointed at anyone in particular, the report also had not said it was an accident and Ann remained the prime suspect. TJ ignored the nudge and continued on.

'Also, we are now members of the Fort Saturn detachment officially – but for how long I couldn't say.'

'When do we get to retake the Grey, sir?' asked a young trooper who had come up with Commander Martel. He went by the call sign of *Blender* but his real name was Doug Jackson and his rank was Corporal. Despite being involved with various paramilitary organizations early on, the military was clearly not his cup of tea.

'At this time Corporal, there are no plans to send us home. They want us to go to the Miles Research Station to see what kind of numbers we're dealing with. Command feels that that is the area where the Bregan threat originated. While we are gone Fort Saturn will also set a watch on the Landran's forest,' Daniella said.

'This will be a recon mission only.' Sighs seemed to echo through the catwalk enclosure. 'I know we haven't had any luck on these *simple* missions and that's why a squad from Fort Saturn will be joining us.' TJ added.

'Great! So now we have to baby sit as well,' the medic Private Slotsen moaned.

'They can fight, which is why they're coming with us. It will be the Fourth Encounter Team. I'm sure you've all met one of them by now. I know Paul has.' TJ said as the squad laughed at Paul's expense.

'So, we are babysitting, then,' Paul chuckled.

'Let's get our gear and move it all to Bay Six. We'll meet the Encounter team there.'

The squad split up with the troopers headed to their barracks, or straight to the vehicle bay if they were already armoured up, and the officers went to theirs. When the officers entered the barracks, Ann, Sam and Paul started for the lower halls while TJ and Daniella started for the second level.

'Paul,' TJ shouted from the staircase, 'could I talk to you about Mike?'

Paul hung his head and turned away from the other two junior officers. He stepped up to where TJ was standing, expecting to get a strip torn off his hide.

'Relax, Paul. I don't really care what you do to Mike. It's about Ann. We need to keep an eye on her. Her reaction to the news was off. She was more upset that we were going to possibly engage the Bregan than she was that we weren't going to go for the Grey.'

'Maybe it's nerves. Can't say I'm thrilled about either idea,' Paul said.

'That's just it, though. She almost seemed happy we weren't going back to Fort Grey.'

'I see where you're going with this,' Paul said after a moment's thought. 'I'll set a watch on her.'

'Thanks. Now, go get ready,' TJ said patting him on the shoulder.

An hour later, like a scene out of a movie, TJ emerged from his room with his gear and in his full armour. As he walked down the hall, Daniella came out of her room and fell into step. At the bottom of the stairs Paul, Sam and Ann came up behind them. Making their way through the base, the five of them were quickly and silently joined by the rest of the squad.

The squad of fourteen drew many odd glances while they passed in their battle armour. A couple of MPs in light armour moved to enforce the no-armour law, thinking better of it when they noticed the beam cannons and bolt rifles indicating an *armed* status.

The squad passed effortlessly through the security of the vehicle bay at the north point of the fortress. The guard all but jumped out of the way when Captain Marso flashed his orders at them.

'Stuck-up recon. They think they're so much better than us,' snarled a guard under his breath.

'Those first ones are,' snapped the watch commander.

Lieutenant Alexandra Brodie, Alex to her friends greeted them at the entrance of Bay Six in her deep green battle armour. She was a short woman even in her power-suit, but full of energy. She saluted TJ quickly before she spoke.

'Fourth Encounter Team is ready and waiting. Your vehicles have been prepped as per your instructions, sir.'

'Relax, Lieutenant, we're not that formal,' he smiled.

'Yes, sir,' she smiled warmly and with some relief.

Daniella saw the smile and glared at her with such malice only Bane itself could match it. She managed to hold the stare until TJ turned around to address the crowd of troopers and glanced at her. Her face flushed in an instant and she looked away. TJ looked at her for a moment longer before speaking. His voice rose for everyone to hear.

'Okay, we have three GCRs in slots Six-One, Six-Two and Six-Ten. Get your gear into one of those vehicles. Warrant Officer Nivek has your assignments.'

'Listen up! This is how it's going to work,' Paul started. While Paul read the duty assignment sheet and troopers walked off to stow their gear, TJ, Daniella and Alex stepped aside for a briefing of sorts.

'We've seen these things fight in a siege action but we need to know how they operate in an open situation,' Alex said.

'It's essentially the same, but they seem to play with their victims more,' Daniella sneered.

'They appear to hunt more than actually attack,' TJ added.

'So then they're slightly more intelligent than wolves,' Alex concluded.

'You had best curb that thinking in you and your troopers, Alex,' TJ snapped, '…or your squad won't be coming home, understand?'

'Uh, yeah. They can't be that bad, right?' she asked Daniella.

'They wiped out my squad in less than an hour. They gave us no warning at all,' Daniella said on the verge of tears.

'Alex, the Bregan adapt faster than humans do. Much faster, so it's best to think higher of them than they really are. And no long distance communications.'

'Right. I'll pass the word,' she smiled again.

Alex turned to leave the pair to get her squad set and to let them know the new information. A tap on her shoulder from TJ stopped her before she got too far. He motioned for her to come closer, looking around cautiously before he leaned in to whisper, 'One more thing, Lieutenant.'

'Yes, sir?' she whispered right back.

'This stays between us, not even your XO can know. Do you understand?' TJ asked seriously.

'Positively, TJ, not a word.'

Alexandra's smile widened as she leaned closer to hear what her Captain was about to tell only her. Daniella knew what TJ was telling her even though she was not a part of the conversation and she could see in Alex's smile what she was expecting to hear. She was looking forward to the disappointment about to creep over her overly pretty face.

'Watch carefully now,' TJ started. Alex caught her breath. 'There is a good possibility that there is a mole in Kain's squad and I need you to watch them discretely for signs of treachery.'

Boom! Like a bomb hit. Her face changed from the secretive smile to one of shock. 'Yes!' thought Daniella, barely concealing her enjoyment of the situation.

'That's it? That's all you wanted to say?' Alex spouted.

'I'd like to know what you were expecting.' TJ said, playing up a little anger. 'Get your squad ready to move now, Lieutenant!' he ordered.

Daniella recoiled in shock at the harshness in his voice as did many of the techs and troopers milling around. TJ had never snapped at a subordinate that way before – at superiors sure – but never a subordinate. When Alexandra walked briskly away, those in the immediate vicinity made themselves scarce as well, in the event whatever she had done was contagious.

'Jeepers sweetheart, you don't have to fill Amanda's shoes now that she's gone,' Daniella said.

The procession from the east doors began at two minutes after noon and consisted of five GCRs and a BRAT. The five officers walked ahead of the lead vehicle, with four troopers escorting them and three more bringing up the rear. As the force marched between the two rows of thirty to forty-year old buildings leading straight to the northeast inner exit, the occasional citizen would stop and wave. When TJ and the other officers began to salute the waving people word spread like wild fire of the miniature parade.

Before they could clear the inner wall, the route they were taking was edged by a solid double line of civilians and off-duty military personnel. Cheers and well-wishes echoed throughout the city as the two squads moved toward the east exit of the outer wall. TJ and his entourage continued to salute the people and they continued to cheer wildly each time.

Officers and soldiers who were on duty began to join the crowd and even returned the salutes with smiles of encouragement. The troopers at the gate were surprised by the gathering and some of them got caught up in the excitement of the send-off.

The column stopped at the gate before they left the protection of Fort Saturn, allowing the officers to put on their armour. TJ and the others stepped into the guardhouse to change, away from the cheering crowd. Outside the troopers were waving and shaking hands with the hundred or so people sending them out.

When TJ came out, the travel group entered into the airlock and waved at what could be their last look at a human settlement, certainly for a while anyway. The inner doors closed seconds before the purified air was expelled and replaced with the mildly uncomfortable atmosphere of the Eden peninsula. The outer doors opened to the sharp sunlight of the unprotected world. The troopers and officers who had been walking now hopped into the vacant vehicles before setting out.

'Arrowhead formation drivers, let's go!' TJ said on a closed-band frequency.

The GCRs swept into a delta pattern to provide decent cover for the BRAT which slipped into the space provided at the rear. The vehicles raced across the lush grass, maneuvering perfectly through and around small stands of trees. They blasted over several small streams annoying several small, mostly furry creatures.

They traveled for a couple of hours after dark to reach their first camp site on the western side of a small stream, the same one Commander Martel had made several days before. The east side was also the beginning of the cracked marshes and they would need daylight to traverse them with any success.

'Mr. Cooper here has the watch assignments,' TJ said to the gathered troops once the sleds had stopped. 'Listen closely and stay alert.'

'TJ,' Kain said after the troopers had been set to their tasks, 'I have some news about Ann.'

'Just a minute, Paul. Daniella, you and Alex oversee things. I have to go check on the BRAT's cargo,' TJ called to the Lieutenants.

TJ and Kain began a show of inspecting the outside of the BRAT before they ducked inside to talk.

'Don't let that new rank go to your head, Ken,' Ashley warned with a smile after he had jokingly ordered her to pitch a tent for him.

'I know you're still my lieutenant' Ken smiled.

'And don't you forget it,' she laughed.

'Hey you two!' Erik whispered as he ran up to them.

'What is it, Corporal?' Ashley smiled and punched him lightly on the shoulder.

'Heh, yeah,' he smiled. 'But no, … it's Ann. Look, she's watching the BRAT like her future depended on it.'

The two senior troopers turned silently to peer

around the corner of the GCR at Ann. She was standing with a ration pack, almost burning holes in the side of the BRAT with her stare. None of the other troopers even looked twice at the large vehicle.

'That's too spooky for me,' Ken said turning back.

'Well, she's the spy in my books,' Ashley said, going back to work on the tent.

'Oh, man, say the word and I'll just… Kapow!… take her down!' Erik said energetically.

'Whoa there, big fella,' Ashley counseled, turning from her job again.

'She is a legitimate Blademaster, you know,' Ken smirked.

'Yeah, well, still,' Erik puffed his chest out, 'I ain't letting her out of my sight.'

'Go easy on her, big gunner,' Ken smiled as Erik slunk off.

'You get too much pleasure out of playing with him, Dolly,' Ashley said with an amused look on her face.

'That's Sergeant Dolly to you! I mean, Sergeant Michelson,' Ken said seriously.

Ashley began laughing, hard enough she was virtually useless in trying to put up the tent. Even with Ken's help, they both had difficulty working through their laughter. The two troopers continued their jocularity well into the night, oblivious to the goings-on around them.

'You mean to say, she actually sent out a transmission?' TJ asked.

'I couldn't say for sure,' Kain said, 'I just said, I saw her messing with the communications equipment in the GCR. She could have just been checking the frequencies. Regardless, she looked nervous about whatever she was doing.'

'Who's on her watch tonight?'

'I'm not entirely sure, my list is with my gear, but I know Ashley's with her.' Kain said.

'Alright. I'll have a talk with Ashley later. Get some rest now, bud.'

'I'll try.'

They stepped out of the side door of the BRAT into the perfect blackness of a night about to see a storm. Switching on the light intensifier display allowed TJ to watch Kain return to his final duties for the night. The camp was quiet and motionless except for the occasional pass of one of the watch. The quiet provided easy passage to where Ashley and Ken had set up the tents for their team.

About five yards from the smoldering fire; TJ was approached by an armoured trooper who prevented him from entering the site.

'Please identify yourself,' the young woman said.

'It's Captain Marso.' TJ smiled at the woman's nervousness.

'Sorry, sir, I was just...' she stammered.

'Following orders. I know. Keep up the good work, Private Der Mar.'

'Yes, sir.' she whispered before returning to her well hidden position.

TJ watched after her for a moment. He always marveled at how much courage it took to be a private in troubled times and how often the newest recruits had more than their fair share. TJ felt he might come to want to be a private again someday soon.

'Ashley,' TJ called, above a whisper.

'What?' she replied from the center tent.

'Get out here, will ya?' he said.

'Man! You're very annoying.' she said, pushing through the pressure lock a moment later.

'It comes with the rank,' he smiled, 'Listen, on your

watch tonight; I want you to keep an eye on our friend.'

'I was going to anyway… sure, chief. Anything else?'

'No, I'm good. Thanks.'

'Smart-ass!'

'Yeah and you love it, now get some rest.'

TJ chuckled to himself as the pressure lock resealed. He was amazed at the mix of loyalty and friendship the squad showed him every day. He was a long way from his day as a simple squad lieutenant. His head hung, weighed down by the new stresses of captaincy. Rest came eventually and images of carefree days long gone filled his dreams.

*****

CHAPTER XXIII
Saturday, 14 April, 2251

They did not wait for the rise of their Mother star before the two squads broke camp and began their trek through the Cracked Marshes. The night had passed in silence which was a pleasant change from the chaos that had punctuated their previous outings. Sleep had come easily to most and had hopefully prepared them for the day to come. Though groggy when they first woke, spirits were high, even jovial in some cases.

'Eden calendar 25.04.16, Captain Krushell's log. We set out today from TG-141 in the hope of settling a border dispute with the Bregan Empire.' Erik broadcast to the GCR and troopers ahead of him from the BRAT on a narrow band. Snickers and giggles echoed through the vehicles during his short speech. Some troopers even applauded his effort at comic relief if they managed to catch the dated reference.

'Captain, eh?' Daniella snickered, 'don't expect me to salute, sir.'

'I will crush dissidence wherever it may be found!' bellowed Erik in his role.

'Hey, pipe down, Emperor,' Ann said in a monotone.

'He's just playing, Ann. Lighten up!' Kain snapped.

'Let's all cool down and start watching for signs of our friends,' TJ interjected before things got too out of hand.

'Hey Erik, what was TG-141?' Ken asked from his position in the marching order beside the BRAT.

'I don't know man,' Erik chuckled, 'I just made it up.'

Before the solar system died, the Eden peninsula had

been relatively flat compared to the rocky-red outlands and deep purple ocean now. It was in every sense, picture perfect with its spanning play of grasslands, growing forests and magical water features. Until the gas planet's core slammed into Mars. That day, the Comb Plateau and the Cracked Marshes were formed in a violent birth.

The Eden Peninsula was entirely man-made. Originally, the colony was to be placed on an island to contain both human and vegetative growth until the planet was stabilized. The scientifically created crater in which the island was to be made was placed in the middle of a dry ocean bed. The crater walls were shored up then the hole was filled in with dirt from the *ocean* floor. Because the walls of the crater needed to be left to harden, a land bridge was built to carry the vehicles transporting soil and rocks.

The water was then added to a predetermined level around the globe before the land bridge could be removed. Fortunately, the water reserves on Mars were not as large as predicted so the extra land mass was welcome to compensate for what would have been a significant lowering of water levels and became a permanent feature.

During the aftermath of the core impact there was significant tectonic activity. The major fault line in the area was located on the mainland side of the land bridge. The resulting plate shifts sent jagged mountains soaring into the sky across the entire span. So while the colony was not on a contained island as originally planned, they were still isolated since there was no way for the hovercraft to sail over the rocks.

When the plateau appeared, the land to the east sank to a single foot above sea level and in some cases, was actually below. Scientists from the Miles Research Station, which was located in that area at the time, studied the cause. They found the planetary turmoil had cracked the wall of the crater. Most of the dirt had settled by that time which prevented the underground flooding from devastating the entire peninsula. Plant life flourished in the marshes and animals of all species flocked to the buffet of plants. There were few trees in the marsh, but the shrubbery was tall and thick enough to force the vehicles into a single file. First thing in the morning a rich fog wafted through the plants, obscuring them. Vehicle sensors had a tough time in this area beyond the norm. Some thought it was the fog or maybe the plants causing the interference. Either way, TJ's vehicle could only scan to a hundred feet ahead, although they could only see fifty feet if the fog thinned.

The landscape around the convoy changed by the hour – from overgrown areas of dark green grass to black swamp and barren red sand dunes rising over the blue canals to towering stands of large green and blue trees. The pilots of the GCRs snapped many computer images for those back home that may never get to see the marshes.

Aside from the sightseeing, the trek was uneventful and they figured it was time to stop just before D400 for a rest. Currently, they were under the lofty canopy of a small forest of trees, giving the air a sweet freshness for those who dared open their visors. After D400 the fog had begun to lift, providing the full visual range for scanning but still limited by the foliage. There was an average-sized hill located just a mile off from the trees that had shown up during their scans. TJ figured the rise in the horizon would make an excellent base of operations and ordered a set-up at the top. Their vehicles moved easily up the slope and formed a semi-circle around the hilltop while the squads ate in shifts.

The other oddity of this area was the abundance of breathable air. The large numbers of oxygen-producing plants and filtering leaves, as in the Sky Trees, allowed the troopers to switch off their filters and take in the common odours of their surroundings, though they kept the particle filtration running at least on a minimal level.

'It seems almost wrong to have this many smells in one area,' commented Art McKee, a private in the Fourth Encounter Team.

'Reminds me of Earth, it does,' added Drew Webster, also of the Fourth Encounter.

Out of the group of twenty-five humans, Sergeant Webster was the only one who had any real memories of their home world. He never talked much about those memories since his occasional statements of Old Earth usually stopped the conversation. This time, it merely killed their enjoyment of the fragrant aromas.

'It looks like we've already come halfway since last night,' Warrant Officer Rayner said between mouthfuls of rations as he sat down heavily in the circle of command officers.

'Where do you think we'll stop, TJ?' Alexandra asked playfully.

'The map shows dry ground in that area,' Daniella pointed to the shimmering blue digital map displayed in front of them. Her growing annoyance with the other lieutenant seemed to be ignored by everyone.

'Yeah,' TJ started out, 'That sounds about right by the looks of it. Kain, what is your operational status?'

'As before, chief,' he replied, looking at the confused faces around him, 'it appears that the time is not yet right to act on the issue.'

'What the hell are you talking about?' Martin Rayner spouted.

'I think your helmet's on too tight, Paul,' Alex said.

TJ and Kain smiled smugly at their confusion, while Daniella was slow to join them in understanding she did smile eventually. The two Encounter officers got up and sauntered away, shaking their heads rather than trying to figure out these recons. The remaining three were silent until they had moved off, then they began the real conversation.

'We're getting awfully close to the Bregan's probable lair, TJ. Don't you think we could put a guard on her or something?' Daniella asked.

'We need all hands in this operation – we can't even spare one trooper to guard her. Besides, she's a Blademaster; regular troopers wouldn't be a match for her, anyway.'

'I see what you're saying,' Kain put in.

'But we have to do something with her,' TJ said.

'We could put her in a vehicle.'

'No, 'cause she'd shoot us,' Daniella said.

TJ added, 'But she could drive one.'

'Yeah, she couldn't get very far that way,' Kain smiled.

'Okay. I want you to tell her, it'll look better coming from you,' TJ said to Daniella.

'Got it.' she stood to leave.

'Also you two, I think we should hit the trails again.'

'No problem, Cap'n.' Kain saluted in an exaggerated manner.

'Knock it off, buddy!'

The three of them walked off chuckling to one another, even if it was forced. Their laughter put the rest of the squad at ease, despite the danger they could face in the near future. Conversations sprang up throughout the previously silent camp now that a course of action had been determined. The troopers were friendly and the talk was humorous – yet they still managed to clean up the site in a professional manner and in less than half an hour and were on their way ten minutes later.

The convoy swept from their lofty perch at a leisurely pace of twenty-two miles per hour. They drifted into two columns in the slightly thinning foliage of the more eastern marsh for greater protection. From a distance, one could imagine these vehicles were sailing through a sea of green in tides of red, yellow and violet. Slowly as the day passed into twilight, the landscape passed from lush fields and sparkling canals to sparse vegetation and cracked mud, then on to the red dunes.

'This planet never ceases to amaze me,' Dolly said, shaking his head.

'That doesn't seem too hard to do,' Viper quipped.

'You're a pain, you know that?' he sighed.

'Yeah, and you couldn't live without me,' she smiled.

'Heads up, joker. TJ's stopping.'

The convoy glided to a halt on the west side of the first large dune in this out-of-place desert. TJ hopped out lead GCR as it settled down and sank a couple inches into the soft sand. Within minutes, everyone except the vehicle gunners were standing outside, surveying the area.

'Lieutenant Brodie, send a team to the top of the dune. We should be able to see the Station from here. Kain, get your team to swing these vehicles around in case we have to make a hasty retreat,' TJ ordered.

Orders were barked and four members of the Second Recon rotated the vehicles to face in a west-south-westerly direction.

'Daniella, the rest of your squad is to secure the area.'

'Sure thing, TJ,' she smiled before taking the last five members out on a perimeter patrol.

The team on the dune was not yet back when Kain's group emerged from the vehicles. TJ had almost sent them on an advance recon when he noticed one of the team had not returned. 'Kain, where's Steve?' he asked.

Kain spun around to see that, indeed, the sixth member of the team was absent.

'He went to the BRAT, it's spun around, and so he should be here. Oh, there he is, coming out if the thing now. Get your butt over here!'

A nonsense transmission blared from the BRAT on an open frequency. Private Gallagher smiled and waved before the gunner came storming out of the vehicle.

'The bastard overloaded the reactor,' Jack Cotton cried.

TJ and the seven troopers surrounding him were stunned. Steve was the turncoat, not Ann! Before any action could be taken, a screech blasted over the airwaves. Steve spun around and impaled the unprepared private, dropping him to the ground and kicked him into a convenient crevasse. After the violent death of the traitor, hell broke loose.

'They're coming!' Mike shouted as he and his team ran down the dune.

'Son-of-a-bitch,' TJ cursed.

Steve cocked his head toward TJ and smiled before darting off toward the north. A medic ran to Jack's aid next to the BRAT. 'Get out of there,' Kain yelled to the medic.

His cry was cut short by the detonation of the BRATs reactor. TJ, Kain and the others were hurled against the other row of GCRs while the unfortunate medic and Jack's body were incinerated. The scout team descending from the dune was caught in the blast wave of the GCR at the rear of the row next to the BRAT. It was also blown to pieces as a result of the BRATs detonation. The lead GCR was scorched to the point where no paint or coloring was visible. The back of it looked like an Old Earth train had hit it.

The gunners from the vehicles still intact jumped out and ran to the aid of the scout team. TJ and his group of flattened troopers were helped to their feet by Daniella's team. Since they were too shaken to stand on their own the dented sides of the GCRs was the only way to support their bodies.

'Frag the prick,' TJ said painfully to Sam.

'My pleasure, sir,' she said as she turned to run after Steve.

'Kain, you and Ann make sure she gets back.'

'Yes, sir,' they said together.

The three of them ran north hunting the traitor, at the same time as the gunners returned with three members of the scout team of four. They were in a similar condition as TJ's people.

'Mike, where's Jamie?' Alex asked.

'He was too close to the gopher. The blast shredded him. Not much left...' Mike said as he winced from his own injuries.

Brodie was taken aback by the news. She was now down two troopers in less than two minutes. Her distress was obvious to those around her. Daniella walked to her side and placed a comforting arm around her.

'Sometimes, squaddies die, Alex. Nothing anyone could do but make it worth something,' Daniella said as she tried to comfort Alex.

'We have to get out of here. Alex, get your other gunner out of that wrecked sled and have your other medic load her patients into the middle GCR,' TJ said as he stood up straight, stretched stiffly and began to walk off with a limp noticeable.

Sam Cornwall crested the copper coloured dune ahead of the two Blademasters, who were coming behind her at a brisk walk, and got the first look at what was once known as the Miles Research Station. Though the structure was two miles off, she could still see the Bregan swarming over, around and from it with her targeting optics and a favourable atmosphere shift. She hesitated before running back for cover when she saw Steve Gallagher talking with a trio of armoured Bregan off to the east.

'They're swinging around south. They'll cut us off,' Ann pointed out as she got to the crest of the dune.

'Cut him down, Sam, and let's get out of here!' Kain said urgently.

No sooner said, than the emerald beam streaked forth from Sam's class-3 cannon. She swung the beam across the foursome, catching two Bregan off guard. As the beam cut toward Steve, Sam switched it to pulse mode. Steve and the other Bregan had drawn their blades to deflect the beam but they proved to be incapable of handling the multiple shots of the pulse cannon.

The first few shots were neatly turned aside, lighting a few clumps of marsh reeds on fire, then they started to miss the pulses. Once the hits started coming, it was only a matter of time. The pulses peppered the two until they finally fell to the ground.

'Let's go, Sam. You got him.' Kain said half-dragging her back. The light had virtually disappeared by the time the trio made it back to the vehicles. The troopers had salvaged what they could from the crippled GCR and were finishing the loading procedure as darkness enveloped them. People were still shaken up but were walking better, still were not a hundred percent.

'Good, they're back. Let's go home, everyone,' TJ said and twirled a finger in the air.

'We can't,' Kain said, stopping all activity. 'They've circled south. We're cut off from Fort Saturn.'

'Then we run to New Venus. How much time do you think we have?' he asked.

'I'd say none,' Ann said indicating the top of the dune.

Luck was on their side for a change. The two of Mars' own natural satellites, shone brightly in the night sky, allowing the light intensifier displays to show everything in perfect green-colored detail, sadly also meaning they could see the Bregan's hideous faces and bright green eyes with disturbing clarity.

'Drivers to their vehicles now!' Brodie ordered.

'Why are we always fighting in the dark?' Erik pondered.

40

'Ask the guy who wrote the script,' Dolly said, running to load the injured gunner, Heather Campbell, into the GCR.

'Script?' he paused, '...what script? What are you talking about?'

With nine people in the GCRs, and twelve walkers escorting them out of the valley the unit was in sad shape compared to how they started. They made it a mile and a half before the Bregan descended from the east and south and were seen flying in the west. They were trying to pinch them off.

'Take those vehicles ahead. Cut a path for us,' TJ said, waving them ahead.

The GCRs slipped out of the assault path with seconds to spare. The twelve troopers on the ground were in the fight of their lives. Blades erupted and burned to life as if to welcome the combat, though their light barely compared to the pulsing of the Bregan's wings.

Blades met either blades or arm scythes in a spectacular release of destructive energy. The humans in this combined squad were veterans and summoned all their fighting skills to deal with the threat. The Bregan found out quickly that these were not going to be easy kills, the snap of the humans' blades was a constant reminder.

'They're trying to separate us from the gophers,' Dolly yelled above the din.

TJ blocked a triple slash attack and followed it by decking the Bregan with a right hook before he turned to look north. The creatures were working their way around the grove to the west of the GCRs. If they got cut off, he knew they would not see daylight.

'Let's pick up the pace, people!' he shouted.

So far none of them had fallen. That luck could not hold long. The squad of humans surged northwards, swinging madly to keep their escape route open. The class-3 beam cannons were simultaneously switched to their pulse mode and began to sputter their deadly deterrent.

Despite the emerald energy bolts impacting their armour or their bodies, the Bregan continued to close the gap. As the swarm of Bregan continued their sweep north, the squad's movements pushed them into range of the waiting GCRs. Blue shafts of death sprang forth from the three sleds and cut down a dozen unsuspecting gargoyles.

Now fighting on two sides, the Bregan momentarily faltered in their attempt to surround the humans, or so it seemed. The squad quickly capitalized on the arrested assault and with equal haste ran to the cover of the vehicles – unfortunately, right where the Bregan wanted them to be. A division-sized group had raced ahead of the vehicles and now moved in to close the trap.

'Nowhere out, guys,' Der Mar cried.

'Keep it together, pilot,' Kathy Fredricks called from the gunner seat.

'She's right, TJ!' Dolly yelled, 'These boys are going to dice us if we don't do something soon!'

'Give me a minute, will ya,' TJ grunted as his arms absorbed a hit from his opponent.

'Keep cutting the path,' Viper suggested from the second GCR.

The turrets spun around and commenced their deadly barrage in the forward direction. Bregan fell or were simply incinerated where they stood by the class-5 beam cannons. They had actually begun making headway until a courageous Bregan pealed in front of the lead GCR and redirected its beam back into the vehicle. The GCR did not detonate but was rendered useless as the beam pierced both occupants.

'Who the hell taught them to do that,' Daniella cursed.

Now, with a large obstacle in their path and the reduction of fire power, the squads were trapped. The Bregan regained confidence in their victory over the lead GCR and intensified their attack. They jumped from the crippled GCR to another and began cutting at the turret and windshield. 'I'm out of here,' said the pilot, Robert Balm.

'Good idea,' WO Rayner agreed.

The two troopers bailed out of the GCR in record time and from different exits. Martin Rayner rolled out of the back of the sled into a pack of Bregan and was ripped apart in seconds. Balm fared better as he dove into the middle of the squad's defensive ring.

'Okay, this is going from bad to worse,' Kain sighed.

Sam's cannon began overheating again from the intense release of death so after a couple of parting shots she tossed it into the pack of Bregan. A couple of warriors in the group were obviously at Fort Saturn in that previous attack and soared into the air to safety. The others, clearly rookies, hovered over the discarded weapon with curiosity. They had come to the conclusion it was not dangerous when the weapon went critical. The blast was as fantastic as a fireworks display with smoldering Bregan sailing through the air like smoke-trailing flares. One of the *smoking flares* was accelerated to break-neck speed and sent straight at Sam. The impact drove Sam into the back of another trooper. The pair then tumbled into the pack of Bregan. 'Flash balls, now!' Mike yelled.

Doug Jackson and Erik stepped off the battle line and retrieved one flash ball each. They lobbed them to roughly where Sam and Gibson were last seen. The two balls detonated on impact right next to Sam. The two spheres of energy from the balls threw Bregan out and away from the immediate area. At the centre of the twenty-foot clearing was Sam's battered form.

Dolly swept the legs from under his opponent and ran out to grab the motionless form. While there, he quickly scanned for signs of Crystal, the other trooper, but found nothing. He took Sam by the foot and dragged her back into the circle. Once at the centre of the defensive ring, the medic looking after Heather jumped from the last sled and began checking Sam.

'Can you get her into the gopher?' the medic asked.

'Yeah, sure. Stand back a minute,' Dolly responded.

Around them blades met blades and armour and splintered everything else into shards of metal and sparks of discharged energy. Despite the light show, Dolly tossed Sam into the GCR rather unceremoniously. Swain jumped in the instant Dolly stepped out of the way. She promptly closed the door and set to work on her new patient. Before Dolly could return to the fray, the Bregan pulled back over the nearby dunes and into the valley beyond.

'We're screwed, chief,' Kain puffed.

'Always the optimist, eh Paul?' TJ smiled.

'Why do you suppose they've stopped?' Erik asked.

'They could be re-evaluating their strategy I'd say. I mean, there are only a dozen of us or so and they can't make any headway,' TJ responded.

'Perhaps we could use the time wisely as well,' Dolly suggested solemnly.

'Good idea,' TJ started, 'Ashley, let's move out quietly.'

The GCR slid silently over the north ridge and into the valley, which was conspicuously devoid of Bregan. Tension amongst the escorting troopers was extreme and the cooling systems in the suits were working overtime to bring the occupants back to a reasonable boil at least. Nothing good ever came from a superior force withdrawing from combat. The red sands of the micro desert quietly covered the footprints of the squad with the slight breeze that had picked up since fighting began.

'Stay alert, everyone,' Alex said.

'Don't have to tell me twice,' Richard muttered, visibly shaking.

The squad managed to travel two miles before the reason for the sudden withdrawal of the Bregan became apparent. Swain had opened one of the GCR's doors to speak with Alex when there was a powerful flash behind them, indicating a contained nuclear detonation. Snap reflexes was the only thing giving them enough time to turn away before the shock wave hit them. Shock waves on Earth were destructive enough but here on Mars, with the denser atmosphere, the wave hit the squad like the same train that destroyed the other GCR earlier. At the same moment the wave hit, controls on the GCR went haywire and it began to tumble.

Under normal circumstances, when a tactical nuclear bomb is dropped near a GCR-305, it is knocked around but otherwise fine. This time, when the side door was opened, the electromagnetic pulse shielding was effectively removed. The troopers were blown north from ground zero at an astounding pace, led by the crippled GCR. The force of the blast slowly dissipated pushing them northward, then an inland storm picked up the energy from the blast.

They tumbled and rolled for hours seemingly and occasionally one or two of the troopers were lifted into the air briefly before crashing into another dune. TJ caught a glimpse of the cause of their hazardous movement when the sled spun on its axis. The lights shone to the southwest momentarily and illuminated a massive twister. TJ presumed the atomic blast had something to do with this rare phenomenon.

TJ and the entire squad decided to use this time to rest since they had no control of their movement. The bumping and rattling made it difficult to drift off but he managed to doze intermittently while he and the others continued their tumble north.

*****

CHAPTER XXIV
Monday, 15 April, 2251

Morning was a painful experience for everyone. Daniella was the first to rise if not actually wake up after the tumultuous travel of the night before. Slowly, she looked around at the strange landscape, looking nothing like the dunes and crevasses they had been in before the storm. At first glance, she did not see anyone or anything manmade, in the tall grass now browning from a once powerful green. When she looked again, she saw glints of light bouncing off the pieces of several mangled suits scattered over the field she was sitting in. She also noticed a small grove of trees not far off had been drastically bent out of shape, most likely because of the GCR resting on the fringe of them.

'Oh man, we are definitely nowhere close to Kansas, Toto,' Erik moaned, lifting his head gingerly, his love of the classic movies obviously intact through the events of the night.

He was ten feet away but until the Corporal had moved, Daniella had not noticed him. She decided now was as excellent time to perform a system diagnostic on her own suit. The results were shocking – her suit was crippled. Actuators and servos were flashing warning messages faster than she could cycle through them. At least that meant something was still working.

'Mr. Krushell, status of your armour, if you please.'

'Yeah, sure, give me a sec,' he paused. '…not good, Lieutenant – forty percent at most. It's not going very far any time soon.'

'Is everyone else conscious yet?' Daniella called over a low range frequency.

'Yes, but I'm not enjoying it,' Dolly moaned.

'I am,' Kain said, 'Where are we anyway? And what's with the nukes?'

'No idea to both.' Mike said. 'By the way, my armour is trashed. How'd the rest of you fare?'

Slowly the rest of the squad checked in, most with negative reports on the status of their armour Daniella called the roll and found only thirteen troopers had reported in, including her. Notably absent from the list was Alexandra Brodie and TJ Marso. Among those reporting in, four suits were in working order – not nearly acceptable for fighting the Bregan again.

'What do we do now, Lieutenant Klon?' Richard Nevel asked. The trooper managed to retain a functioning suit through the adventure last night.

'Get the Blademasters and the medic into working suits. Everyone else will have to do without,' TJ yelled emerging from the stand of trees near the GCR.

'Captain!' Kain replied with more than obvious relief.

'TJ,' Daniella whispered.

She was so relieved she almost fainted. Somehow she managed to twist out of her suit and ran to embrace him. Her lungs ached on her first breath with the effort to breathe through the crystal dust. She struggled through the resisting air, still making it to him in a couple of minutes. It was not until she had her arms wrapped around him that she realized he was not wearing his suit.

'It's good to see you, Dani,' he smiled and kissed her.

The squad moved to the GCR, trading armour for standard uniforms while Dolly made field repairs on the suits for the three Blademasters and the medic from the other disabled units. Once repaired, the medic began to distribute air filters to the now unarmoured troopers and administer injections to reduce muscle fatigue.

'Has anyone seen Lieutenant Brodie?' TJ asked.

'No sir,' Heather responded while leaning against the side of the GCR.

'Alright then, I want the Fourth Encounter Team to get us ready to travel; the Second Recon will search for all missing personnel,' TJ announced. When he saw a unsteady Sam Cornell trying to stand, he made an amendment, 'those that are able-bodied, at least.' He smiled at Sam as she lowered herself back down to the ground. Sam gratefully returned his smile and gave him a weak salute.

The Second Recon fanned out through the marshy terrain and began their search. Several pieces of metal were found along the path of destruction, nothing larger than a couple of feet across. They found TJ's armour at the edge of the larger grove of trees behind the GCR but nothing else in two hours of searching.

'There's nothing in the fields, sir,' Doug Jackson said, who had insisted on being called *Blender* from the moment he was permanently assigned to the Second Recon.

'Thanks, Doug,' said TJ, 'Ken, Ashley and Paul, come with me. The rest of you get back to the sled and help the others.'

The majority of the squad was now huffing and puffing because of the strain involved in physically pushing through the heavy air, and having to breathe through the unpowered air filters was not helping either. In addition, without the suits to cool them, they were exposed to the above ninety degrees Fahrenheit temperatures, common in the eastern part of the peninsula. They were uncomfortable, to say the least.

'Never thought it got this hot out here and so early in the day,' Ashley moaned, wiping the sweat from her brow.

'Now would be a good time to have a look through the forest here,' TJ stated.

'Second that, big guy,' Ken said, making for the trees.

The foursome walked into the shade of the large leafed trees and began a leisurely search of the thick underbrush. Within this rich vegetation the air became slightly easier to breathe, providing the three troopers not in armour with an energy rush, but it was a placebo effect in reality. With new found energy and cooler temperature, the three unprotected people were able to perform to almost the same capacity as Kain in his armour.

They combed through the three acres of trees and thick ground-hugging underbrush efficiently. Even without the armour, the team finished their sweep in less than half an hour. Their search pattern was in an inward spiral to ensure every square foot was covered.

'Here! Here!' Ashley shouted as they moved into their second last lap. The other three rushed toward her and found her kneeling over a suit of armour. The armour was more damaged than many of the others, probably because of its passage through the trees. Since the rest of the squad had managed to escape injury there was no reason why this occupant would not be in a similar condition, except for the young trees resting across the armour. 'Well, hello, Ale,.' TJ said, slightly out of breath.

A muffled response could be heard from inside the suit. Judging by the lack of movement and the damage to the power pack, he assumed the suit was currently unpowered. TJ and Kain began the process of extracting the Lieutenant while Ashley went back to the squad to retrieve the medic. Dolly stepped back from the rescue operation and finished the sweep of the trees. He made it back moments before the medic came trotting up with Ashley lagging behind, clutching her aching chest.

'How long has your oxygen been out, ma'am?'

'About three hours,' Alex replied as Swain slipped an oxygen mask over her head and cranked up the flow.

'Cap'n,' Ashley puffed, '…supposed to tell you that the GCR is totally fubared.'

'Damn! We're in the middle of nowhere with no transport and maybe five suits of armour,' TJ said trying to clear his head.

'Um… I'm gonna have to…' and Ashley went down.

'Oh great, another one out,' TJ sighed.

'I'll get her back up and running in an hour or so, sir,' Swain said.

'Okay, Swain, take Ash to the sled and Kain take Alex. Dolly and I will salvage what we can from Lieutenant Brodie's suit.'

'Oh gosh, could I?' Kain asked slightly sarcastically.

'Don't get smart, armour boy.'

Once TJ and Ken had struggled back to camp and had rested from their journey, it was time for a strategy session. As best they could guess, it was D400 hours when the group sat around to discuss travel. TJ faced the crumpled remains of the GCR. Daniella was to his right while Alex stayed to his left, nursing a badly bruised shoulder.

'Ladies and gentlemen, we need to leave this place before the Bregan find us,' TJ announced to start the meeting.

'We're not going to get very far,' Richard mumbled.

'First, how bad is the GCR?' TJ asked, ignoring the grumbling.

'The propulsion drive is scrap. We still have power but it doesn't move,' Erik said.

'Okay and how are we all doing?'

'Two with significant injuries, but we're fully mobile,' Swain replied.

'Right. There's our status, everyone. Any ideas?'

'We could get the armoured troopers to drag the rest of us on a gurney of some kind,' Erik proposed.

'And just how are we going to build a gurn – the GCR! It can still hover, right?' Mike interjected.

'Yeah, sure it can,' Ken said excitedly.

'We aren't going to fit inside, the outside's no handholds left,' Erik stood to ensure his objection got heard.

'I think we've got a plan going,' Daniella smiled, turning to Erik and put a hand on his arm, 'We'll figure out seating in a moment.'

'I think so. Mike and Kain need you boys to grab those trees that landed on Lt. Brodie and bring them back. Ann, Swain and Ken, get the GCR ready to clamp onto these poles. The rest of us will finish salvaging the area and ready the sled to carry the other twelve of us.'

'You got it, TJ.' saluted a few of the Second Recon as they hurried to their new duties.

The two armoured Blademasters ran off into the stand of trees on their acquisition mission, while the rest of the group circled the damaged GCR. Ann, Swain and Ken began to work on shaping the armour plates at the front of the sled to attach to a tree Mike and Kain would be bringing shortly.

TJ organized the unarmoured part of the group into two teams, tasked with removing the top off the sled, effectively chopping it in half. Four of the team worked inside the sled slicing apart mouldings and internal framing. Two more worked at the front around Ken's team separating the roof and sides from the windshield frame. The remaining six worked in pairs in a tag team effort, taking turns to slice through the tough side armour

Surprisingly, the operation only took an hour, which was enough time for Mike and Kain to return with two fairly thick tree trunks. Each was approximately fifteen feet long, a foot in diameter and clear of any branches. After turning their prizes over to Dolly, they used their power armour strength to remove and re-position the now-severed roof to the back of the lower half of the vehicle and in an upside down position.

Two techs began to move some of the grav-plates from the bottom of the GCR to the *new* bottom section of the sled. During the transfer, Mike, Kain and Ann held the transplanted section steady while TJ's group welded the two sections together. This had the effect of opening the combat vehicle in a clamshell fashion and increasing the sled's total length by forty percent.

Once Swain and Ken put the finishing touches on the wooden pole at the front of the sled, they went to the back of the new section to repeat the process. It was getting dark when the project was finished but the group voted in favour of heading out without delay. To where was entirely another matter.

'So, where to, chief?' Kain asked the obvious question as he positioned himself on the front left pole.

TJ sat in what used to be the pilot seat, staring at the flickering scanner image. He had spent so much time planning the sled conversion he had not thought of where they would go when it was done.

'We have to go to Fort Saturn. The Bregan must think we're toast. Besides, command will want to know what we've found,' Ann said leaning on the front right pole.

'We can't,' Viper cut in from the sensor seat next to TJ.

'Why not?' Dolly asked from behind her.

'For the same reason we need to get moving, now! Sensors show a group of contacts moving in from the south, west and southeast.' she replied.

'Why can't they leave us alone for one day?' Daniella moaned, behind TJ's seat.

'That settles it then,' TJ said, 'we have to go to New Venus. It should be a couple of days run from here.'

'Sounds just ducky to me,' Kain said signaling the other suits of armour to begin pushing.

'We're going to New Venus,' Daniella announced to the rest of the crew on the sled although her voice did not carry too far through the mask, 'but we've also got some shadows. Keep your eyes and ears open. They'll likely see us before we see them.'

As the sled slowly began to move under the foot power of the four armoured suits, Sam and Drew Webster readied their new beam cannons taken from the GCR's turret. They sat across from each other practically on top of the joint but on the rear half of the sled. Sam watched the left side with a pair of salvaged night goggles while Drew scanned the right with a motion detector.

The sled reached a speed of fifteen miles per hour as it entered the *creased* meadows north of the Cracked Marshes. The creases were folds in the land caused by an impact of a large object, probably the same object that had formed the comb plateau. These creases averaged twelve feet in depth while being only two or three feet wide. The four on foot casually jumped the smaller ones and leaned over the poles as the sled drifted across the larger ones.

'This is kind of fun,' Mike laughed at the right rear as the sled glided over a ten foot crease.

'Yeah, maybe if you're wearing armour,' Richard Nevel said.

Progressing in this fashion, the Recon group out of Fort Saturn hopped and glided their way north at a good pace. It was not until D700 that Viper noticed the group from the south had remained where they had woken the day before and their western *escort* should be coming into visual range by now.

'Heads up, Sam. You should be able to see our glowing green friends soon,' called Viper.

Alexandra and Erik also turned since they too were on the left side and tried to see if they would have to fight any time soon. The three of them were unable to see either the glowing green of the Bregan eyes or the rhythmic pulsing of their wings. Even with her night vision goggles Sam could not make anything out from the passing landscape.

'Are you sure?' Alex asked as she turned back to Viper.

'Yeah, they're less than a mile off.'

'Maybe it's those Landran you folks keep talking about,' Rob Balm mocked.

'They can't move that fast,' Ann stated matter-of-factly.

'We can't say for sure,' TJ said, suddenly suspicious.

'Maybe they have a sled of their own?' Heather asked.

'They don't have … um. I mean, we didn't see any vehicles while we were there,' Ann sputtered.

A loud blast shook the hover barge and sent Erik flying across the sled and out of the right side of the skiff. Obviously the makeshift grav-plates had not fared well. The back half of the skiff crashed into the ground and broke the non-industrial grade weld. The unexpected separation sent both sections tumbling. With no restraints for the riders and no prep time for the pushers, the entire group ended up on the ground.

'I'd say, whoever that is, they have at least one vehicle,' Dolly groaned after everything and everyone had come to a rest.

'Let's get some cover, people,' TJ ordered before running behind the overturned forward half of the sled.

'Roll call!' Daniella shouted.

Slowly, the troopers began to report in, once they had secured cover for themselves. Daniella counted off the troops as they called in – she was short one. She quickly ran through her mental list to find who they had lost in the attack.

'Swain,' she muttered, 'has anyone seen Mercer?'

'The blast took her,' Erik moaned crawling through a crevasse toward the group.

'What's happening?' TJ asked from behind the wreckage.

'All accounted for, but we lost our Medic.' Daniella reported.

'That's just great,' TJ muttered a mite sarcastically. 'Can anyone see who's shooting at us?'

'I ain't puttin' my head up to find out.' Webster replied.

'Get your butts out here!' called an electronically filtered voice.

'Yeah, we'd like to know why you civvies are fluttering around our turf,' said another.

TJ was stunned! These were human military personnel, or at least formerly military, firing on what seemed to be a civilian target. A plan to exploit this misidentification formed in TJ's mind.

'Ann,' he said to the armoured trooper sheltering beside him, 'tell the other suits to stay down, until I give the signal.'

'Yes, sir,' the Blademaster sneered.

TJ was not sure where that tone came from, but now was not the time to go into it. He would try to remember to get back to her later. For now, though, he had to make sure he did not lose any more people. He was getting ready to stand up when another shot pulverized part of the wreckage.

'Whoa! Whoa! We're coming out and we're not armed.' TJ shouted.

Slowly, the unarmoured group emerged with their hands raised. While the armoured troops remained hidden in the crevasses, the *civilians* moved out to the area of mostly flat ground their captors had designated. Once the roundup was complete, they were ordered to their knees with their hands clasped behind their heads.

There was a full squad of these guys and two GCRs. TJ racked his brain for a way out of this mess but every scenario ended badly. There had to be a way! Any plan germinating faltered with the sight of the second vehicle.

*****

CHAPTER XXV
Later Monday, 15 April, 2251

'Fine mess this is,' TJ said, 'If only the Buzz was here.'

Instead of Buzz there were a dozen armoured troopers loading his unarmoured troopers into the two GCRs. He was running out of time – if they could distract these mercenaries, for even a second, his people could clean up.

The squad was half loaded when the first shot hit. Although he had been hoping for this type of event, TJ was momentarily stunned. The mercenaries were obviously well trained and formed a skirmish line facing the source of the shot within seconds. Despite leaving two troopers to guard their prisoners and another slowly getting up from the hit, they made for an impressive sight.

The barking of orders from the mercenary commander only intensified when another of his men was thrown to the ground by a second blast of lethal blue energy. Half a second later, TJ could make out nine figures racing toward the scrimmage line. The three Blademasters figured this was a good sign as any and emerged from their cover with their shimmering blades at the ready. TJ gave a quick nod to Viper and the others being loaded in the other GCR and the fight was on.

Seven mercenaries from the battle line sprang forward on the newcomers while the other five met with the three Blademasters. This left TJ's people free and clear to commandeer the vehicles. Two of the newcomers stayed back from the fight for some reason TJ did not have time to contemplate.

Six of TJ's people advanced into battle while the other four remained inside the sleds and secured them. Although the Blademasters were holding their own, the mercenaries were getting the better of the *rescuers*.

TJ saw a mercenary kick his opponent's blade aside, then kicked the trooper ten feet away. While he was momentarily unopposed, he engaged a comrade's opponent and together they took him down. Now it was seven to six. A shot from one of the two figures standing back temporarily evened the odds but it was only a matter of time. They could do nothing because the fight had moved off and they were having trouble breathing and moving through the atmosphere. As they passed the wreckage of their sled, Dolly noticed their bag of flash balls – now they could play without getting close! He knelt down, lifted the sack and caught TJ's attention.

'Think it'll work?' Dolly asked.

'Never hurts to try,' TJ smiled.

Dolly quickly selected a ball and set the timer to a ten-second delay. He handed the sack to Robert then threw the ball into the fray. It landed and rolled next to a couple of pairs of combatants.

'A bit close to the good guys, don't you think?' Lieutenant Brodie asked.

'You may be right,' Dolly replied.

Froomp! The ball detonated, sending the two mercenaries flying back toward TJ's group, and the two rescuers, who had already been beaten to the ground, tumbling several feet. Because of the differences in dispersion methods, the two rescuers were able to rejoin the fighting a few seconds later. TJ dispatched Robert and Rich to guard the two shaken mercenaries who had landed nearby.

The fighting stopped only a few minutes later with four mercenaries taken prisoner by the rescuing squad and with the loss of one more rescuer. The rest of the mercenaries had quickly been taken care of by the Blademasters, leaving them with two prisoners as well as the two being watched by TJ's two unarmoured troopers.

Only when the commander of the rescue force gave the signal did the two observers approach the battlefield. TJ noticed one was obviously the heavy weapons expert for the group since the steaming beam cannon was usually not carried by anyone else. The other person wore a civilian-styled armour suit. After a few brief words with the squad, the civilian and the commander approached TJ and his people.

'I am Colonel Cheryl Fredrickson assigned to the former Miles Research Station. This is Dr. Miles Romaluk, director of the same facility.' said the commander.

'Captain Trevor James Marso, Second Recon, Fort Saturn,' TJ saluted.

'What are you doing out here with only three suits of armour, Captain?' asked the doctor.

'We got caught in that tornado a couple of days ago and the rest of our suits banged up pretty good.'

'Okay – what were you doing out here in the first place?' Col. Fredrickson asked.

'We came out to reconnoitre the station. We knew it was probably under control of the Bregan and we weren't sure how badly. They jumped us east of the station and drove us north, and then the tornado came,' TJ responded, beginning to sweat under the questioning.

'Captain!' hollered Viper from one of the GCRs.

'What is it, Ash?' TJ asked.

'Someone just transmitted a long-range signal!'

Terror or something similar filled the faces of both the armoured and unarmoured personnel of the Second Recon and Fourth Encounter Troop. They knew now the Bregan knew where they were and would be on them soon. The troop out of Miles Research Station showed only confusion at the others' change of emotion.

'What's the matter, Captain?' Dr. Romaluk asked.

TJ did not answer; he was too busy searching the faces of the armoured troopers for anyone who looked even partially guilty. His eyes fell on Ann last, and though she showed no guilt, he studied her anyway. A second later she lit up her shimmer blade and went into a battle-ready stance.

TJ's reflexes kicked in and he readied himself for a fight with the Blademaster. He knew he might need to run so he checked around quickly for possible escape routes. When he saw the real threat things made a lot more sense. The two mercenaries who had been thrown by the flash ball were now on their feet, standing over the crumpled bodies of TJ's men.

The two waited a moment before charging the group of officers with their blades ready to cut them down. These two must have called for reinforcements, at least that made sense to TJ.

The next thing any of them knew, the entire squad was sprawled out on the ground with scratches and/or dents from flying debris. TJ looked back to see what happened to the mercenaries without finding a trace. What he did see was the two badly beaten up bodies of his troopers. Around them was a massive field of debris. Looking up, he saw steam rising from the barrels of the two GCR's cannons.

'Everyone okay?' Daniella called over the loud speaker, primarily concerned about TJ, although she did care whether the others were hurt or not.

'Call in!' Dolly boomed running up to TJ's side.

Daniella could see TJ shaking his head and moving around unencumbered. He was okay, she thought, breathing a sigh of relief.

'Captain! May I see you over here for a moment?' asked the colonel as she picked herself up some fifteen feet from where she had been before the attack.

TJ made his way to the Colonel's side and provided the best salute he could. He was unsteady from the blast and the breathing assistance drugs wearing off, but he still managed to stand at attention. Somehow, in spite of what he had been through, he managed to keep a decent appearance. He was quite handsome, thought Cheryl, but now was not the time for thoughts along that line.

'Captain, it appears that you've lost control of your situation here,' she said mildly.

'Ma'am, things rarely go according to plan in combat,' he replied.

'Sometimes true,' she said thoughtfully, 'but this lapse of yours lasted longer than the combat and cost the lives of two of your people.'

'Without armour, anyone would have been taken by those two.' he said, indicating the blast area that used to contain the two mercenaries.

'Exactly my point, Captain,' she snapped, then lowered she voice again. 'You should have reassigned guard duties to armoured personnel the instant it was possible. You may retain control of your people for now, but you'll direct any tactical or strategic thoughts through me personally from now on. Understood?'

'But, Colonel…' TJ began to protest.

'I could remove command functions altogether, Captain,' she cut off his protest.

'Yes, ma'am,' TJ responded, 'Understood.'

'Good! Now, salvage what you can and get those GCRs loaded. I want to be out of here by first light.'

'Excuse me, Colonel, but I think we should head out sooner than that.'

'Why's that?'

'I believe the mercenary commander sent a transmission before we could stop him,' TJ started.

'We can handle the reinforcements, Captain.' she said confidently.

'Honestly, Colonel, it's not them concerning me – it's the Bregan. They hear our conversations and can track us down with only one transmitted word.'

'Are you sure?' she was concerned now.

'One hundred percent, ma'am.'

'Then we had best make ourselves scarce. Everyone, listen up!' she commanded. 'It has come to my attention that we may be attacked by the Bregan shortly. We need to pack up and beeline it for New Venus. One hour, folks!'

The group of twenty humans raced into action before she was finished. The thought of facing those creatures in battle and in their condition was decidedly unsettling. Save for the light from the GCRs, the night was as pitch black as ever there could be since the moon Deimos had set yesterday and was not due to return for another day and a half and Phobos was not set to rise for another three hours, the troopers moved as though it were full light.

Most of the unarmoured troopers formed a line from the destroyed GCR to the nearest functional sled to transfer the salvage carried by the vehicle. Four uniformed soldiers manned the controls of the GCRs in case they were attacked before the rest were finished.

The troops in the environment suits scoured the battlefield collecting weapons and armour components. She did help with the task at first, Colonel Fredrickson spending most of her time with Dr. Romaluk or paying special attention to Captain Marso. He was going to be interesting to have under her.

Daniella took a moment to glance over at her newest CO and caught a glimpse of something she did not like. The Colonel was actually scoping out her man! Higher rank or no, that sort of behaviour did not sit well with Daniella and she made a mental note to keep an eye on her new rival. Apparently, it was not enough to have Alexandra after TJ.

'Everything easily salvageable has been loaded, ma'am,' Lieutenant Linda Cherwinski saluted.

'All unprotected personnel have boarded the vehicles,' Kain added.

'Wonderful,' she smiled, 'let's head out. Danielle, keep an eye on the radar. I don't want any surprises on this trip.'

'It's *Daniella*,' she muttered, 'Yes, ma'am!'

The squad was on the move a good fifteen minutes before the Colonel's deadline. They moved along at their best possible speed, which brought them to the northern edge of the Cracked Marshes by dawn. By this time the members of the Second Recon and the Fourth Encounter Troop were tired – troopers inside the GCR were beginning to nod off. It had been a long time since their last rest stop. Although the armoured troopers were better off, they too began to show signs of fatigue.

Weeks of warfare had begun to hone the skills of the veterans but the sleeping and eating habits were still those of a lightly trained civilian militia. TJ found himself in the gunner's chair when Daniella had noticed the previous occupant's deteriorating condition. He could not even hold his head up and had to be rolled out of the way so TJ could take over.

'This is ridiculous!' TJ muttered only loud enough for Daniella to hear.

'The rest of the group is out too,' she said, motioning to the back.

TJ looked over his shoulder to the group of three sleeping men and women. 'And I don't think it will be a matter of an hour or so before we start snoozing too.'

'I don't think she'll let us stop, TJ,' she yawned.

'We'll see about that.' He switched the communications button to external, short-range broadcast. 'Colonel Fredrickson, my people are passing out in here. We need to stop for...'

'Keep this channel clear, Captain! Your people will be fine,' she fired back.

'Told ya,' Daniella smiled weakly.

'Oh crap!' TJ said as he watched the lead GCR begin a slow drift to the right. The armoured troopers were taken by surprise and a couple of them barely got clear before the vehicle raced past where they had been walking.

In the lead GCR, Alexandra struggled to get Drew out of the pilot seat so she could take over the sled, she was obviously having difficulty. Halfway out of the seat, Drew's unconscious hand knocked the throttle control and sent the GCR racing ahead. One final pull freed the sleeping heavy weapons specialist, landing partially on top of Alex. She could hear the Colonel barking orders. She could not answer with the two hundred pound man pinning her to the floor.

A brief and awkward struggle gave her the superior position on top of the limp trooper and allowed her to scramble into the pilot's seat. She slipped on the headphones to the ranting of the Colonel. By the time she glided the GCR to a halt, the main group was a mile away.

'What the hell in going on in there?' the Colonel yelled.

'My pilot passed out, Colonel, just like TJ's people,' she replied.

'Hold your position, Lieutenant, until I get there.'

TJ could feel an *I told ya so* building inside him but he knew he would catch hell if he let it out, especially with the mood she was in. From his seat in the second vehicle, TJ could see into the lead GCR. The Colonel and one of her henchmen were roughly reorganizing the sleeping troopers so they fitted and one of her people could pilot. They closed the door just as the *contact alert* went on.

'Where are they?' Cheryl asked.

'South-south-east, about twenty miles and closing fast!' Daniella replied, the sleep leaving her considerably faster than it had come on.

'Mercenaries again?' asked Cheryl's HWS Yvonne Bailey, almost pleading.

'If it is, then we have at least thirty hover vehicles bearing down,' Cpl. Skye replied from the lead GCR.

'Okay, I want the Bregan then,' she laughed dryly.

In answer to her request, the southern sky became an eerie hue of pulsating green light, quickly dissolving into tiny specks, flashing green on both sides. The Bregan had found them.

'Form the line!' Cheryl ordered, 'Bailey, you may fire when ready.'

Even before the first shot was fired the Bregan ceased their flapping and went to ground. The tall carpet of still darkened grass completely covered them from the squad's enhanced vision.

'I suggest we move ma'am. They aren't...' TJ started.

'Let's back it up, people! They don't move fast on the ground,' Colonel Fredrickson interrupted.

'I'm sure I don't like her now,' Daniella mumbled.

'We can discuss it later, Dani. For now, do as she says.'

The squad began to move north once again, this time at a much slower pace. While the GCRs slid along with their turrets facing the last location of the Bregan force, the troopers outside walked backwards as fast as they could. Each one of them expected an attack any second. The group continued as they were for a mile or so with no noticeable advancement from the Bregan.

'Okay, I'm nervous,' Kain admitted when no attack came.

'Time to run,' Cheryl said as she spun around.

'Right behind you, ma'am,' Mike added, relieved beyond belief!

The squad picked up the pace, accelerating to fifteen mph in an instant in hopes of leaving the Bregan behind. Those hopes were only partially realized as a dozen creatures jumped to the pursuit, now half a mile behind them. The proximity to the group was surprising. It appeared as though the ground travel had slowed the Bregan very little, at least they were still behind the group.

The GCRs began firing to cover the armoured

troopers as they regrouped. The blinding green light streamed from the plasma cannons of the vehicles, hitting nothing. The creatures had either become too quick for the beam cannons or the gunners were too slow to hit them.

'Track back and forth from the right,' called TJ to Viper in the other GCR turret, 'Wait for my shot to fire five degrees left.'

'Copy that,' she responded stifling a yawn.

TJ fired his shot directly where the target Bregan should have been but was not. A split second later, Ashley let off her shot as ordered, and without much aim still managed to clip the target three inches in from the right shoulder. The remains of the Bregan spiraled into the ground.

A cheer went up from the humans the instant the shot hit. The congratulations were short-lived when Cpl. Skye called out that another group of Bregan was approaching from the west. Efforts to reposition the scrimmage line to cover the second group as well faltered when a third group began its approach from the east.

'I'm not having fun anymore,' Dolly said.

With the two GCRs side-by-side and facing north, the eight armoured combat troopers formed a semi-circle with the vehicles' backside as a backdrop. In mere moments forty Bregan surrounded the group. They stayed clear of blade range while still managing to block all routes out of the battlefield.

'Colonel, we need a plan here!' Erik said urgently as he continuously shifted his position inside the mercenary GCR in an effort to keep the Bregan in his field of vision.

'I'm thinking, Corporal!' snapped Cheryl aloud, eyeing three of the nearest attackers. 'What the hell am I going to do?' she muttered to herself.

A half dozen Bregan swept forward from the group before she could formulate a plan. Contrary to their usual attack methods, they ran across the opening to close the gap. The pop-up manoeuvre was certainly not an animal-style attack. It was apparent from the combat stance most of the troopers from the Colonel's squad still thought of the Bregan as mere animals.

Though the Bregan tactic was brilliant, the implementation was short-sighted. The initial ground approach had prevented the vehicle cannons from wiping out the attackers, but their leap above the ill-prepared troopers put them point blank in the cannon's sights. Even though the average Bregan soldier knew how to evade these cumbersome weapons, these six individuals suffered from a brief bout of tunnel vision and consequently did not dodge the cannons.

Though their reflexes were slowed from a lack of sleep, TJ and Viper managed to get their shots off at a perfect angle. TJ's beam cut through the legs of one of the advance soldiers and tore into another of them. Viper's shot missed its mark entirely, her sweeping action to try to compensate diced two in the barricade force.

If there was one, the Bregan's plan fell into disarray. The southern blockade faltered with the gargoyles rolling or flying away from the shots. The two side groups shuffled around to strengthen the weakened section so their siege could not be broken. The northern unit became visibly nervous at being essentially abandoned.

'Viper! Fire north! Maybe we'll be able to get out of here!' Daniella called.

TJ overheard the suggestion and swiveled around to add his firepower to the opportunity now presenting itself. The northern Bregan seemed confident the battle was on the other side of the vehicle and did not notice the turrets spin around. The combined shots ripped into the smallest group and made smaller bits and a carpet of green blood out of four unfortunate creatures. The two vehicles surged ahead when the sides of the circle flowed in to close the newly formed gap.

Meanwhile, when the partially stricken Bregan fell out of formation from his five fellow attackers, he landed in front of the human defensive line. Over anxious to begin the fight, Lieutenant Linda Cherwinski dove on the creature and sliced at it with her blade. She was completely oblivious to the other five Bregan now descended from their deadly height.

'Lovely!' shouted Cheryl's Blademaster, Chris Onaga.

Linda's reaction was fast enough only to block the first attack. She turned the lead Bregan's scythe slash aside with enough force to throw the big creature to the ground. Only one other gargoyle was in range to attack her as she fought off their assault. Its blade swing came as Cherwinski finished her block. The emerald blade ripped a line across her right shoulder, disabling her entire arm.

The third gargoyle to attack had landed out of swing range, positioning itself between her and the staggered scrimmage line. As Linda was still recoiling from the gash in her shoulder, it dove at her, caught her full in the torso and rolled to the ground. Somehow it managed to regain its footing, while at the same time, maintaining its solid grip on Linda.

Realizing it would soon have to fight more humans, the Bregan flung the five hundred pounds of flesh and flex-steel that was Linda off toward the gargoyle army. Contrary to past tactics employed by the Bregan, they subdued the injured trooper then carried her away from the battlefield.

The already faltering scrimmage line was stunned to see the abduction and momentarily lost what control they had in their formation. What would become of her? That was the silent question running through everyone's mind when the Bregan attacked again.

The armoured squad would have been smashed if the back doors of the GCRs had not sprung open and released the nine unarmoured soldiers. The troopers had been sleeping until the turrets began to fire. Unanimously, they sprang into action and were out the door with their blades buzzing.

The Bregan did score a couple of good hits in before the humans rallied. Fortunately for the Bregan, the couple of shots making contact did so against Master Sergeant Susan Damian, Cheryl's other Blademaster. The damage inflicted on Susan's armour seemed to concentrate in the area of her filtration unit. The damage seemed insignificant for the time being so she ignored the warning alarms and rejoined the attack.

The new surge of human troopers actually startled the Bregan, causing some chaos. With blades swinging in pure defence, the gargoyles fell back and into the arc of the beam cannons. In their confusion, the Bregan's dodging ability that had served them so well initially, failed them.

Blasts from both vehicles and Yvonne Bailey's portable unit began tearing into the gargoyles and sparked a full-scale retreat. The two GCRs started running a drive-by action, catching a few gargoyles as they tried to flee.

'Come back and fight, like a *whatever-you-are*!' shouted Doug Jackson as he chased an injured Bregan.

The Bregan was hurt so badly it could not get away, Doug was too badly injured to finish it off. Yvonne saw this scene and decided to end it. She drew bead on the gargoyle and fired, striking it squarely in the lower back.

The reserve power unit on the armour torso protecting the Bregan was fully charged. While the resulting explosion was limited, it was big enough to finish the creature. Unfortunately, it was also large enough to send shrapnel through the pursuing trooper. Without the environmental armour, the damage to his body was severe. Yvonne was silent as she stood, looking through her scope at the convulsing body of the dying human trooper.

'Medic!' Doug wailed softly, even as TJ's GCR pulled

alongside. He died before he was loaded on the stretcher.

As the squad regrouped and began to take inventory, TJ noticed Susan wobbling toward him, unsteadily. Not overly concerned with the condition of the Blademaster at this point, he walked over and nudged her to get her attention. 'Too much to drink?' he asked, teasingly.

When she turned to face him, he saw her eyes were rolling back and foam oozing from her gaping jaw. In the reflection on the whites of her eyes he could see a warning light was flashing from her heads-up display.

'Shit!' he said loudly enough to attract attention.

Acting quickly, he lit his blade and brought it up and across Susan's visor. Startled shouts rose from the converging crowd as a two-inch sliver was shaved off her helmet. The force of the hit sent Susan onto her back.

Two of the big, armoured troopers grabbed TJ and disarmed him while Cheryl and Dolly knelt to attend to Susan. She was out like a light and a noxious odour wafted up from the inside of her helmet. Before he could back off, the odour overtook Ken and he rolled to the ground next to the trooper.

Even Cheryl's armour began to give warning messages as the filtration system in her suit began to filter the pungent odour. Cheryl looked to the side of Susan's neck and saw a gash next to the purifying filter. The filter was a chemical agent reacting with the atmosphere and made it breathable. The chemical itself was toxic, a situation of two bad things together equaling good.

The gash at the neck link had ruptured at the storage tank and leaked its contents into the air supply at a considerably higher rate than could be handled. It was likely this poisoning would put the Blademaster in a coma.

'How many swings did Captain Marso take?' Cheryl asked the crowd.

'Just one, *fttt* up the visor,' Erik said sweeping his hand up in front of his face.

'Yes, Colonel, I saw him walk over. He said something, then pow!' Dr. Romaluk agreed. A chorus of agreements rumbled through the semi-circle of troopers. Colonel Fredrickson ordered the troopers to release TJ and congratulated him on his quick thinking.

'I doubt she'll be any good to anybody again, though,' TJ said.

'We'll see, Captain,' the Colonel replied, lightly patting him on the shoulder.

The troop loaded its cargo of dead and wounded and set out for New Venus during the next hour. Even though the trip would be long, they had nowhere else to go. They stopped early that night to give everyone extra rest.

The troop traveled the rest of the way to New Venus in relative silence. They did not see another single soul, save for the herd of oddly shaped deer they saw the second day. Their blood red fur and purple antlers were likely due to environmental contamination since they did not come over on the transport from Earth in that condition. It was day four of this long march when they arrived at New Venus.

Although Colonel Fredrickson had assured Yvonne no charges would be laid in the death of Doug Jackson, she resigned her commission that night.

*****

CHAPTER XXVI
Thursday, 18 April, 2251

The squad arrived at New Venus in the late hours, in bad shape. Cpl. Jackson's body was sent to the morgue while Susan and the unarmoured troopers spent the night in the environmental exposure recovery unit of the Medi-Centre. Most of the patients would not be released for at least another eighteen hours.

Colonel Fredrickson was not happy to be stuck in the town for that long; at least she could use the time to organize for her return to Miles Research Station. Twelve hours later, she was most of the way through a marathon effort to try to convince Ms. Bailey to return to active duty.

'Come on, Yvonne,' Cheryl pleaded, 'it was an accident.'

'Don't tell me *it could happen to anyone*,' she sneered.

'That's right. No one could have known that pack was charged. Besides, what are the chances that it would explode when the shot hit it?'

'I know all the arguments, Colonel, but it doesn't make it easier.'

Yvonne turned her back on the senior officer and peered out the window of her temporary quarters. She had been thinking all night about what had happened in the field. Images of the explosion raced through her mind to the point she could not function.

'I'd like to be alone, please,' she said quietly.

'Fine, but I'll be back,' Cheryl agreed before leaving the small apartment.

Dr. Romaluk was busy in the first laboratory he had

seen in two months. He was happy to be useful again. Running through the fields with ego-maniacal infantry, slicing up every moving thing was not his idea of a good time.

He spent the first half of the day after arriving familiarizing himself with the city's main military lab. It was sub-standard compared to his lab at MRS but there was some potential. He had managed to bring his data with him and was anxious to finish his current project.

It was N400, on May first when he set to work. 'This will definitely change the balance of power,' he laughed enthusiastically.

TJ woke in the Recovery Unit, still tired and thought through the events from the past week. He had lost control at some point, and he needed to be in control of his people again for their sake if nothing else. The senior officers did not know what to do with the troops and had got them killed.

'TJ,' Paul called as he entered the room.

'Yeah?' he said, snapping back to the present.

'Colonel wants everyone to assemble at the south training compound first thing tomorrow,' he said casually.

'Sweet!' TJ replied sarcastically. 'Paul, get the others together in the lobby at N5 tonight.'

'Got some kinda scheme going, chief?'

'We have some plans to make. I'm sure the Colonel wants to go back and we need to be ready,' TJ replied sombrely.

'You got it.' he paused. 'How're you feeling by the way?'

'Still a little tired but healed. How's everyone else recovering?'

'Coming along nicely, except that Blademaster. She's still in a coma. Doctors don't think she's ever coming out if it.'

'And Ken…?'

'He's awake but the docs don't want him stressing himself.'

'Okay, see if he thinks he can make it. If not, I'll fill him in later,' TJ said, 'I think I'll get a few more winks now.'

'Cool, chief, take it easy. I'll see you tonight.' Paul saluted and strolled out.

TJ rolled over and sighed. He was still the leader of his squad and his people might actually survive if he could think of a way to keep command decisions away from certain brass. The Colonel did not seem quite right in the head. For now, he had to get a plan that would prevent more deaths.

*****

'TJ,' a soft voice called to him. TJ slowly opened his eyes. The world around him was different. No solid lines could be seen on anything and the colours were faded. He was no longer in the recovery unit at New Venus, but on the Comb Plateau. He could only see the area he was in and nothing below but somehow he knew it was the plateau. This had to be a dream, he thought.

'TJ,' the voice came again.

It seemed to take forever for him to turn around but it was worth it. The vision standing a short distance behind him was the only thing in this world in focus. A shining halo, like the sun itself, surrounded the woman as she seemed to hover a foot off the blurry ground. She stood proud and tall, casting a beautiful light on TJ.

'Amanda?' he asked, more to himself than aloud.

'TJ, trust only what you know. Trust your instincts,' the woman said softly.

'What?' TJ's head started to hurt. 'Amanda, wait!'

'You know the answer to your question.'

Either TJ or the woman began to move away from the other. TJ tried to close the gap making no progress. 'What do you want?' he cried.

The image changed from the beautiful woman to a crouching Bregan. Its eyes flared to life in an instant but emitted a powerful red light instead of the usual green glow. With its gaze firmly locked on TJ, it rose up then sprang toward him. TJ braced himself, no longer sure it was a dream he was in.

As the creature was about to hit him, it shouted at him, 'Go from here!'

TJ bolted out of bed and rolled to the ground. The light outside was fading but it still illuminated the room enough for him to be sure there was no menacing Bregan, ready to pounce on him. He slowly stood and leaned back on the end board of the bed. He glanced at the bedside clock and saw it read D700.

'I really need a vacation!' he moaned, rubbing his neck.

'Not for a long time, Captain,' came a formal reply from the doorway.

'Good evening, Colonel,' he said without looking up.

'Aren't you going to dress?' she asked.

TJ looked down and noticed he was only wearing his briefs. She had already seen what he had in terms of physique and he was still groggy from his bizarre dream. Not worth it, he decided.

'Too late, I think,' he said before turning to face his superior officer. 'How may I help you tonight?'

'Just wanted to, ahh,' she stuttered, 'to, um, let you know to meet in the southern training compound in the morning.'

'Yeah, okay. Paul already told me. I'll be there.'

'Of course, yes. Well, goodnight, then,' she said.

As she left, TJ could have sworn she was blushing – another oddity from an odd woman. He would have to think on that point later, one of a growing list, for now he still had plans to make. He grabbed his robe and quickly threw it around himself before heading to the nurse's station. He acquired a journal pad and a hot tea from the overly muscled nurse observing the patients' monitors then raced back to his room.

Upon returning to his room, he found Daniella sitting on the edge of his bed. She looked tired but happy to see him nonetheless. They embraced without saying a word, simply holding each other for a while, enjoying the comforting touch of a warm body.

'I missed you,' she said, leaning back.

'Me too,' he replied.

She smiled. 'Paul says we're going to have a meeting before the meeting.'

'Yeah, I feel a war brewing. We need to be prepared beyond what the Colonel might have in mind.'

'You're not going to disobey her orders are you?'

'I'm going to preserve the lives of the people under my command the best way I know how. For all I know, Cheryl may have it all under control but I want to be sure.'

'Okay,' she said soothingly, 'You know we all trust you.'

'I know, that's why I have to do this.'

'Okay,' she said, patting him lightly on the chest, 'Mind if I doze off in here? I kinda like your company.'

'By all means. Take the bed; I have some thoughts to sort through apparently.' They shared one lingering kiss before she climbed into bed and he went to his chair beside it. Daniella kept TJ in sight while she fell into a pleasant sleep. TJ kept at his journal pad, tapping away at the electric blue line trying to figure out tactics and strategies for the days to come. They stayed that way until Paul arrived to collect them hours later.

After rousing Daniella and quickly dressing, TJ led the other two down to the lobby where the remnants of the Second Recon and the Fourth Encounter Team were waiting. He quickly checked with everyone to make sure they were at one hundred percent. Ken managed to attend even though he was still in the low nineties.

'It's good to see all of you,' TJ said, 'I didn't think there was that many of us left.'

'What's the plan, TJ?' Ashley asked.

All eyes turned to him and he could see the sparkle of loyalty in their eyes. 'Now, I'm sure the Colonel is a good person but she doesn't have the experience that we do. I fear that this may get us killed.'

'What do you mean?' Ann asked, showing more concern than the situation called for. There was more than loyalty in her eyes but TJ, once again, did not have time to delve into that subject, plus one to that damn list.

'I'm almost positive that she'll request our unit for her next command. Combine that with the fact that the High Command will likely order an offensive against the Bregan if they can get a transmission through and you can see the trouble we're in.'

'So, what do we do?' Ken asked as he shifted his weight to get comfortable.

'I've spent the last few hours trying to devise a suitable plan that wouldn't cause too much disruption in whatever force goes out there but…'

'Nothing, right?' Ann sneered. 'Well, that's just great!'

Watching her storm off down the hall, TJ noticed the scientist that had been with Colonel Fredrickson was shuffling toward them. What was his name again, TJ thought, Dr. Ramblebeau? Whatever it was, he was in a hurry and heading straight for them.

When the Doctor saw TJ had noticed him, he began to wave his arms around in a *come here* motion. His shouts echoed throughout the corridor and stopped Ann for a moment. 'Captain Marso!'

'Yes, doctor.' TJ responded, smiling in his amusement at this funny little man.

'You absolutely must come with me!'

'Calm down, doctor. What's the trouble?'

'Trouble,' Dr. Romaluk was honestly perplexed.

'There's no trouble. No, no, no, I have something for you! Come, I must show you.'

'Okay doctor. Look everyone; be extra careful tomorrow and the days to come. Get some sleep and I'll see you at the meeting. I'll go over the details I've worked out after the Colonel has her say.'

'Yes, yes! Talk tomorrow. Come, Captain, you are going to love this!'

Daniella gave a quick wave and a silent goodbye before she turned toward the stairs. TJ could feel the eyes of the Second Recon on him as he followed Dr. What's-his-name to who-knows-where.

'A little strange, don't you think?' Paul asked to the troopers around him.

'It's a strange world, Paul,' said Ken.

'Only since we left Fort Grey,' Ashley muttered.

'Well, I don't know about you folks but I'm curious as to what's so damned important. I'm going to keep an eye on the big guy,' Erik said.

'He'll be fine,' Ken said.

Erik ignored the assurances and quietly moved off on the trail of his CO. The others shook their heads, leaving him to his spy games.

Dr. Romaluk led TJ to a hastily assembled lab in the medical centre's basement. The security on the room was intense. The two fully armoured troopers standing by the door were what truly perked TJ's curiosity.

'Do you really think whatever you've got in there is worth this many resources?' TJ asked.

'Oh, definitely!' the excited man replied. 'Worth more if I could get them!'

TJ turned to watch the Doctor engage the locks and noticed a head duck behind the nurse's counter. He made a move to notify the troopers but the door sealed first. His training in the Recon forces allowed him to identify the spy.

'That had to be Erik,' he muttered.

'What was that?'

'Nothing. What did you want me to see, Doc?'

Miles Romaluk shuffled to the steel closet in the far corner and opened the doors. Inside the closet stood a black suit of environmental armour, though it had noticeably less armour than the troopers usually wore.

'So? It's a civilian protection suit,' TJ pointed out.

'No! Can't you see, it's a military suit?'

'I'm sorry, perhaps I'm too tired. Why don't you just explain what it is, and save us a whole lot of time?'

'Clearly,' he sneered at his game being cut short, 'It's an environment suit that's phase-armour equipped.'

'And what is phase armour?' TJ's interest began to perk up a bit.

'How you became a Captain, I'll never know.'

'You and me both. The armour?'

'The armour plates have inside them phase alignment modifiers and a phase detection program in the sensor suite. The program can easily identify the phase alignment of any matter, or the frequency of any energy attack. That information is fed into the modifier in the plates, which then re-aligns the suit and its occupant to match.'

'Okay. I know a little bit about this stuff. You're saying any attack on this suit will pass right through?'

'Yes, but just one attack at a time,' his pride faded a tad.

'That's incredible!'

'What is?' Erik asked.

The two men in the room spun in the direction of his voice. Shock mixed with anger could be seen on both their faces. Erik was halfway out of the ventilation shaft with as many pearly whites showing as his face allowed.

'What the hell are you doing here, Corporal?' TJ said as calmly as he could.

'Who are you? You know him? I should get the guards!'

'Just a minute now,' said TJ, 'First I need to know why this young man felt it necessary to follow us.'

'We're all just grunts, sir. No one wants to show us anything, especially, not with as much enthusiasm as that guy has. I got curious and wanted to make sure my favourite captain was safe.'

'Cut the crap, Erik!'

'Sorry, sir.'

Dr. Romaluk shifted his weight from one foot to the other, clearly undecided as to whether he should call for help or trust these barbarians. It was unsettling how they seemed to pop up everywhere. They do serve as a means to achieve his ends, irritating as they are.

'I think we've found one volunteer to test your suit, doctor,' TJ said, 'How many more do you have?'

'T-two others,' he said before he regained his composure, 'but I must keep one to further refine the design, just in case.'

'Wonderful,' TJ smiled. 'I'll use the other one.'

'Captain, what did I volunteer for?'

*****

CHAPTER XXVII
Friday, 1 May, 2251

The southern compound of New Venus was likely the highest concentration of people on the planet. All of the troopers that had stumbled into the city the day before were gathered in front of a central raised platform. Three additional squads of personnel were assembled around them. Thousands of other base and city residents ringed around the compound to celebrate. As the next mission was not going to be a secret, the command staff did not mind.

Everyone in the inner compound snapped to attention when the base command staff arrived on the platform exactly at D200. After a rather lengthy speech of welcome by the base commander the meeting was turned over to Colonel Fredrickson. She outlined at great length what TJ had feared. These four squads were to return to Miles Research Station and remove the Bregan threat.

The three other squads were still cheering when the gathering was dismissed, eager to go to war. The Colonel had asked for TJ's command to remain behind. They were not cheering or eager for a return engagement with the Bregan.

'Colonel, I respectfully request that my command be allowed to have at least rest a few days before they're sent back out there,' TJ requested.

'This is war, Captain!' snapped Commander Tremont of New Venus. 'You and your people have to do your duty for their race and follow the chain of command!' He wheeled around and marched away so the special briefing could start. Cheryl and TJ watched as the Commander finished his dramatic exit. A moment of silence followed before anyone spoke.

'I know you guys are tired,' Cheryl said, 'but this is really important. There was another attack on Fort Saturn last night.'

'We aren't just tired, lady. We're not even healed,' Erik cut in.

'Erik, stay out of this,' Daniella said.

'Yeah, shut up, dude,' Drew Webster added.

'What's happening with us?' TJ asked.

'We need people with experience as squad leaders, and that means you people. I've been authorized to give field commissions to promote Sam Cornwall and Mike McMillan to Lieutenants and Ann Huston to Warrant Officer.' She put away her list. 'TJ and I will lead a five-squad force to engage the enemy at MRS.'

'Five squads? I only counted a total of four squads in the compound here.' Ken said.

'The four squads here were the shock units,' said Cheryl. 'The fifth is an armour division that happened to be here on exercises from Port Mars. They will return from training tonight so we leave tomorrow.'

'Armour division!' a few of the troopers bristled at the notion. Coming from the small Fort Grey base, as well as an out-of-the-way city like Fort Saturn, few of them had ever seen the most powerful weapon in mankind's arsenal – the hover tank.

'That's right. Now, this group will be splitting up for the most part,' she continued. 'You'll find your assignments posted at the quartermaster's depot. You will form up in your new squads at D1 hours tomorrow.'

'Yes, ma'am,' they saluted.

'Oh, man, we're toast!' Brent Skye moaned.

'What do you mean?' Erik asked.

Like the rest of the squad, Brent and Erik were packing the few personal items they were allowed to take with them. They were not accustomed to military protocol yet nor were they mentality prepared like the other veteran troopers were.

'The only reason they even send out foot soldiers with tanks is so the bad guys have something other than the precious tank to shoot at.'

'That's an insane idea and you know it!'

'I'm telling you man, we're all gonna get slaughtered! It's a historical fact.' he said, shaking his head.

'I stand corrected, you're insane.'

'You just wait. I'm right – you'll see.'

'Okay,' Erik decided to end the conversation there. He was getting scared, though. What good would tanks do when the GCR turrets could not hit anything? Brent was right; this was not a good sign.

The formation time came for the squads on a dim morning thanks to some heavy cloud cover. They assembled in front of the main entrance for New Venus. Cheryl moved through the group and conducted a brief inspection. She paused for an equally brief conversation with the armour division commander, Lieutenant Charles Brower, before moving to the head of the column of vehicles and troopers.

The column consisted of six hover tanks located at the rear, eight GCRs and two armoured BRATs. When Cheryl gave the signal to move out the troopers jumped into their assigned rides. The hum of the repeller engines in the main corridor rattled anything not secured down.

The last time this many vehicles were in one spot and combat ready was during the last battle of the pirate wars in year 8 NEC – New Earth Calendar. The fight, not surprisingly, was over quickly, resulting in the loss of only one of the original vehicles. Those who could remember that far back were hoping this fight would end at least as well.

TJ and Daniella's units were packed into two GCRs and a BRAT. Sam Cornwall had been promoted to Lieutenant and her new unit was packed into only two GCRs. The Fourth Encounter Team under Lieutenant Brodie was jammed into one GCR and the remaining BRAT. Mike McMillan, now also a Lieutenant, commanded the fourth squad which occupied the last three GCRs, along with the Colonel.

Once clear of the walls of the city, the formation shifted into a combat ready position. The two BRATs lined up at the centre, while the GCRs flanked them, four to a side. The tanks drifted into a hexagon pattern around the lighter vehicles.

'We're going to make camp south of the Caminar forest,' Cheryl called to the unit commanders on a tight frequency. 'I want a fresh group of people for the fight.'

'Isn't that a little close to the location?' Brower asked.

'We'll be fine. The Bregan don't use long range patrols.'

'Maybe we should scout ahead so we aren't surprised when we get there,' TJ said falling back on his recon experience.

'Good idea. Fourth Encounter, you'll head out after a perimeter has been established.'

'Yes, Ma'am,' Brodie replied.

'Excuse me, Colonel, but the Second Recon unit is a better choice for the task,' Daniella said.

'I have another assignment for your people, Lieutenant.'

'Oh, goody!' Dolly mumbled.

'Ma'am, I really do feel that I have to point out that the Second Recon is much better suited for a reconnaissance,' TJ said after a few awkward seconds.

'Their skills will be used elsewhere, Captain! I want radio silence from now until we reach camp.'

Cheryl wanted to tell her command team what the

plan was, especially TJ, but she had her orders, too. Worrying about who liked who was a game for those who did not need to lead. Despite that, she wanted TJ to like her. All she needed was some time alone with him without Daniella around. Fortunately, her plan just happened to separate the two lovebirds.

'What the hell is going on, TJ?' Erik asked.

'I have no idea. This is probably the first time I've gone into a fight with no plan. Everything I thought of is out the window once those tanks glided in'

'Oh, there's a plan,' Dolly said, 'but we're just players today.'

'The plan is, or part of it is, Cheryl wants TJ for herself and with Daniella off with the Second Recon, she'll have him,' said a huddled trooper from the back of the GCR.

'That's nuts! Who are you?' TJ asked.

'It's me, sir, Yvonne Bailey.'

'I thought you resigned your commission,' Dolly said before TJ could open his mouth.

'Yeah, well, I figured if I can help out a little, then maybe that would make up for what happened,' she said.

'What makes you think the Colonel has the hots for the big guy here?' Erik asked.

'She told me. On the way back from our run-in with those mercenaries or pirates or whatever those guys were.'

'I find it hard to believe that she would let her personal feelings interfere with the operation of the unit.' TJ said.

'You don't know her like I do, Captain. She'll do whatever it takes to get what she wants personally and professionally.'

'Even sacrifice an entire squad?' Dolly asked.

'Whatever it takes,' Yvonne replied coldly.

Before the camp had even been established on a small

84

rise above the near black marsh, the Fourth Encounter Team set out to have a look at the Miles Research Station. The Twenty-first Encounter squad led by McMillan and Lieutenant Corwall's Eighth Scrimmage Unit set up the camp and basic automatic defenses including beam cannon turrets while Colonel Fredrickson chatted with TJ and the Second Recon Squad.

The Seventh armoured division made their camp on the top of a second rise to the east of the main camp. For reasons unclear to the majority of the foot troopers, the *tankers* preferred to stay out of sight unless they were escorting or called into action.

'At first light tomorrow, I want the Second Recon to sweep around the east portion of the Cracked Marshes and engage MRS from the north-east, while we attack from the west,' Cheryl said.

'Yes, ma'am', Daniella agreed.

'And no vehicles. They'll give you away.'

'What!' TJ and Daniella said in unison. TJ continued, 'They could be slaughtered without heavy support!'

'Tone it down, Marso,' Cheryl snapped. 'We'll be making plenty of noise at their front door to keep them busy.'

The rest of the meeting progressed with considerably less emotion, although Cheryl did have to field several more questions than usual. There was something about these militia folk a professional military officer did not like. At the end, the squad dispersed through the camp, conversing about everything except the suicidal mission.

TJ sat with Daniella for a while and talked idly about his new suit and various rumours involving other squads. An hour after nightfall came TJ left the small camp fire and went to have a chat with Cheryl. He was determined to find the underlying cause of this mystery.

'TJ, come in. I was hoping you'd come to see me,' she smiled.

'I bet,' he said, 'Listen, I have to clear something up.'

'What is it?' Cheryl leaned back on an comfortable couch, showing off her full figure.

For extended operations such as this one, officers above the rank of lieutenant were given pressure tents to use as planning rooms, medical facilities or resting chambers. Environmental controls were not required inside the walls because of the airlock-equipped entranceway. Cheryl was making full use of her turf and relaxing without her suit on. Instead, she wore her civilian clothing, specially selected for this part of her plan.

Although TJ was not wearing his helmet, he was still wearing his phase armour in the late day suns. Watching her lounge in that inflatable chair, he would be lying if he said she was not appealing but he had the perfect girl, and he was not there to admire his superior officer.

'I heard that you're ordering Daniella away for personal reasons,' TJ said.

'I have nothing against her. What possible reason could I have?' she said, getting to her feet.

'You want me and she's competition.'

She laughed. 'My, you are full of yourself, aren't you? But I won't deny that I find you attractive, Captain.' She moved closer to him.

'So it's true.'

She wrapped her arms around his neck and kissed him. 'Partly, I suppose.'

'How can you do that? These are good people you're sending off to die!'

'We all may be about to die, TJ, my dear. So why can't we give ourselves as much pleasure as possible?' She kissed him again.

'Now? When we're about to go into battle? Now, you put your moves on me?'

'You're saying I should have done this earlier?' she smiled.

'Damn!' he said before he stormed into the airlock, then out into the camp.

'So much fun,' she smiled to herself for a few minutes, not moving an inch. Then she wrapped her arms around herself and slumped back into her chair, still smiling.

*****

CHAPTER XXVIII
Later Friday, 1 May, 2251

The Fourth Encounter Team moved swiftly across the flowing fields of grass and flowers south of the camp. Their two GCRs crossed into the Cracked Marshes shortly after Sol set beyond the horizon. Brodie figured the squad would be in visual range of the station by Bane-set.

'Stay sharp... we're in enemy territory,' Drew Webster said over the comm. channel, narrow band.

'Anything on radar yet?' Alexandra asked.

'Nothing for miles, Lieutenant, but these cracks are pretty deep,' Sergeant Drunan said.

'Understood. Distance to disembarkation?'

'One mile,' Ann Huston replied.

'Squad ready!' Alex ordered.

'Ready!' They all replied in sync.

The gophers stopped with a floating, one hundred and eighty degree skid bringing the tail end of the vehicles to face the distant station. The rear doors flew open even before the end of the skid, allowing the troopers to spill out onto a large section of unmarked ground. They stayed low and moved off in groups of four.

They were not more than three hundred yards from the waiting vehicles when a scrambled signal was sent on long distance channels. The eerily familiar screech of the Bregan followed in the same instant. Shocked, the troopers froze and waited.

'Get back to the GCRs now!' Alex yelled, 'We've been compromised!'

'Damn!' Drew muttered.

Several Bregan appeared on the horizon, moving fast. The brilliant green pulsing of their wings could be seen clearly in the last remnants of light from Bane. The troopers would be pounced on before they could get back to the vehicles.

'Unit Two, stay with me. The rest of you get back to the camp,' Alex ordered.

'Yes, Ma'am.' Ann smiled.

'You'll be killed,' Heather Campbell started.

'So we won't. Now go!'

The two retreating units made it to the GCRs as the Bregan descended on Brodie and her three companions. Their escape went unchallenged.

'They know we're here,' TJ said as he entered Colonel Fredrickson's pressure tent.

'What?'

'The Fourth just came back minus four. Apparently, someone sent a long-range message just as they were headed out. Lt. Brodie, Sgt. Brunan and Pvt. Jackson and Bestt stayed behind so that the rest could get away.'

'Well that's just great!' she said, pacing. 'I don't suppose we're lucky enough to have had the sender killed out there.'

'I don't believe so.'

'We'll have to step up the operation. Get your people ready and tell Lieutenant Brower to have his tanks in formation within the hour. Looks like our rendezvous will have to wait, Captain.' She smiled after that last bit.

'Ma'am,' TJ saluted, with little emotion showing.

'You may go, and send Lieutenant Klon in when she has a moment.'

'Yes, ma'am.'

At N700 the Second Recon went out on its assignment. They would be at a constant march for the next five hours. TJ was not happy with the plan, he was going to have to make some changes of his own. Half an hour before muster, he gathered the Eighth Skirmish squad around his Second Recon.

'I have some special orders for you people,' he said in a whisper.

'Anything you need, TJ. We're with you.' said Sam.

'This is going to sound stupid but I'm pretty sure it will work. I want your vehicles to be the lead.'

'No way, man!' Corporal Craig Zimmerman moaned.

'This strictly a volunteer action. Those who wish to fight in the main group report to Huston.'

Five of Sam's troopers left the circle and marched off into the darkness to the Fourth Encounter's temporary CO. The remaining troopers all professed loyalty to TJ's method of combat before he continued.

'We're going to go on a rescue mission for the Second Recon. Our gophers will plough through to their location. I have a hunch the Bregan won't be ready for an assault of that sort,' he smiled.

'Are you sure this will work?' Blademaster Chris Onaga asked.

'No, but I'm not letting twelve good men and women get slaughtered because of the romantic feelings of one person,' TJ said.

'Sir?'

'Never mind. Stay with the formation until you get my signal, then we'll break for the Second Recon's position.'

'Yes, sir,' they saluted.

At N730 the entire division was ready. The camp was neatly stowed and the hover tanks were waiting patiently in a ring around the convoy of smaller vehicles as before.

'Colonel! We have company,' Brower called on narrow band before the convoy had even started moving.

'How'd they find us?' she replied.

'Not Bregan, Ma'am, at least I don't think so. They're approaching from the west south-west.'

'Power weapons and get those blades ready,' she ordered.

Image-enhancing equipment showed several creatures approaching with elegant movement. Despite the pitch black of the night, they approached the convoy on a direct course. 'Landran, Colonel,' TJ said putting his imaging gear away.

'What?' she looked at him, 'How'd they get here?'

'More importantly, how'd they know where we are?' Sam asked.

'Stand down,' ordered Cheryl, 'Let's see what they want.'

'I've got a bad feeling about this,' TJ muttered.

The human army only had to wait a few minutes before the first of the Landran came into speaking distance. TJ recognized the leader of the force in a flash as Kraston. The mystery seemed to deepen though it was of some relief this was not a different group of Landran.

'Well met again, Lieutenant Marso.' Kraston bowed.

'Captain now, Kraston,' TJ returned the bow.

'Excellent! Rewards to the true warrior,' he smiled.

'Thank you.'

'I hate to interrupt this reunion but may I ask what brings you to our camp?' Cheryl asked more angry than shocked at the sight of another alien.

'This must be Major Harte's beautiful successor – a pleasure, Lady. Sorry to hear about the loss of a fine officer.'

'Marshal Kraston, Colonel Fredrickson,' Ann said.

'Marshal?' TJ asked.

'We have come to offer assistance for your mission,' Kraston smiled.

'That would be great. Thank you, Marshal Kraston,' Cheryl said.

'What do you know of our mission?' TJ muttered, his

comment unheard by the two Commanders.

They walked off to the center of the human formation to revise tactics while TJ contemplated his next move. Something in that exchange bothered him. He decided to double-check with the Eight Skirmish squad to be sure his plan would still be followed.

By N800 hours the combined force of humans and Landran made its first step toward their joint destiny. Troopers and serpent riflemen interacted easily during the march as had been done back in the Landran city. It seemed long ago now. TJ kept his unit close behind the lead tank and away from the Landran. He was uncomfortable with the way those riflemen stayed one step behind the troopers.

Heavily armed troopers stood at every entrance to the primary hangar of the Port Mars military air base. Unarmoured techs scurried from offices to aircraft to strange piles and inventory rooms then back again. Many of the techs were too busy to notice him as he walked among them but the troopers snapped to attention as he passed them. To the techs seeing him, he was nothing more than another pilot but the troopers saw a Captain of an air wing.

'Sir, a communication for you,' puffed a young private from the comm. station as he came running across the steel compound at full speed.

'Thank you, private,' said the Captain, 'just a moment.'

The private had started back to his post when he was caught in mid-stride. The Captain quickly scanned over the message for any hidden codes or trickery.

'Signal my wing. We go airborne in one hour!'
'Yes, sir.'

The Captain moved to the flight room to get ready. Within a minute, the first of his unit began to file in.

The activity at the airfield was generally slower around N900 hours but today twelve Raven Heavy Fighters were in line for lift off. Each fighter had a crew of three – a pilot, a weapons officer and a systems engineer and everyone was on-board, ready to go.

These classified aerospace fighters had three class-3 beam cannons, one fixed forward and two turret-mounted, one up and one down. The weapons officer controlled the turrets and the dual missile launchers while the pilot used the forward fixed cannon. The Ravens were as yet untested in combat situations, though the firing range tests were promising. The pilots and crew scored highest grades of all candidates – the best of the best. The engineer of the first fighter handed the Captain a systems report before they boarded. The Captain read it over then signaled the other pilots and climbed in his own fighter.

'Everyone set?' he asked through his helmet communications system.

'Affirmative,' replied the other eleven pilots in sequence.

'Let's go save our friends.' he smiled.

He slipped his shiny black helmet visor down and hit the throttle controls to begin his ascent. The visor was linked to the ship's computer system remotely and gave him all the info he needed to fly the sleek machine. Also, in the down position, it exposed his call sign stenciled in white across the forehead of the helmet. The call sign read, *Buzz*.

*****

CHAPTER XXIX
Saturday, 2 May, 2251

An uncommon dawn rose on Eden Peninsula with the blinding light of Sol slipping through the cloud cover and grey haze. The human and Landran army was in position north west of the Miles Research Station – they had been there for more than an hour. By all calculations, the Second Recon would be in attack range in a half hour.

'Are we ready, Captain?' Cheryl asked.

'Yes, Ma'am. All units report green status,' TJ replied while looking behind him inside the GCR to his crew for confirmation of their status and understanding. All members nodded, they knew what was coming.

'Then, I believe, it's time that we made our intentions known!'

'For a home world!' Kraston cried.

Kraston's war cry sent a chill down TJ's spine. Something in those words spelled doom for Man. He knew it was too late and all he could do would be to save his friends and as many other troopers as he could. He hoped Cheryl had the same sense of the situation as he did. Battle ready troopers clung to the sides of the GCRs and the combat BRATs, ready to jump into battle once the combat zone was reached.

At first, it seemed the Bregan had left MRS to the humans but as TJ's three GCRs raced ahead the wave of gargoyles finally hit. They were still within the protection range of the massive hover tanks, a fact the Bregan were apparently unaware of or they simply did not know about the tanks. The highest creatures soared a hundred feet above the ground creating almost a full curtain of pulsing green. The Bregan force blocked out the sun with thousands of individual soldiers racing toward the

Human/Landran army. The green glow of their wings replaced the comforting yellow light of Sol.

TJ was signaling a turn around when the Bregan entered the optimum fire range of the tanks. Pieces of the living tidal wave were smashed to atoms as the tanks' class-8 plasma pulse cannons began to fire what looked like flaming red rain. Seconds later the smaller vehicle's beam cannons joined the fight with their blue lightning.

The Bregan counter-offensives faltered, if there had been any thought of that, receding before TJ's vehicle. As he passed the target combat zone another assault started – this time a verbal barrage from Colonel Fredrickson.

'Where the hell are you going?' came the first call.

'I have to rescue my people.'

'You have a duty here, Captain!'

'Ma'am, I'm going to save my friends and there's little you can say to stop me!'

A pulse cannon shot rocked TJ's sled, not a direct hit though close enough to send a message. He began to sweat as he continued his charge. He brought up an aft display and saw the Bregan converge on the Colonel's army. Cheryl would not chase him but the gargoyles were now in hot pursuit.

Bregan tried furiously to rip the troopers off the three GCRs. Blades met with scythes in showers of released plasma and crystal but the troopers hung on. Beam cannons ripped through the Bregan not paying attention around the charging vehicles. Shot after shot hissed from the turrets yet there was no noticeable reduction in numbers. In less than fifteen minutes of fighting, TJ noticed some of the Bregan were not facing him yet were not running either.

'Looks like we've found our people!'

The troopers detached from the now slow-moving sleds and raced into the fray ahead of them. Bregan howled and scattered in confusion as the Eighth Skirmish fought their way to the Second Recon. Blades were buried into the backs of some of the massive creatures while other Bregan soared into the air to avoid the onslaught.

'Sir, I have a problem here,' called the pilot of the GCR to the left of TJ.

'What is it, private?' he had to raise his voice above the almost constant hum of the cannon.

'I'm registering a weapon's lock on me.'

'Are you sure?'

'Yes sir. It says…' The transmission ended as a smoke trail burst from the mass of Bregan soldiers and detonated the vehicle.

'Missiles!' Warrant Officer Effort cried from the other GCR.

'Get out! Everyone get away from the sleds. We're not equipped to repel missile fire!' TJ cried and punched the eject button.

His sled blew apart a second later as another missile came streaking in. TJ's gunner had not cleared the blast area in time and was thrown into the main body of the Bregan army. A fate similar to that of Linda, days before, took the gunner as he was carried away by the enemy.

From his sky-chair, TJ saw the other GCR crew dive out the rear hatch before a third blurry missile fragmented the last sled. Apparently the Bregan were not concerned with their own casualties. As the explosions of the vehicles tore into their numbers, they still kept the pressure on. Clearly their intent was an attrition battle but it would not be won this day if TJ had a say in the matter.

TJ caught movement out of the corner of his eye as his ejection seat reached its highest point. An airborne gargoyle slashed at him before he could react and since his phase armour was still reeling from the blast, the hit once again removed his shoulder deflector plate. A miscalculation on the part of the Bregan soldier meant it was moving too fast and sent it crashing into TJ before further dueling could occur. The two plummeted to the ground and landed with a powerful thump. TJ, having been on top at the point of impact, was winded while the Bregan beneath was taken out of commission indefinitely.

'Son of a...' he wheezed and got to his feet with a wobble.

Without giving it much thought, TJ activated a flash ball from his pack and slow-pitched it into a rather shocked looking Bregan force. The ball impacted squarely on the lead creature's chest and went off. The blast caved in its chest and threw it into the crowd of other creatures while the already wobbly TJ was tossed up and over the Bregan and Second Recon skirmish line.

'Morning, Captain,' Erik said as he defended himself from his opponent.

TJ could only gasp for breath and look around him at the fight. Breathing was his first concern for the moment. He saw most of the Second Recon and what was left of the Eighth Scrimmage fighting in a tight cluster. Their thundering footsteps would normally be the most noticeable thing for miles but the screeching of the Bregan and the violent swordplay drowned out any signs of dominance.

'You okay, TJ?' Kain asked after dispatching his opponent in a shower of bloody green rain.

'Yeah,' he said after a moment, 'everyone, get ready to use the flash balls. We have to get back to the others.'

'It's nice to see you again,' Daniella said as she helped him to his feet. He hugged her as best he could before moving toward the edge of the trooper cluster nearest the direction they had come from. He was prepping his last flash ball when a shrieking Bregan descended on him. The emerald green of a personal beam cannon lit up the creature and shot it back into the waves of soldiers. He spun around and saw Sam give him quick wave before turning back to her own fight.

Without pausing to aim, TJ spun and lobbed the ball into the pressing crowd. After a brief pause, as in the movies, the ball detonated in its fantastic blue light and blew a hole in the crowd. Before the Bregan army could compensate, the human squads rushed into the opening.

In his eagerness to join the charge, one soldier dropped his guard too soon. His opponent attacked as he turned his back. The forearm scythe ripped apart the trooper's arm and knocked him down. The other gargoyle joined the attacker and jumped the fallen human. The rest of the force had to continue. To stop and help would seal their fate but Kain took a swipe at the group as he passed. The slash ripped open the Bregan's neck and killed it instantly.

'Flash ball!' Daniella cried once they had regrouped.

As the systematic use of the balls continued the human force pushed on with relative ease. Occasionally, a zealous warrior would jump on the group but would be quickly dealt with, barely slowing down their progress.

With little effort, the troop crossed half the distance across the raging battlefield to the main group. A quick inventory at the halfway mark revealed they were out of flash balls. The Bregan had begun to avoid the expected blast of the grenades and actually opened a gap ahead of the squad. Because of this, the troopers gained another hundred meters before the Bregan could adjust their tactics.

'We'll have to fight the rest of the way!' TJ said.

'It's going to get nasty, chief,' said Dolly.

'No cannons!' Sam called as she drew her blade and stepped over her steaming and powerless beam cannon.

'Last push?' Erik asked.

'Yep,' TJ said then he and the others let out a primal battle scream.

As if on cue, the mass of Bregan ahead of them was torn apart in a rapid series of explosions. The ground shook as if a building had fallen. The Bregan shrieked in surprise and anger, their cry drowned out by the sound of two Ravens ripping the sky overhead.

'Those must be Terran,' Viper said.

'I didn't know we had jet fighters,' Erik turned to watch the planes arc away.

'Technically not jets. You see in order to be a jet they would have…' Dolly started.

'Shut up you geek,' Ashley laughed

'Or they're bad guys but just lousy shots,' Chris Onaga said ignoring the routine beside him.

'Somewhat cheery thought. Thanks!' Sam said.

The attack had little effect on the Bregan save for wiping out thirty or forty warriors while the remaining army still had a few tricks up their sleeves. The Ravens were fast, though still unable to evade a missile strike from the ground. The lead fighter banked to avoid a missile but was clipped by a second. It was apparently a minor hit, enough to send it toward base with a smoke trail.

The wingman seemed to be unaware of the deadly projectiles sent to meet it. Two missiles struck it amidships and split the hull at two angles. The crew ejected but the wind was carrying them into the main body of the Bregan force. A few gargoyles even raced into the sky to meet the parachuting humans. directing their catches toward MRS.

Past the clearing made by the Ravens, TJ could see large explosions and more Ravens in the sky. The air was too hazy to actually make out what was happening but the blasts were bright enough to mirror off the sleek hulls.

'Something doesn't look right,' Kain said without glancing away from the surrounding Bregan soldiers for more than a second.

'What do you mean?' Yvonne shouted.

The din of battle around them had increased significantly once the Bregan had re-grouped. The squad was being herded closer together by a vicious assault.

'If those fighters were truly ours, they'd be doing strafing runs. Those guys are essentially dog fighting by the looks of it.'

'Doesn't matter if they were just doing an air show,' TJ grunted under a powerful hit from his opponent. A blaze of green plasma fire lingered over a scratch on one of his shoulder plates where the scythe had glanced. 'We can't stay here any longer.'

'We'll never make it!' shouted a trooper from across the cluster.

'Watch what you're doing,' Sam ordered.

Too late the trooper saw a second Bregan dive at her from the crowd. She deflected the first two swipes, got flustered and began swinging wildly before she was quickly taken down. The gap from the fallen trooper let in a surge of Bregan taking several other troopers by surprise. The two troopers next to the gap tried valiantly to close the opening and were torn to ribbons for their effort. Sadly, they were the second officer and third in command of the Eighth Skirmish.

'That's it, we're leaving now!' TJ ordered. 'Blademasters take point and get us out of here!'

Two more troopers were taken down before the retreat started. Kain and Chris led the way with Jen Ferny of the Second Recon and Wallace Smith of the Eighth Skirmish flanking them. The rest of the remaining troopers followed close behind. They made remarkable progress through the mob. The squad was moving so fast the Blademasters were using their blades defensively for the most part and knocking down anything in the way with fists and kicks. More Bregan were incapacitated by trampling them than by the crystal shimmer blades.

The sounds of combat ahead of them steadily became louder despite the furious shrieking in their wake. An alley appeared in front of the charging humans as dozens of Bregan took to the air on either side.

The thought of a trap occurred too late when a solitary Bregan stood in their path. It held a device none of them had ever seen before. The plume of smoke announced what was about to happen, giving little time to adjust for it. The missile corkscrewed slightly and blasted past Kain, who got knocked over by the sonic wave, and careened into Jen. The blast was powerful enough to incinerate her and the trooper behind her and knock the rest of them down. There was no time for the airborne Bregan to attack as missiles from the Ravens cleared large holes in the sky. Green rain was added to the grey haze in the air, painting the area as a lush green field instead of a killing ground. Ground-based Bregan were thwarted in their offensives by a hail of energy bolts from behind their scrimmage line facing TJ's group.

'The Landran have made it here!' Chris said getting to his feet.

'Ann's with them,' Viper added.

'Hi!' Ann smiled as she walked up to Chris and lopped off his head!

'Motherfu… Get ready, the Bregan aren't the only ones here to kill us!' TJ said as he readied himself for the attack.

The barrage of bolt fire continued ahead of them but now it was directed at the squad of humans. Ann lunged for TJ. She was, instead, intercepted by Kain. He wore the biggest smile anyone had ever seen on his face.

'Long time coming,' Ann said.

'An expected pleasure, bitch!'

It quickly became impossible to identify whose blade was whose as the two Blademasters engaged in fierce combat. Their blades blurred together with only a rapid series of sparks to indicate they had even made contact. Occasionally, a bolt would rocket toward Kain and would be deflected way. One or both of the combatants did not want outside interference.

The rest of the squad was beaten by the Landran rifles as were any Bregan warriors foolish enough to try and take advantage of the fray. Several hits were taken but none were getting through the armour. TJ and Erik began to engage the closer riflemen when they realized the phase armour they were wearing was working as intended.

Stunned Landran began to retreat from the two advancing troopers. Shock clearly showed on their reptilian faces as the energy bolts sailed through the two with no effect at all. A couple of brown guardsmen turned tail and ran from the human squad but were cut down by the nearby Bregan.

TJ and Erik had engaged the first Landran that stayed to fight and had managed to boot them to the ground when their opponents and several other dragons were blasted from the planet. Their suits registered a massive energy surge and reported an imminent shut-down of the phase shield.

Two beaten up hover tanks drifted into view along with the remains of the human army. The surrounding Bregan and Landran were scared off by the show of force and began to engage each other as the mortal enemies they seemed to be.

Dusk began to settle around the last of the human squads. With Bane casting its blue glow above them the tanks continued to fire as hugs were exchanged below them. TJ noticed Kain standing a few feet off and called to him.

'She's gone, TJ,' he said.

'Who?'

'Ann. That blast from the tanks knocked us over and by the time I got up she was running to join her friends.'

'I have a feeling we'll see her again,' TJ put his arm around his friend, 'but for now we have to leave.'

'TJ,' Cheryl called.

'Oh, no!' he said hanging his head.

'I want to thank you for going after your friends,' she said.

'Ma'am?'

'It's true I wasn't happy about you taking off like that. However, you created so much havoc that, in retrospect you probably saved all our hides.'

'I don't understand,' Daniella said, stepping into the conversation.

'Ploughing into the Bregan army split their forces into three groups and prevented a full-scale assault. Also, I think it confused the Landran and delayed their attack.'

'Ann also took several of those dragon creatures on a hunt for you as well, chief,' Drew said.

'Yeah, figures. She never did like you,' Erik said with a smile.

'That weakened them a whole bunch, too,' Cheryl said. 'You've got a good man there, Lieutenant Klon.'

'Thank you, Colonel.'

'Colonel, they're coming back!' Conture said from the nearest hover tank.

'Okay, people, let's move! MRS is a lost cause – let them have it,' Cheryl said.

The squads picked themselves up and ran off to the west. Their intention was to sweep around and go back to New Venus, it was a sound plan. The group of Bregan following them from the northeast had other plans for them.

The chase lasted until nightfall. Two hours after dark, when they were sure they were not being followed any more, the humans made camp and posted a guard. Those allowed to go to sleep had no trouble doing so after the day's events. No fire crackled for their comfort since they were still in open ground, the Bregan would have been able to see any spark in this moonless night.

Erik was looking for a place to sleep when he came upon an injured trooper lying on the ground next to one of the tanks. He recognized him as Brent Skye. He knelt beside him, 'Hey, bud.'

'Hey man,' replied the trooper, 'You made it.'

'Some didn't. We lost Lieutenant Cornwall about thirty minutes before you guys saved us.'

'Sorry. They also got Lieutenant McMillan and Lieutenant Brower in the first attack,' Brent grimaced.

'That's a lot of officers. You hit bad?' Erik asked.

'Yeah. They got me stabilized and say I should be alright if we can get to New Venus. Hey, I told you we're just fodder!'

'We'll make it,' Erik said.

'Hope so,' said Corporal Skye before the sedatives took him again.

Erik stretched out beside his friend and waited for sleep. It was not long before he was dreaming of the Earth in the textbooks his dad had made him read – filled with only one sentient life form, Man.

*****

CHAPTER XXX
Monday, 3 May, 2251

Dawn of Sol came to the camp site at the same time as the Bregan assault. The only glitch in the sneak attack was that the victims were not there. The shadows they saw with their keen eyesight were in reality cleverly sculpted figures of mud and grass. The detonation of several pounds of high explosives confirmed that they had been duped.

The gunner of the hover tank sitting a mile to the west switched off his image-enhancing equipment and signaled to the pilot and smiled to himself. Quiet repeller engines pushed the massive vehicles down the small hill to rejoin the two remaining squads of troopers and the second tank.

'Operation complete, Colonel. Estimates place the toll at sixteen casualties,' Warrant Officer Conture said.

'Well done,' she said.

'I don't believe that we'll make it back to New Venus,' TJ said.

'I agree. That's why we're going to Port Mars by way of Fort Saturn.'

'Bad idea,' said a trooper in black armour that had until now stayed to the rear of the formation.

'Who are you?' Cheryl asked calmly.

Some of the troopers tensed noticeably when they realized there were actually six of these troopers among them. A few even readied their blades, though if asked at that moment, none save the Blademasters would have said they were confident fighting these people.

'Captain Zedluk, Colonel. At your service,' he bowed theatrically.

The members of the Fort Grey squads let out cheers of delight and ran to Buzz for a group hug. All of the black armoured soldiers were snared up in the surging swarm of Fort Grey troopers for the massive hug. Troopers from Fort Saturn and New Venus originally jumped at the sudden outburst and show of affection.

'Captain Marso, explain!' Cheryl said in a not quite calm fashion.

'Sorry, Colonel. This is my former Warrant Officer from Fort Grey. He got re-assigned after the battle of Fort Saturn. Buzz, this is Colonel Cheryl Fredrickson, my commanding officer.'

'A pleasure, Colonel.' Buzz saluted.

'Captain,' she returned the salute. 'I suppose I have you to thank for keeping Mr. Marso alive long enough to come into my command.'

'Doesn't sound like there was a *thank you* in there,' he smiled.

She smiled back politely, 'What were you saying about Fort Saturn?'

'Oh, right. Fort Saturn fell to the Landran two days ago.'

'Damn!' Dolly said.

'How do you know that, Buzz?' Daniella asked.

'We got the report at Port Mars not long after. The message came in with a bunch of refugees,' Buzz replied, his smile gone.

'So that's north out, east out and now south out. Too bad the plateau is to the west,' Brent said.

'Guess that means we're headed up and over,' Viper said.

'That is the only route left,' Cheryl said. 'You were the crews of those flying fighters we saw I take it? Can you take any of my people with you, Captain?'

Buzz said, 'Sorry no. The Raven has a max crew space of three.'

'We have an injured trooper here. He needs to get to a medical facility,' Daniella said.

'Let me see what I can do.'

'Thanks Buzz.'

Buzz took one of his troopers aside while TJ looked on with a mix of pride and sadness. It was unlikely that the two of them would ever be in the same command again. TJ noticed the tank commander staring at the glowing plateau in the distance.

'What's up, Luke?' he asked.

Luke looked down, then back at the plateau. 'We can't do it.'

'Do what?'

'We won't be able to get the tanks up the cliff. Not unless there's a thirty degree slope to the top. We'll have to scuttle them,' he said with a touch of sadness in his voice.

Buzz came back to the group while his men went to the injured trooper. He was smiling, as always. 'My Lieutenant will take your man back, Colonel. And I'll give you a loaner until you folks get to Port Mars.'

'Thank you. Is your trooper good with a blade, just in case?' she asked.

'I'd say I'm pretty good,' he laughed.

TJ cracked up after Kain quickly shot in, 'You always were a loser, Buzz!'

Buzz pushed the Blademaster into the side of the tank, 'I guess I should have seen that one coming. Being in charge means you aren't razed too often, unless you're TJ.'

TJ stopped laughing for a moment but started again when Buzz started laughing too. Soon the airmen had carted off Brent and the ground bound troop was headed west. Even though it had only been a week since they parted ways, Buzz and the Second Recon talked and reminisced as if he had been gone for years. Sol knows they had been through a lifetime of crap in that time.

By the time Bane showed itself to the Eden Peninsula the human army was at the base of the Comb Plateau. The troopers milled around getting climbing equipment from the tanks ready while the senior officers planned the ascent and what was to happen to the hover tanks left behind.

Buzz, TJ and, Daniella surveyed the towering cliff rising one thousand feet into the air at the lowest point. Because the plateau's formation had occurred literally overnight, the sides were practically sheer and rose at a ninety degree angle at the majority of its surfaces. Climbing technology combined with the armour suits enabled the troopers to climb with a minimal amount of effort, all they needed was handholds. There was always the danger of equipment failure.

'Should take us an hour or so to get to the top,' Buzz said.

'Do we have enough personal climbing repellers?' Daniella asked.

'Yeah, seems that these tanks are nicely equipped,' Buzz said.

'These cliffs look awful!' TJ said.

Buzz replied, 'Not that bad.'

'There are too many cracks. I'm thinking we'll need ropes between everyone in case there's wind at the higher altitudes.'

'I doubt we have enough.' Daniella waved Kain over.

'Buzz, get yourself outfitted. We'll be right there,' TJ said.

'What's up, guys?' asked Kain.

'How much rope do we have?' Daniella asked.

'A couple hundred feet, why?'

'That won't be enough,' TJ said shaking his head.

He turned to look back up the cliff face and the jagged spires that formed the few outcroppings there were. Movement out of the corner of his eye drew his attention to the approaching Colonel and her four companions.

'Are we ready to move out?' Cheryl asked.

'Yeah! What's happening with the tanks?'

'We've set them on auto for a tour of the countryside on the way to New Terra. We'll set a short range message so that someone there will know to collect them. We'll also set the security system so that none of our friends try to take them before they get to the destination,' Luke said.

'Let's get you folks hooked up and then we'll go,' Daniella said.

TJ was the last one to attach a climbing repeller once he had checked the rest of the pack then the entire group started up. They had attached a rope between the twenty-three troopers in groups of three and one pair. The climbing repellers were simply anti-gravity generators, negating ninety percent or more of the weight of the power suit and wearer. Since the troopers trained regularly with the suits on, this massive reduction in weight combined with the power-assist features of the armour allowed the troopers to crawl up the cliff with ease. Even though it was easy to climb, a misstep still meant death.

The ascent was almost like play, with troopers bounding up the side of the red stone plateau like vertically oriented squirrels. The first of the squad crested the top of the bluff with joy and was hit by a projectile of some kind! The hit did not kill Freeman but it did knock him off the edge. He swung out on the rope that was tethered to Sergeant Roberts and Colonel. Fredrickson. His arc brought him hard into the cliff face and damaged the climbing repeller.

The gyro that allowed the repeller drive to counteract gravity locked into an *up* position. Unfortunately, this drove the corporal down. The force was too great for the other two repellers. Terrance Roberts grunted as his grip on the rocks faltered.

'TJ!' Cheryl yelled when her engine cut out from the strain. TJ reached for her but she was too far. The screams of the three troopers echoed through the radio, seemingly forever, before an eerie silence abruptly followed.

'What the hell was that?' Kain asked.

'Don't know,' TJ said, looking down a moment longer, 'but we can't stay here. Detach, get ready to fight!'

As a group, the twenty troopers pulled themselves up and activated their blades. They sliced through the rope like cutting water. Once up they were set upon by a flock of large *birds*. Claws and beaks scraped at the armour, doing little damage. These creatures seemed more interested in flying around than actually attacking which left a gap close to the ground.

'Crawl out, keep low,' TJ ordered.

The squad quickly crawled for a hundred yards before the attackers yielded. Once the birds retreated, TJ stood to get a better look at the creatures that had taken three of their comrades.

'Those ain't birds, chief,' Erik said.

The birds had four wings and six foot-long tails. They eyed the troopers suspiciously from their nests. The leading edges of their wings and their beaks had a shimmer around them like these animals were generating magnetic fields to enable flight.

'They were just protecting their kids,' Viper said.

'We should nuke 'em,' Mason Smith said.

'That wouldn't matter to them or us. Absolutely no effect to this whole situation,' Dolly said.

'This whole planet is getting weird,' Buzz said, studying the birds.

'Let's go! We've got a long walk to Port Mars,' TJ said.

*****

CHAPTER XXXI
Late Monday, 3 May, 2251

TJ wanted to give those bird things plenty of space after they had killed three troopers in his squad. Sure, those animals were defending their young, that did not mean they did not have a dark side inclined to attack. With the squad's camp ten miles away it was unlikely that there would be a repeat occurrence.

Many of the troopers remaining after the disaster in the valley below sat silently in the camp surrounded by sporadic clumps of dry and drying grass mixed into the broken red and dark brown rock thrown up during the creation of the Comb Plateau. The landscape was the perfect mirror to their morale. If TJ's feelings were a match for his squad's, he was sure they were sick of watching friends and comrades in arms die.

'Hey TJ,' Buzz waved at him from the north side of the camp.

TJ stood and walked over to the Air Captain through small clusters of troopers who looked as though sitting where they were, in their dusty, silver armour would be a nice way to spend their last days. For many, yesterday had been their first battle of this war and their first loss. A one hundred percent failure rate was hard to take. The remnants of TJ's original squad had a better record so they were in a better mood. He could still remember that first day, seeming ages past, when the First Recon out of Fort Grey had been slaughtered. It was only a couple of weeks ago now but the looks on all these troopers' faces brought it all back.

'Yeah Buzz?' he said as he melted into the formation of dulled armour and only slightly brighter faces.

'We've been going over our supply situation and it's

not good,' Buzz scrolled across his data pad before handing it over to TJ with a sigh.

'What do you mean?' he asked before looking at the shimmering numbers on the pad.

'Fuel is low but we might be able to make it to Port Mars, if all we do is walk,' Ken cut in before Buzz could answer.

'Food is critical so we'll have to ration,' Daniella added right after.

'And water will not last, no matter what we do,' Ashley said with a hint of something TJ could barely make out and never expected from Viper, resignation.

'And, and, those New Venus military are moving like anchors,' Erik piped up from his leaning post of a rock.

'Alright,' TJ stopped scanning the inventory and handed the pad back to Buzz, 'I'll admit it to you guys. We're screwed, but I think we can still make it out of this. Everyone take a moment to think of solutions. If we keep thinking and keep moving we'll pull out of this one like we have all the others.'

A few moments passed in silence before the first of the ideas began to roll in. TJ could see all their faces in the soothing combination of fading blue light in the sky and the sharper rainbow of colours from the HUD flashing messages across their faces. Some had ideas early but thought better before vocalizing. TJ wanted to involve his people in this decision if for no other reason than to give them something to do.

'TJ,' Ken stood and half raised a hand like he was still in primary school. 'There is an option, how about Combtown? It's on the north side of the plateau but the cliffface is lower on that side.'

'Why not go to Fort Saturn if we're talking alternate destinations, it's closer,' Erik said from the clump of dirt he had slumped against.

'I think I may have mentioned, while you guys were

marching into one of your wars the Landran took FS,' Buzz said. The statement dimmed the light of hope but TJ could see the gears start turning faster in the minds of his people.

'He has a point, Erik I mean, it is closer. What are the chances that the Landran are still there?' Ashley asked with a bit more excitement than she had a moment ago.

'Another point would be that we know the ins and outs of Fort Saturn. Who knows Combtown even a little?' Kain asked.

'There may, at least, be people in Combtown,' Daniella offered.

'The real question is water guys,' TJ cut in, 'Do we have enough to get to either of those places on what we have?'

Buzz looked to Ken who had already started the furious tapping to recalculate the duration to both of the new end points. The news did not appear to be good when the Sergeant tossed the pad to the ground, 'Combtown is a no. Fort Saturn is manageable with light rationing.'

'So that's the tipping point,' Buzz said.

'Right, Fort Saturn it is. We'll leave at N13 tomorrow,' TJ picked up the discarded pad. 'Try to sleep.'

The troopers moved off to their rest points in pairs or alone, all silent. Now this elite portion of the plateau squads looked as defeated as the rest. Daniella stayed with TJ while the others left and had a private talk as they settled in.

'TJ, we're going to have to be so careful when we get closer to Saturn. We don't know what's there,' she started.

'I know but the Landran don't seem to be the occupier types or they would have made a move a long time ago,' he worked into a position where Daniella's and his suits sat close to each other, visor to visor.

'How many times have we been fooled since all this

started?' she leaned forward until their helmets touched.

'Too many. We'll set extra watches until we get to Port Mars, Okay?'

'Okay, I know you'll do everything to keep us safe.'

'Wish we could get out of these suits for a few minutes. That seems like the right thing to me,' he said switching gears.

'One more thing that will have to wait until we get to Port Mars,' she smiled playfully.

N1200 came with a jolt as the last watch started kicking boots to rouse the squads. The blackness was pure at this hour except for a display few on the planet had ever seen. Stars, not the multitude described in the books from Earth but a twinkling show, filled the sky with light and the emergence of the moon, Phobos on its breakneck, westward trek added motion to nighttime painting, while Deimos hung almost motionless though some knew it was gliding to the east. Up on top of the plateau they were above the vast majority of the crystal and dust haze. Troopers each took a few moments to take in the sight. Consequently, the start up on this day took longer but TJ was not going to push it too much.

'We're missing one TJ,' Kain reported as the Captain finished what washing up he could manage while encased in his power armour.

'A trooper you mean?' he asked while locking his second glove into place.

'Yeah, a Private Raemance from the New Venus squad,' Kain read from his notes to be sure the information was correct.

'Was it a fatality?' Daniella asked as she stepped closer to the pair from the dark.

'No sign of a scuffle anywhere. Just gone.'

'I've heard of people going crazy when the end is near,' Erik added, sipping his morning ration of water.

'That only happens when you are near,' Buzz laughed.

The troopers gathered around TJ chuckled lightly. There were no deep belly laughs but he could feel the tension ease, if only marginally. Troopers out of earshot continued tromping around in a brooding storm that was their misery, performing their duties around this light-hearted eye in the storm. Everyone's mood dimmed when the fires were kicked out and the southwest march toward Fort Saturn began. News of the disappearance of one of the soldiers was not well received but it was unlikely anything could bring these men and women down any further.

*****

CHAPTER XXXII
Tuesday, 4 May, 2251

When the sun rose a few minutes before D100 and an hour after the march started TJ called a stop to the procession. The fire of yellow and white of the saviour star lit the sparse haze and cloudless sky. Dark rocks around the group flashed over to a light rust colour like a light switch had been turned on. More green leaves of grass fluttered and shone in the early sunlight but ground cover still consisted more of rock and dirt than vegetation on the plateau. Like the star filled night before, the troopers were in awe of the relative clarity of the sunshine up here. Clouds from a far off storm had made the sun a fuzzy ball in the sky but it still held a painful quality to eyes that had never seen it like this.

'Let's keep moving everyone,' TJ twirled a finger in the air. 'Buzz, take point from here.'

'Yeah, no problem boss,' Buzz said while staring at the solar display having forgotten his own rank.

'Hey, you're a pilot now, bud. Haven't you seen that before?' Kain asked.

'Not really. They like us to focus on the flying.'

'Probably safer for you,' Erik smiled.

'Oh! Come back for the kid!' Ashley laughed.

'Not bad, rookie,' Buzz gave Erik a pat on the shoulder.

With lighter hearts and a chuckle the group resumed their march. Mile after mile passed beneath their heavy boots with little changing other than the rusty rock they walked by on the left was now passing on the right. The green speckled landscape was gladly tolerated by the parade since it provided them the glorious view of the sun as it too paraded across the sky. At this altitude and with nothing else to do, it was hard to avoid the sight of Banerise.

'I'm going to build a house up here I think,' Buzz said after a few hours of marching.

'Think we need to take a break, I'm sore and Buzz is hallucinating,' TJ held up a hand to bring the group to a stop. Even though the armour was doing most of the walking, the uneven ground jostled them around inside their suits like a maraca.

'It's a nice dream though,' the Air captain replied as he dropped to the ground in his black armour turned grey-brown.

'I'll take one if you're going to sub-lease,' Kain said.

'How are we doing for distance and time then Ken?' TJ asked as the shuffling armoured forms came to a stop.

'We made real good time, chief. Without landmarks it's hard to be sure but we should be maybe ten miles north-northeast of the descent point.'

'Excellent,' TJ took a moment for himself. He looked around the landscape and imagined it was what the early terraforming appeared to be like for the peninsula. Mankind had built so much from much less than this. He was determined not to lose it, not lose their only home.

'Penny for your thoughts,' Daniella came up beside him.

Impact sensors on his right arm indicated she had placed a hand on his arm. Fortunately, the phase sensors did not register it as an attack, letting the hand actually make contact which was good because he really needed it, even through the armour. He turned toward her with a thankful smile and was mesmerized by Daniella's own smile, bright enough to rival the sun. It seemed to TJ there was something besides home that he would fight to the death for.

'Dani, I gotta say…' he started.

'Captain!' a trooper from the current watch cycle called in. Since the closed circuit message was not specific, Buzz jumped to his feet as well. The maneuver grabbed the attention of many troopers who sensed the urgency of Buzz's rise and TJ's twirl.

'Report!' TJ replied on the same channel. He raise a hand to settle the troops.

'I've got contacts closing!' the young woman was almost screaming.

'Deep breath, Private. What's the direction?'

'Form the southwest, coming up fast.'

'Fantastic,' Viper said, drawing her weapon but not triggering it.

'Get ready,' TJ said to Daniella before turning to the squads, 'We've done this before people. We are better, we are stronger, we will remind them who's planet this is. Blades ready, get low. Kain take three and swing wide to the north.'

'Yes, sir,' Kain pointed to three random troopers before running to his position.

'We don't have any cannons, Captain,' Yvonne Bailey called in from behind her cover.

'Understood, I don't think their Bregan so that won't make that big of a difference.'

'Visual range is a lot better up here and I don't see any flashes,' Ken confirmed the theory.

'Could they be on the ground?' Buzz asked from the front of the crouching formation.

'They don't usually register on the tracker when they're ground bound,' Viper said.

'And it's unlikely we would have any units up here besides us,' TJ considered all possibilities. 'Could they be more of those bird things?'

Silence filled the channel as the troopers waited on a report from the scout that had originally called it in. Seconds turned to a minute with no report only rusty dirt and yellow sun. When their gaze eventually locked, Buzz motioned to TJ he did not know what was happening.

'Private, report!' TJ called at last to the distant scout but received no reply.

'We're going again, aren't we?' Ken asked though he knew the answer.

'Looks like it's coming this time,' TJ said, 'Erik, Viper, go see what happened to our watch.'

'Yes, sir,' they replied in unison.

'TJ,' Ken waved. 'She was on the south perimeter. Those contacts are too far west to have gotten to her.'

'Okay. Viper, watch yourselves.'

'TJ,' it was Kain's turn to call in. 'We're set up.'

'Good, thanks,' TJ again took a moment to look to the sun above. While the evil, that was Bane, was in the sky it was Sol's light that was at this moment no longer comforting but instead a blazing spotlight on their position. TJ knew these approaching contacts were not birds, but rather he was almost convinced it was their latest enemy, the Landran.

'Okay, people, we're going ahead as if these newcomers are not Bregan but Landran. Remember your training for ranged combat and get ready. Wait for the signals,' TJ placed a hand on Daniella's armoured shoulder in a subconscious move. She was crouching beside him behind a three foot high boulder.

Buzz waved one hand behind his back in a subtle gesture to the squads that he could see the approaching opponents. His black armour was a glaring contrast to the tan and red striped rock pile he had chosen for cover. It was almost as bad as the shining silver of the armour the rest of the troopers were wearing, all but TJ and Erik in their phase armour.

Among the rocks, hills and divots along the southwest horizon small shapes began to appear, moving with confidence. The rays of both Bane and Sol sparkled off the scales of six approaching Landran. TJ thought of the couple concerts he had gone to when he was younger except there was constant light reflection in front of each of the creatures that was no guitar but a lethal bolt rifle.

All the troopers tensed in their armour but kept their blades off until needed. To the right of the incoming Landran TJ could make out four silvery spots closing in. Clearly Kain had determined his services would be needed sooner rather than later. Another sparkle appeared to the left of the Landran further away and much closer to the enemy. As soon as it popped up the lizards stopped. Their scale sparkles visibly turned toward the new dot then stopped all together. No plasma shots were seen but TJ was sure it was an armoured person. Maybe it was one of the team he had sent south.

'Ken,' he called over to his sergeant, when he did not answer, 'Dolly! Any contact from Viper or Erik?'

Ken grumbled when he heard his call-sign, 'Gimme a second,' the pause was too long for TJ but he waited and watched the commotion in the field. 'Viper's checked in. She and Erik found Private Siddleman's body.'

'So that's not her,' Daniella sighed, mirroring TJ's frustration with another mystery. Someone was out there and the Landran were not killing them.

'Okay, Ken. Call those two back. Dani, get everyone ready. This is going to get nasty.'

The calls went out among the crouching troopers while the light show in the field resumed its approach. Now the rhinestone-like show was turned down. They seemed to consciously restrict their movements, to limit the light reflection, but their dark colour betrayed their position almost as well. While cautious they were still confident in their ability and closed the gap quickly.

TJ kept all six Landran in view while they weaved their way through the rocks. In his periphery he kept Kain's approaching group in mind as they moved to intercept. That horrid pause in events came when both groups were in a position where nothing seemed to happen and TJ hated it.

Debatable fortune took over when a hail of plasma bolts showered the rocks to TJ's left. He looked to see what they were shooting at and saw Viper dive for cover after a snap deflection. Erik was slower to move for cover and took a shot to the helmet. Fortunately his phase armour worked as intended and let the shot pass straight through with no ill effects. He jumped for cover behind a pile of black rocks before his armour would have to compensate for another shot.

'Good thing he took the shot in the head,' Buzz quipped.

'Oh no! Aha ha ha,' Ken burst out.

The entire squad began laughing and ducking as the Landran now directed their attack at the peanut gallery. While the bolts failed to impact into the armour of the troopers each shot blasted a portion of their cover.

'TJ, we'll be on our stomachs soon,' Daniella shouted from beside him.

'Just stay low. The moment's coming,' TJ stole a quick glance to gauge where Kain's group was and got a bolt to the helmet for his trouble before he managed to duck back. His own phase armour negated the hit, similar to what Erik's had done.

'Good thing…' Buzz started.

'Stuff it, Captain,' TJ smiled and the squad laughed again.

The deadly rain sputtered and stopped on their location, though rifle fire could be heard in the distance. TJ popped his head up to see the Landran firing on Kain's group, which had moved in close. This was the moment. TJ waved a hand to signal the charge. Two dozen troopers erupted from the rocky ground and charged the Landran patrol. They closed the gap in a flash but not fast enough to prevent two of the riflemen from turning their rifles on them. The shots came quick and brought down two troopers with undetermined injuries.

A third rifleman spun, its scales firing off a disco ball affect as it began to fire at Buzz. The Air Captain deflected the first two shots with a clockwise sweep of his blade then a third with a forearm shield. The movement was clean but put him off balance and he fell behind a small boulder, under the next four shots.

These rifles that this patrol was using had a higher rate of fire which they used to pin several behind cover. TJ and a couple troopers made a flanking maneuver around to the south and drew the fire of one of the riflemen. The split in coverage opened a path for Daniella to charge in. Her first swing was too hasty and missed her target, cutting off the top third of a four foot wide boulder. The targeted Landran reacted quick and fired at her point blank. Daniella's swing left her arm across her body and put her forearm shield unit right in front of the Landran's rifle. The shot hit the shield and rebounded back into the creature's chest. The wounded lizard stopped all action and fell to the ground without a peep.

Commotion to the north drew most of the attention on the battlefield as Kain's group made their move. His left-flank trooper took a hit early and stumbled to the ground while the remaining three crossed the rocks fast. Kain deflected everything shot at the center of the attacking wave but the other two were having some difficulty. As he became fully engaged he noticed one of the Landran actually focusing on aiming at his right-flank trooper. The next shot directed at Kain was purposely deflected into the left leg of his fellow trooper causing him to stumble and fall. The fall took him out of the firing line as a fresh burst sailed over where he would have been standing.

The stunned rifleman was caught fully unprepared for the attack of the third backup trooper in Kain's group.

A single motion from the Corporal ended with a blade buried to the hilt in the green scales. Kain's own charging of the Landran firing group, broke their braced firing position and any chance they would have of hitting anything easily. The Landran began moving away from the multiple troopers closing in on them. With no time to aim, their shots began to fire wide, more often into the dirt than close to a trooper. Kain ended one Landran's frustration with a sweeping slash diagonally across it from its left shoulder and out the right side.

Now with only three riflemen remaining the shots became more like spraying paint than shooting enemies. Troopers formed a wall of shimmering blades, deflecting bolts or even absorbing a hit in order to maintain the barrier. With four of their own troopers down they were not going to be making any risky moves.

One of the Landran decided it had had enough and broke formation in a dash for freedom. It ran to the southwest, which had not been fully secured yet. A single trooper stepped in front, a single trooper in dark armour. The Landran raised the rifle while at full charge to blast its way past. At this range the green bolts of plasma easily found their destination. To the Landran's surprise the shots sailed clean through the armour without a mark. Before it could react to the phase armour display TJ swung hard and planted the blade more than halfway through the lizard. He let go of the hilt as the body fell and stepped around it to address the last two Landran.

TJ was taking a huge risk by being unarmed but he felt it was a good risk, 'Honorable Landran, lower your weapons so we can forego the ugly business of war.'

'Forego the, what?' Buzz shook his head.

'I'm going for diplomacy.'

'Alright,' he raised a hand, 'Just don't get any of that stuff you're shoveling on me.'

A few of the troopers around them laughed but all

remained focused on the aliens in front of them. The Landran had stopped their firing as soon as they saw TJ's trick with the armour. The odds they would survive continued conflict was certainly zero and they knew it, especially with a Blademaster in the ranks of the enemy. They slowly lowered their rifles and surrendered them effortlessly when the troopers came in to collect them.

'What will you do with ussss?' a darker green Landran asked with a heavy accent.

'You will be prisoner, naturally,' TJ said, 'Have a seat while we work out the details.'

TJ pointed to three pairs of soldiers and assigned them to watch the Landran who were now sitting on the battlefield. He ordered Ken and Yvonne to tend to the fallen troopers while Kain was ordered to set a watch around their little gathering. With that, TJ was left with eight troopers around to figure what was next.

'Okay, speak up,' TJ said to the group.

'We need to get rid of those things,' the former tank driver Luke said without hesitation.

'We aren't going to kill prisoners,' Daniella snapped.

'Right, they'll have to be taken to a base,' TJ scanned the faces around him.

'Supplies, chief,' Ashley said, 'We don't even have enough for ourselves.'

'What if,' Buzz stepped forward, 'What if we take them to Combtown. It's clear that Fort Saturn is lost and the town is between us and Port Mars, more or less.'

'That seems pretty risky, TJ,' Daniella shook her head a little.

'TJ,' Ken called out as he ran to join the group.

'Yeah,' TJ turned to the incoming trooper.

'Casualty report, we lost two and have one in serious condition.'

'Didn't we have four go down?'

'Yeah, but thanks to Kain it was just a scratch,' Ken smiled.

TJ looked to the Blademaster who looked to the dirt but clearly had a smirk on his face. 'Okay, we need to get medical for that one and while Combtown may have prison cells they probably won't have doctors if the Council has ordered a retreat. Kain, pick out four troopers to take our friends to their new spa. We'll have them carry our fallen as well. They did the deed so they can clean it up.'

'Yes sir,' Kain nodded.

'If we go along the north shore of Saviour Lake, then Kain's picks can stay with us for three-quarters of their trip,' Ashley offered.

'Good point. Let's work that plan. Redistribute the supplies and get those Landran set for their new job,' TJ ordered, he was glad to be done fighting this day.

*****

CHAPTER XXXIII
Wednesday, 5 May, 2251

For the next day of marching the humans on top of the plateau enjoyed a restful night even with enemy in the camp. At least they knew where the threat was. The day's march was a peaceful romp over the rocky plateau with the Landran keeping their own complaints to a background hiss.

The combination of thinner air and power armour made short work of the miles of walking. Camp was made on the third night on the plateau on the coast of Saviour Lake. The water in this half mile high lake was fed from an underground spring giving the water a peaceful demeanor. Many members of the parade indulged themselves with ideas of opening a resort up here after the war.

TJ was solely concerned with getting himself, his friends, his command and more importantly Daniella through to the successful conclusion of the war. Too many had fallen including the two the Landran would be toting away. This night he made plans to split the squads the best possible way. The time to rest came quickly, maybe it was the last time he would have to sleep in his armour.

Thursday morning, with the sparkle-free rays of Sol washing over the camp, the two groups parted ways. One of the groups consisted of four soldiers from New Venus assigned to escort the two Landran prisoners. Those Landran were tasked with carrying the bodies of the two troopers killed in the latest engagement. The other group split off to the west heading for Port Mars. They tracked the north shore of the almost forty-mile long lake. Next to the Inner Rim Sea which sat to the northeast of the plateau, Saviour Lake was the largest land-locked body of water on the peninsula.

Shortly past the west end of the lake the land began to slope down for the first time in three days. The ground itself slowly transformed with emerging grass filling in the cracks of the harsh rocky terrain. Minutes later the ground cover grew into a lush carpet above the top of the thick atmospheric haze.

TJ opted to make their last camp in the clearer night. The haze they had all grown up in hugged the ground like a fog through it never dissipated below eighteen hundred feet. While he noticed the grass up here was not any different than the grass below, he did see a difference in his people. Even suffering losses a couple days before, the troopers were in good spirits. Down in the soup the troops would often be in a foul mood even after a victory or on a three-day leave.

'I think we'll have to leave,' he said to no one in particular.

'We just set up camp,' Erik moaned from a comfy spot in the grass.

'I don't think he meant the camp,' Daniella stepped closer to TJ with an unspoken question of concern.

'No, sadly I wasn't in the present. I was thinking of the future. Unless the Council has something up their sleeve we'll have to consider evacuation.'

'You're giving up?' Erik stood.

'Just getting ready. At every turn we've been attacked by Bregan, Landran or even other people. The odds aren't looking good.'

'True, but Port Mars has an actual army!' Buzz pointed out.

'The question is, will the Council use it though?' Kain asked even though no answer was needed.

'That will be up to them. I am prepared for war or

retreat though. Hopefully the Council won't split our forces whichever way they go.'

'Right! We can take out these things if we get everything together,' Erik all but cheered.

'I like the enthusiasm,' Ken chuckled.

'We need more like him,' Ashley smiled.

'One is plenty,' Buzz said.

With a chuckle in their throats they retreated to their bed-down spots as determined by Kain's watch schedule. Some would dream of victorious battle, others a flawless retreat to somewhere else, TJ's mind was filled with the same haze covering the planet below them. Their future was uncertain and if he was being honest, he was tired of fighting.

Friday morning came and the troopers with more energy than they'd had in days. Personal energy anyway since their armour was almost drained. They broke camp quickly to avoid bleeding out any more power than they had to. Reserves were low forcing Ken to take the fuel cells from the injured trooper to top off a few of the suits with lower tanks. He had to leave the wounded soldier with an open visor and a manual respirator.

The grass grew slick as they descended into the haze but not because of the floating crystal shards. Their path brought them to the magical edge of the Channel. This was the massive seam in the peninsula marking the point where the gas planet core drove into Mars. The seam split the peninsula fifty miles in from the coast and ended where the plateau began. They could not see into the channel even though they had dropped almost a thousand feet in the first couple hours of marching.

Soon trees began to dot the horizon in a pattern indicating there was some farming in the area. This had to mean they were close to Port Mars. The two GCRs bursting from those same trees over a half mile distant confirmed the suspicion. Unless they were pirates again, this would be the perimeter scout.

'Hold up everyone,' TJ raised a fist, 'Kain stay sharp, never know.'

'Got it,' the Blademaster said and took a few subtle steps away from the main group.

A couple minutes passed with TJ standing at the head of a column of worn out troopers in the middle of a field of long grass. The GCRs slowed their approach at the point they would have received the ID signals from the power armour. They converged as friends would have pulling into the driveway.

Once settled the rear hatch of the lead sled opened with a hiss that, while normal made a few troopers jump. The patrol leader emerged a moment later and introduced himself after giving TJ's group a quick once over.

'Commander Ramirez, Port Mars,' the tall man in armour said.

'Captain Marso, Fort Grey,' TJ shook the man's hand.

'We heard you'd be coming this way.'

'You heard? How?' Daniella asked from beside TJ.

'Your advanced scout told us. It will be getting dark in a couple hours, captain. We should be going,' Ramirez swept a welcoming arm toward the city.

'We have wounded Commander. Could we load them into your sleds to speed things up?' Ken asked from a few steps back.

'By all means,' the commander waved to his people to take the hurt trooper to one of the GCRs.

'Commander, we didn't send an advanced unit,' TJ said as he and the newly formed convoy began their trip home.

'Is that so? Well, that would explain why Private Raemance couldn't say when your patrol would be coming in.'

Great, another mystery. TJ was pretty sick of them.

He and the rest of the walking weary finished the last miles of their trek bracketed by the GCRs and in total silence. They simply watched their feet beat down the perfect green fields of the Port Mars peripheries.

Two hours later in the fading light of Bane, the crystal-like domes of Port Mars appeared through the darkening haze. They knew beyond that city lay the wide purple ocean but could not bring themselves to get excited about it. This was the funk TJ knew had been awaiting them while they had been on the plateau.

The night of the fourth day, the squad approached the gates of Port Mars. Buzz identified himself to the guards, who then released the seals and opened the gates. No hero's welcome greeted them, only an escort to a secured barracks.

'Less than a dozen left,' muttered Walter Martel.

'Sir, count is twenty,' said the aide at his side.

'Less than a dozen of mine,' he replied.

The lift doors opened to the secure barracks where the newcomers to the city were held. TJ and the others sat in a spacious common room and rose to greet Commander Martel.

'So good to see all of you,' he said. 'I've read the report concerning events following your departure from New Venus.'

The men and women in the room shuffled around uncomfortably under his gaze. The memories of the last week were tough to dwell on.

'What's our next move, Commander?' Erik asked.

'The plan is a pull out,' he said.

'Right, right. So we regroup and hit 'em.'

'No, Corporal, we're leaving Mars.'

The room fell silent at the impact of Walter's words. No one knew what to say about the loss of their home world again. Some of the men and women had tears in their eyes and a few retreated to the couches to be alone with their thoughts.

'Why is the Council giving up?' Daniella asked.

'Where are we going to go?' Paul asked.

'How do you propose we get there?' Ken was next.

'Whoa, people, let the man talk,' TJ said.

'We've analyzed all reports since that convoy went missing at the end of March and the Council believes we will lose a full-scale war. Numbers for the Bregan are around five hundred thousand, given their estimated dispersion.' Walter read from his clipboard.

'Five hundred thousand!' Erik whistled.

'Estimates for the Landran are two hundred to two hundred and fifty thousand. That gives us a seven to two ratio against. And we don't have the resources to fight on that scale. These creatures do not seem content to share our peninsula.'

'Sounds right,' Drew Webster said, 'the last part anyway.'

'The Council is evacuating the outer settlements and putting all our resources into escaping to find a home that is only ours.'

'When do we leave?'

'In four months we'll be without a home,' said Martel, 'We've lost Eden and it looks like mankind will need a new garden to call its own, so it's up to us to find it.'

*****

CHAPTER XXXIV
Saturday 8 May 2251

The battle force slipped out in the midst of fight with the sacrifice of only one company of soldiers. With the Bregan engaged with that small group or chasing the last of the humans, Kraston's army had an easy march back to Fort Saturn. Once a jewel in the crown of humanity's Mars colony, it was now a simple forward operating base for the Landran army. 'It's a shame really,' Kraston muttered thoughtfully as he slithered into the former office of the base commander.

'And what would that be?' Ann Huston asked from the map table. She absentmindedly examined the three dimensional topography with her true thought on the verge of burst past her silence.

'That's probably the last time we're going to see Captain Marso and his little band. I was really beginning to enjoy our encounters,' the Landran leader sighed.

A massive crash at the far side of the office failed to startle Kraston, but it did manage to draw his attention. He put down the data pad he was looking at and turned to face the trooper pacing on the other side of the room.

'Did the display offend you, Miss Huston?'

'I'm sorry. I'm upset that the Nivek got away,' Ann put a hand on her hip and hung her head, fuming silently.

'As I said, it would be unlikely that the human force could have gotten away from the Bregan. They had the north and the east of the battlefield covered and our scouts did not find any sign of their southern retreat during our three day relocation back to Fort Saturn.'

'Retreat,' Ann muttered.

'What was that?'

'I was saying, what about a west retreat by the hu… troopers,' she did not want to disconnect herself that much by saying *human* when talking about her own people.

'By the looks of that map there is a massive bit of rock blocking that direction. They would have been trapped,' Kraston returned his focus to the data pad.

Ann looked up and stared at the giant lizard. Evidently the conversation was over according to him, she had other plans. She kicked the already ruined display before striding to the desk. Her tantrum had no effect on Kraston, she would try something else. She swung hard to slap the top of the desk, forgetting she was still armoured up. Her hand, supported by the armour's strength, crashed deep into the wood. Kraston raised his head slowly, his hood barely flickered.

'Did you have another question?'

His calm was maddening. Ripping her hand from the hole in the desk she tried to stare down the alien momentarily, 'They could have gone over. You don't know these people. It's something they would do.'

Kraston put the pad back onto the desk, sliding it away from the wrecked portion, away from Ann. He strode silently around the oversized obstacle, a feat the always amazed Ann. Kraston drew her in next to him with one arm and pointed to the map table with the other, 'Look at this model, Miss Huston. If the scale is accurate the plateau is over one thousand persa high.'

'Persa?' She hated being led around but it was a short walk this time.

'Forgive me, if I am do the math correctly it would be two thousand feet.'

'I still think that Marso would have found a way over,' she pulled away, though her eyes remained on the map. She wished she had her helmet on so she could drop the solar shield. As it was, she could not bring herself to look at the dragon-thing for more than a few seconds.

'If it's any consolation, Miss Huston, I have ordered scouts to patrol the top of the plateau in case the Bregan choose to attack from that direction. They would surely find Captain Marso's group if he opted for that route.'

'When was that? Have you heard from them yet?' Ann brought her eyes up to his.

'There has been no word yet but with the amount of travel required, I don't expect to hear for at least two days.' Kraston motioned at the map, indicating the distance to the plateau and the height.

'Fine. What's the move for us then.'

He smiled that smile she hated. Walking back to the desk, whisper quiet compared to her heavy footfalls, he slid in behind it and picked up the blue-flashing data pad. 'For now, we will relax and analyze the battle data.'

'Great,' she started for the door.

'I will call on you when we have a plan of action.'

Ann could feel him looking at her with that same smirk. She walked out of the office, past the reception station which no longer welcomed anyone, then down the darkened stairwell to the bright, wide open atrium of the main entrance. Action seemed unlikely for the remainder of the day no matter how much she willed it.

The administration building was the central structure of the city allowing for a short walk to all major installations, including the barracks. She made her way across the lifeless courtyard before making her way up to the officer section. She browsed through the open doors, blasted apart by the Landran invaders a few days before. After a couple false guesses she found her target, the remains of the door's name plate could still be made out, Captain Trevor Marso. 'This will do nicely,' she smiled, grabbing the plate and crushing it in her armoured fist.

The door was beyond salvage, offering no chance at privacy as she removed her battle armour but since she was the only human in the city there was no chance of an incident. Flopping back onto the bed in her comfortable night clothes was the extent of her energy after three days of marching. Even with the occasional break the distance was too much without a vehicle.

Ann had an extra sense of accomplishment being wrapped in the blankets that once warmed TJ. The same blankets would again never welcome TJ's woman, Daniella. Sleep came swiftly and was filled with dreams of Ann ramming various instruments into Kain until the Blademaster stopped crying for his mother.

A solid thud reverberated through the former base commander's office when the door closed behind the human Blademaster. Kraston kept his head down until he felt the subtle shockwave on his scales. He did not have to watch Miss Huston leave, the scent of her was easy enough to track. The data pad in his hand was no more than a dead weight since there was no information that could help. He was not going to give the human the gift of his attention no matter what.

Now that she was gone he threw the pad across the office to the map table, he had no use for either. This was the office of the commander, there had to be more memos somewhere. The Landran leader pulled open another drawer even as the heavy thuds from the human's battle armour faded behind the door. Plenty of paper memos and data pads cluttered up the deep well drawer. Kraston pulled out a handful and dropped it on the desk. Pad after pad joined the first during the search. They were probably safer away from the increasingly frustrated lizard.

'You could build a library with all those devices,' said a voice from the dark corner behind the map table.

'If your tongue would spend as much time hiding as you do we'd all be happier,' Kraston said without looking up. He had known of the other Landran's presence since he and Ann first stepped foot in the office. A smile threatened to break his cool demeanour as he thought of

Miss Huston's complaining without any signs she had seen the charcoal grey Landran behind her.

'We should be returning to our own city in the morning, Marshal. We've destroyed this city and helped the destruction of the human army at the hands of the Bregan. Now, we can leave,' the charcoal Landran said, walking out of the shadows, approaching the desk.

'I will not leave now. We will not leave,' Kraston finally looked up, mildly surprised when his company was not where he expected. 'We took the city and we'll be keeping it. Not only did we help the Bregan finish off the expedition force from the humans but we helped them deal a massive blow to the Bregan force. This, right now, is our time! Our time to strike a fatal blow against the foe and take this planet.'

Kraston was so wrapped up in his speech he failed to notice the other Landran had left. He stood for a moment, looking around the empty room. Without an audience, Kraston's fiery energy dissolved, leaving him no option but to return to the desk and continue the search.

Whether it was the break he had taken to address the charcoal, pure luck or it was time but the first data pad he picked up contained an immensely useful communique. As he read it over, Kraston knew these words spelled out his victory. He calmly turned off the screen, stretched his neck and walked out of the office.

His personal guard had held their station outside the office even though there was no way they could not have overheard the commotion. That kind of loyalty was the chief reason for their selection. The Marshal motioned for the lead Gold Landran to come to him.

'Captain, if you would be so kind as to gather the human survivors by the motor pool while I read over this memo. There may be something they would want to hear.'

*****

CHAPTER XXXV
Monday, 9 May, 2251

The light of dawn crept into Ann's newly acquired apartment. Brilliant yellow sunlight from the mother star slipped over the fortress walls before slowly filling the windows as it rose in the sky. Her freshly woken eyes sparkled at the magic morning light. The dome of the city magnified the incoming light well beyond the dimming effect the haze of the planet had. This sun was what she imagined Earth's sun would have looked like.

Ann stretched in the warm sheets. With the sun in her face, amplified enough by the city dome to warm her skin, she knew she had slept in. This was first time in weeks Ann had done that and it was great. When she had gotten enough of the sunlight she would get up and have a talk with Kraston, but not yet.

Not yet did not last as long as she had wanted. Her Blademaster instincts overpowered her desire for a slow paced morning. Someone, or something, was in the room. Her face froze in the admiring smile but she was not happy. Nothing was in her field of vision which meant whatever she was sensing was behind her, near the door. She continued her contented stretch though this time with purpose.

Under the covers the whatever back there could still see movement so she rotated her right wrist as if working out the night stiffness. As she did she extended her arm under her pillow and grabbed the hilt of her blade. When she had a firm grip on the blade and had it rotated so she could activate it, she held her smile and stretch. In a flash she threw off her sheets, up into the air to obscure any attack and rolled out of bed. Once of the floor she tumbled into a crouched position, activating her blade as she finished off. Now she was ready, facing the door and the intruder. Instead of swinging blades or bolts flashing past her head there was only a single Landran, standing inside the doorway. It did not attack, did not move, only let out a hushed hiss.

Ann rose slowly but kept the blade ready. Her guest did not have a bolt rifle with it but that did not meant it still could not come after her. The two studied each other for a full minute before the Landran finally spoke.

'Blademaster, I have come to deliver a message,' it said in a distinctly female tone.

'You have? What is it?' Ann asked.

The charcoal grey Landran moved further into the room. Now in the fullest light, Ann saw the slender yet formidable creature float across the floor, seemingly without effort. She was mesmerized by this creature's movement and felt drawn in when it spoke, 'The Marshal is intending to attack your station again. He will be taking the full army in his attempt to exterminate the Bregan.'

Ann stared at the Landran for a few seconds before the full impact of what she had said sunk in completely. She could not believe that Kraston would even want to go back to the Miles Research Station. Ann lowered her blade and deactivated it. Clearly this creature was not here for an attack. She was not sure what the Landran wanted but she knew what she needed to do, if what it was saying was true.

'Excuse me. Did you say he wanted to go back to Miles? To attack the Bregan? The army that just wiped us out?' Ann said, they were not questions.

'Of course, that seems the sensible course of action. Why would Kraston not?'

She could not tell if the Landran's response was sarcasm or not but Ann was going to assume it was because she had to put a stop to this. There was no way Ann was going to get control of Mars without the

Landran army and it was sure to be destroyed if it went back.

Ann quickly ushered the creature out of her room and dressed. Within the inner city walls she did not need her battle armour since the battles and destruction of the fortress had not breached the environmental containment this far in, but the one piece of equipment there might be a need for was her blade. She was certainly not leaving that behind. The march to the commander's office was a short hop from the officer's barracks and unobstructed by the people that once called Fort Saturn home.

The welcome Ann received to the office was that of Kraston giving a motivational speech to the Landran she assumed were in charge of the army. She wanted to interrupt the second she walked in but these large lizards and their bolt rifles seemed too much to take on in this confined space, even for her. Biting her lip for the last few moments she scanned the room that used to belong to one of the most powerful men on the Southern Peninsula. She noticed a large number of data pads in the far corner that had not been there the night before. They must have been part of the search Kraston had done before deciding to kill himself with an attack on the Bregan.

After a hearty roar in the Landran language, all of the command Landran left. Each one gave Ann a thorough look over on their way out. Every look contained some level of contempt. Kraston stayed behind, as he always did, thumbing through another data pad that was not his a week ago. He waited for Ann to speak first, but there was something not quite right about the overt courtesy he always showed her.

'Marshal Kraston, I don't know what you think you're doing but I heard you were heading back to Mile Research Station. Is this true?'

'Why yes, of course, Miss Huston,' he lowered the data pad to free up his arms. They gestured in majestic, sweeping motions as he worked through his explanation.

'We've decoded some communications that the former commander Norris received prior to our arrival, indicating that the human colonies are to be evacuated back to your capital city. This is an ideal situation since it eliminates the possibility of future interruptions by a human army. The combined human and Landran attack at Miles Research Station appears to have made a huge impact on the Bregan numbers. So, this would be the perfect time to attack, and that is what we're doing.'

'But Marshal, the Bregan seem content leaving everyone alone so long as we stay away from their home and not rip into their crystal supply. To go back is just suicide.'

'I hardly think so. We've been fighting the Bregan for a long time, we know their weaknesses. If we marshal a large enough force before going back there, we will be victorious. We will eliminate the Bregan, and the humans are no longer a threat. No offense, of course.' Ann was sure the Landran leader was smiling.

'I don't know what to say. This is just ridiculous. If you talk to the people you've taken prisoner from Fort Saturn they will tell you what the Bregan are capable of in large numbers.' She started to pace.

'Well, I am afraid, Miss Huston, that will not be possible. Just last night, after I found this communication to your Commander Norris, I ordered the survivors of Fort Saturn be relieved of any further duties.' Kraston made his way behind the desk as he spoke.

'What! Excuse me? You had them killed?' Ann pounded the desk with noticeably less impact on the wood than the night before.

'Yes, I believe that is what I said.' He picked up another data pad and began to skim over its contents.

'Are you actually insane? That's totally unacceptable. Those people you captured when you took the fort were not only military people but doctors. Doctors we could have used to rebuild that prisoner you have frozen back on your ship.'

'Ah yes, the prisoner. We will have to figure out something else to do with her I suppose.'

'So she's going to remain an ice cube. This valuable person who likely has faster-than-light knowledge. She's the only one.' Ann began to pace around the office again.

'Perhaps, but for now we have a military exercise to undertake. Fairly routine I would say.' He stepped around the desk, walking slowly toward the door.

'Fine, you're going to need my help then. Let me get my armour. I'll meet you at the dispatch point.' Ann kicked the pile of data pads before heading for the door.

'That won't be necessary, Miss Huston. For the time being, I would prefer that you remain in the city. That way, I will be assured no harm will come to you.'

'What?' She was stunned. 'You want... you want me to stand down? I'm a Blademaster, I fight. That's what I do.'

'Not this time, Miss Huston. If you're looking for something to do then check in on our scouts we sent to the plateau at your insistence. Perhaps they have news, I doubt it but perhaps.'

With that dismissive statement Kraston bowed ever so slightly and walked out of the office, leaving Ann alone in the large, empty room. She was furious! Not only was the Landran army she had been counting on so badly, marching on the Bregan force but she could not even fight in the battle.

Her frustration boiled over with a flash of fury. She snapped her blade to life and swung wildly at the map table Commander Norris cherished. The blade easily cut through the heavy wooden surface and frame, splitting the table in two. She let it crash to the floor, not even caring about the map, the data pads and the destruction she left behind. Ann stormed out of the office, barely remembering to deactivate the blade before she left.

The march down to the main courtyard was uneventful aside for the occasional fist into a very breakable object that happened to be on a desk, table or wall. By the time she reached the courtyard her left hand was bruised and bloodied. As long as her right hand was fine she was okay with the few drops falling to the floor.

As she rounded the last corner before the main motor pool, Ann found a large collection of sheet covered bodies outside the building. She was touched that the Landran even cared that much about the people they slaughtered. It was not until she had gotten through the maze and into the building that she found the first Landran. It was busily taking parts off an abandoned GCR and did not notice her entrance. She approached from behind, striking the creature on the back of the green scaled hood. It recovered from the hit quickly and spun around, hissing. It did not have a bolt rifle nearby so it could do nothing more than glare at her.

'You there, find out what happened to the scout sent north.' She felt comfortable ordering this thing around. If Kraston did not destroy the army she would have no trouble taking charge.

'Shsss, who are you that orders me around?' it asked in a slow, broken version of Ann's language.

'I am acting on the orders of Marshal Kraston. You will tell me what happened to those scouts and you will do it now.'

'Hshsss... Asss you wisssh,' It bowed in mock courtesy by Ann's reckoning, and made its way out of the vehicle building. She knew it would head to the north end of the city and out the emergency exit. It was the only portal in the walls left intact after the Bregan attack and before the Landran assault. She looked around another empty building she was left alone in. There was nothing to do now and she had no idea how long it would take for that creature to find out what happened to the Landran scouts on the plateau. Judging by the devastation that the Bregan had rained down on the Landran and human assault force she was sure Captain Marso's group could not have escaped.

For the next hour Ann drifted between service bays kicking dirt into the empty stalls and throwing tools or parts off workbenches. Her mindless wandering should have been an action stopping scene but as the city was devoid of human or Landran life, her efforts to draw attention simply faded to nothing. Exhausted and with no one to rant at she wandered the city, going through courtyard after courtyard, peeking into the occasional building until she found herself inside the main hall. The place where TJ had become a captain. Ann hated this place but she felt there was power here, importance on a grand scale. When control of this planet belonged to Ann and humanity was under her dominion, this would be her royal chamber.

She walked slowly through the wide open chamber, envisioning rows of people. The silence the hall currently held was divine but the cheering and chanting that was just over the horizon was intoxicating. Her stride gradually changed to a royal strut by the time she made up to the stage in the center of the hall. This elevated viewing position showed the full size of the room. Ann looked around the magnificent chamber, absorbing the silent cheers. She raised her arms, basking in a glory so powerful it transcended time itself and came to her before the power of total control was hers.

Ann stood like this for a while until the reality to the emptiness of the chamber sunk in. She lowered her arms, looked around one last time and smiled so wide it threatened to split her head in half. Satisfied with what was to come she marched off to TJ's former bedroom where once again she would enjoy the comforts he would never have.

By N400 Ann was immersed in colourful banners and waving crowds for the ceremonies and parades in her honour. The knock at the door of her officer barrack quarters was a huge shock, abruptly waking her, tearing her away from that world. She was not happy at being interrupted at the best of times, in the middle of a blissful sleep was almost unforgivable. She threw back the warm blankets, grabbed the hilt of her blade and ran across the cold steel floor.

Instead of opening the portal to the hall she yelled at it, 'Who's there?'

'It isss I, your humble messenger. I have newsss, on the ssscoutsss, we sssent, to the plateau,' the lizard on the other side called back. A low voice but powerful enough to breach the door.

Ann's mind struggled for a moment. It was not as fully awake as her body. She remembered she had sent a Landran north to check on the scouts sent to intercept TJ's squad, if he had gone up that way. She smiled at the prospect of hearing nothing was found and that human squads had not even tried to climb over the plateau.

She finally opened the door, keeping her blade ready, and welcomed the Landran into the room, 'Please, come in. Tell me what you know.'

The green Landran moved quickly but made almost no sound on the steel floor panels. Ann imagined, in combat, this creature would be incredibly difficult to detect, even fight. Perhaps they were all like this, maybe it was just this one. It turned around in the middle of the room and bowed its head low, a sure sign of respect this time. At least that was what Ann thought it would be.

'Missstresss, it appearsss, that our ssscoutsss, had encountered a bit of trouble. I found two bodiesss, and noted that, there were two missing. Judging by the dissstrubancsssesss, in the ground cover, there wasss a ssspectacular, fight. The woundsss, on the bodiesss, indicate that they were cut down, by bladesss.'

This new information gave Ann pause. It was possible that the Eden Council had sent a detachment over the plateau for defensive purposes. It was possible but in her heart Ann knew that was not the case.

These two dead Landran were the result of TJ's squad, and probably the insufferable Kain. He had climbed the plateau. He had escaped the Bregan, escaped the Landran, they had escaped Ann. She was tired after a day of ranting and tantrums. For now she could no process all the thoughts in her head. With a flick of her wrist she dismissed the green creature and it left without a word. She closed the door before throwing her unlit blade to the bed.

What was she going to do? They had evaded death and Kraston had left with the army, she was stuck here. Perhaps tomorrow would be a better day to think this through. Who knows, they might not make it off the plateau.

Ann flopped down on the bed, falling asleep in seconds. Her dreams picked up where she had been woken. A blissful kingdom, in which she was queen and TJ, and his pet Kain, was dead.

*****

CHAPTER XXXVI
Thursday, 12 May, 2251

Kraston's master plan held firm for the two day march from Fort Saturn to the muster camp site. He chose this spot to camp, in view of the battleground ahead of Mile Research Station, to rest his soldiers and have a spot to examine the playing field. He had explained his plan perfectly to his generals in such a way that any Landran could follow it. The marshal knew his subordinates did not like being talked down to but there was nothing he could do about that, the plan had to be clear. His hope at the time was that the generals would follow the plan and implement every detail as was supposed to be done.

After breaking camp on the morning of the third day, Kraston led his army to the battlefield, from a rear observing position. His generals rallied his soldiers and formed up on the grounds one mile from Miles. They formed into three groups, allowing them to attack the Bregan not just head-on but also from both flanks. It was a pincer trap from which none would come out alive.

Kraston knew the Bregan army had been dealt a massive blow as a result of the last battle. While they still would be holding firm to a lethal fighting instinct, their numbers would have been greatly diminished. By the time his army had formed ranks and started their advance, the Bregan force realized what was happening and charged straight into the trap. It was instantly clear through the dense planetary haze that the estimates of the Bregan army strength were woefully underestimated.

Though Sol was high in the sky and Bane close behind the glare from all the Landran bolt rifles firing at once put the two stars to shame. The ambient stellar light was enough for Kraston to make out all the gruesome details of every Bregan soldier but thankfully the hail of bolts closed in like a curtain.

The Bregan, in Kraston's mind, were superb fighters but they never seemed capable of following the simplest battle plan. This time it was his plan they were not following. Rather than dealing with the three pronged attack, the Bregan opted to sacrifice a few soldiers on their flanks while the main force slammed into Kraston's center column. Maybe that was a plan when facing superior tactics. Since the Marshal's army was divided into three parts the center block did not have the strength to withstand an all-out attack. The Bregan used skills probably learned from weeks of conflict with the humans, relying on stolen armour plates to absorb the hits from the Landran bolt rifles as well as the new to deflect the incoming shots with their scythes or blades, acquired from the fallen human troopers. The result was a center column wiped out within the first hour of the engagement.

Part of Kraston's plan was for him to be in a position to retreat unopposed if necessary. This position behind the center column allowed him to choose exactly when to fall back and that time was now. As the last Landran soldier fell, the Marshal slipped behind a rise in the terrain, preventing the Bregan from seeing his departure. The usual grey-green haze in the air combine with the thick ground foliage let Kraston and his group monitor the progress of the battle in isolation.

The two flanking groups remained intact because of the Bregan's fanatical focus on the middle column but that was about to change. Landran soldiers continued to press the attack, more for survival than supremacy. The light pulsing over the hills and plants told Kraston how the fight was going, after another hour he had seen enough.

'Failed. How could we have failed so quickly?' he asked to no one. The Marshal meandered westward, weighed down by the burden of defeat and slowed by confusion about how his perfect plan had come apart.

'It *had* to be the generals,' said the charcoal grey Landran.

'Of course!' Kraston looked around to reprimand one of his generals then realised they were all dying right now.

The march over the cracked marshes, away from the battlefield, dragged through the hours. Kraston's remaining group comprised of only a few advisors and his personal guard. Observers with this procession kept tabs on the fading light pulses behind them, while Kraston focused on what his next move would be. By the time the group had gotten to a range where the haze of the planet completely blocked any hope of seeing the fight, the light from the bolt rifles began to fade.

Kraston heard the reports and knew that shortly the battle would be over and the Landran left behind would be dead. He would have to return to Fort Saturn, regroup and try this assault again. This time he would lead.

'When are we expecting the reinforcements?' he asked without looking for a recipient. He didn't care who answered and the Landran around knew someone had to.

'Without direct communication with the city it is hard to tell. My estimates put it at three days from now,' said the charcoal.

'Excellent, that should be the day after we return to the human city,' Kraston's spirits jumped at the thought of not waiting around.

The rest of the journey back was as uneventful as the march out, but this time Kraston no longer had his army behind him. Kraston thought a lot during those two days, about missed opportunities peppered with the occasional thought of lives lost. Every plan he could conceive of reengaging the Bregan ended the same way, defeat. To make matters worse, there was no guaranty as to the size of the new army. On the second evening, as the Marshal's entourage entered Fort Saturn through the northern emergency gate, the Blademaster Ann welcomed him.

The hands on her hips and the look she gave him told Kraston that she was not going to talk rationally. He would have to seclude himself in the commander's office if he had any hope of planning out the next step.

Kraston and his men walked past the Blademaster, without a word. The Landran, once sneering at her very existence, now avoided looking at her. She made sure to memorize every one of them, she would not forget. Kraston knew he would have to deal with her eventually.

Ann watched the scraps of the Landran army return with their heads low, she was stunned. A pitiful thirty creatures slinked in from a full division that left less than a week ago. It was unbelievable. The army was gone, wiped out for no good reason. There was no way Kraston could have won and Ann knew that before he left.

With the person guard of the Marshal keeping her away this evening, Ann would have to hold her tongue for the time being. Tomorrow was going to be a different matter. If she had to take out her blade, he was going to listen to her this time.

Ann snapped her wrist as a sign of dismissal, though the Landran were already leaving and would not look back at her for direction. She stood at the gate, watching the sad procession until it vanished into the maze of shops, offices and apartments. What she wouldn't give for an ear to rant into, a person she knew would be on her side.

For the first time, loneliness crept into her mind. As she returned to her quarters she examined that new mental picture. The closing of the door to the officer quarters also slammed closed that pathetic idea. She had no need for companionship only loyalty.

*****

CHAPTER XXXVII
Monday, 15 May, 2251

'Good morning gentlemen,' Ann chirped to the gold guards outside the commander's office. She had no idea if they were men or women but it matter little since she also did not care what kind of morning they had. Ann was here to see the Marshal and use force if need be.

'No entrancsse for anyone,' the one on the left said. It stepped forward to block her advance, leveling the bolt rifle at her chest. She had to admit they were imposing this close in a confined space.

'Oh, I understand, but I'm a special case,' she smiled. Ann gestured widely with her left hand to halt the progress of the guard and to get their attention. While they were following the show, the blade hilt she had been holding in her right sleeve slipped down into her hand. The weapon snapped to life, breaking the trance of the guards. The closest guard managed a shot but it was turned aside by the advancing Blademaster. A blurry wave of light brought both guards to a halt. The rear guard watched and his cohort slumped to the wall then slid to the floor in front of the Blademaster.

'I think he's expecting me,' Ann continued to smile as she stepped over the fallen guard.

Even though it had a rifle aimed at the center of her chest the guard seemed frozen in place. It tracked her as she worked her way to the door and as the portal opened, it remained passive. The door closed between Ann and the guard without it moving another inch.

'Ah, Miss Huston, good of you to join me,' Kraston said from beside the window. His back was to her and her blade was active, even then he gave no indication of panic.

'Your man outside says hi.' She said while walking

toward the Marshal.

'Just one? I'm touched,' he said without turning to face the advancing Blademaster.

'Yes, well it's Monday. I must pace myself.' She switched off her blade by the time she crossed the office and joined the Marshal at the window. She knew, and Kraston too probably, that she was not going to strike him down in the middle of his city.

'I assume you've come here to talk, about the battle most likely. Before you begin, take a look into the city.'

'What am I supposed to see,' she started but saw what he was referring to before she finished. Columns of Landran soldiers were filling the assembly ground. Easily twice the number that left with the Marshal last week, never to come back.

'This is the next phase, Miss Huston,' Kraston finally turned to address her, she was positive there was a smile on his face.

'That's incredible but the next phase of what?'

'Conquest. After a short rest period I intend to return to that Station and finish the job.'

'You've got to be kidding. That's the stupidest thing I've ever heard,' Ann stepped back from the window, juggling the blade hilt in her hand. The temptation to use it was growing fast.

'I obtained some valuable information from the previous failed excursion and I intend to capitalize on it,' Kraston said, still unconcerned with the angry, armed Blademaster beside him.

'Well I'm not...' Ann started before the office door burst open.

Kraston's attention jumped to the rushing Landran, unlike his response to her entry. She would have to try that method next time. The new Landran was puffing from its run up the stairs. It was the first time she had seen one of these creatures winded. Kraston reached for the brown scaled lizard when it finally got to him and steadied it while it reported.

'Marsssshal, the Bregan are attacking the cssity.'

The Marshal's eye grew wide, another first. Kraston threw the brown Landran to the side as he lunged for the intercom controls. He activated the mike and yelled through the city a chain of commands in his own language. Ann could not break out individual words but she hoped the army in the courtyard could.

'Looks like you'll get to capitalize on your findings sooner than you thought,' she could not help but smile.

'You had better get your armour on, Miss Huston,' the words were polite but the urgency behind soured them.

'On my way. I'll lead a contingent out the north side to cover the entrance,' she started for the door as she talked.

'No,' Kraston snapped, stopped her in her tracks. 'You will lead a fire team out the south side to cover the retreat.'

'What? The southern entrance has collapsed, there's no way to get through. And what was that about retreat?' She walked back to the middle of the room.

'My engineers are creating a breach as we speak, that will be the exit point.' He stood to his full height and strode up beside her and gently turned her to the exit. 'My army just finished a three day march with no resting time before the fight, it won't end well. The time has been thrust upon me to consider plan B.'

'And what is plan B?' Ann let herself be led out of the office.

'Plan B is evacuation, back to the forest city to start,' he said, his calm returning.

'Then what?' She stepped away from the Marshal.

'Let's make it out of this city and into mine first. Now go, get your armour and meet my soldiers at the southern gate.' He lightly pushed her further down the hall before returning to his office.

Fine mess this was, Ann thought as she ran back to her room. All her plans were flying out the window before she could make them. At least she would get to kill something now. Once in her room she slipped into her armour in her fastest time since basic training. All systems reported online as she ripped the door off its hinges and stepped into the hall.

She was immediately stopped by that charcoal-grey Landran. Its movements were as effortless as a waving flag, never seeming to stop even though forward motion had ceased.

'Mistress, I've noted that you have developed a distaste for our Marshal,' she said.

'Damn right. That fool is going to get us all killed,' Ann flexed inside her suit.

'Could I then suggest we form an alliance. To better assure our survival and perhaps convince the Marshal of the errors he's making?'

'You're saying you want to stage a coup?' Ann was intrigued now.

'In a fashion, when the time comes I will need you to be as close to the Marshal as you can get. I will give you a sign and you will kill Kraston.' She was still calm and floating.

'So we play along for now? What kind of sign?' the Blademaster started to dance in anticipation.

'Yes, for now. You will not miss it when it comes. As for now, we have a bit of trouble to deal with.' The charcoal Landran turned without a sound and drifted down the hall to the staircase.

'Right,' she punched the wall to release the built up energy flowing through her. She was back on track.

The blast to open the southern gate had to be a big one to overcome the tonnes of rock wall that blocked the way. Shockwaves rolled through the city, cracking the massive glass-steel dome. If Ann was staying she might have been concerned. Instead she raced into the field, snapping on her blade and waited with the fire team for the Bregan onslaught.

Thanks to the explosion she did not have to wait long. Seconds after the last stone fell back to the ground, the Bregan swarm flowed over the city's dome. Kraston led the charge out of the blasted wall with a small contingent of soldiers as the first gargoyle descended. Ann was not sure if he was leading the charge or the first to run.

Ann's fire team started the rising hail of bolts as Kraston ran past. A dozen Bregan fell in the first few seconds before Ann's target landed in front of her. She smiled inside her helmet and readied herself. The pause before this fight could be felt by all combatants. The first contact of blade and scythe seemed to cause an explosion of commotion. Showers of sparks and energy sprayed both sides. Bregan rained down on the Landran faster than the bolts sailed up.

While the Bregan engaged this primary defense line, the bulk of the Landran army filtered out of the breach. Their establishing firing line cut down a multitude of foul creatures and allowed her to finish off her opponent and a second that tried to get close to her. In the calm umbrella of plasma bolts Ann saw the skies over Fort Saturn darken with countless Bregan. There was no way to win this one. She prepared herself to fight, to die.

The Bregan quickly chose to ignore Ann's little team and concentrate on the main force. She was about to charge into the fray when the charcoal grabbed her by the arm. The grip registered as a severe impact on her suit's sensors and it stopped her cold.

'Mistress, we have business elsewhere,' she said loud enough to be heard, though not yelling.

'Where? What?' Ann managed to rip her arm free as she turned.

'The Marshal has made it to safety, now we should do the same if we are to complete our objective.'

Ann looked back to the fight then to the Landran. Her instinct was to fight but not to die. She stepped back from the fight slowly, ready to reengage but the Bregan had their hands full. As the haze filled the increasing distance between her and the battle her anger grew. Twice now that fool had destroyed an army. It had to end.

After the second night, still miles behind the Marshal's group, Ann's ranting got her into trouble. The charcoal slid next to her in the night and took the Blademaster's weapon. She woke shortly after, making every effort to find the lost blade.

'You will not find it, Mistress,' the charcoal said.

'You, you took it!' she fired a finger and the Landran.

'Correct. You will have to calm down before I feel you can handle it again,' she said in that same kind of maddening calm that Kraston used.

'I'll give you calm you scaly...' Ann started to move against the Landran but was halted by four blue Landran. These bodyguards seemed large even for the dragons.

'We have another day's march before we get to our destination. Try to enjoy the trip.' The charcoal turned from the Blademaster and melted into the night.

For the remainder of the march Ann grumbled but with no weapon and no target her energies for destruction waned. By the time they reached the forest city there was nothing left but acceptance. She would have to wait for the sign, whatever that was.

*****

CHAPTER XXXVIII
Friday, 1 June, 2251

'In four months we'll be without a home,' Walter Martel had said. It took two weeks since Commander Martel made that statement for the Eden Council to determine Captain Marso, and those still alive from his command, had nothing to do with the botched battle at the Miles Research Station, in the terms of any criminal charges. Until that had been decided the squad had to remain in the secure barracks located at the west end of the military compound in Port Mars. They had managed to use that time to get some much needed rest. Near the end of their stay they had become increasingly restless.

Councilman Mathew Idolan's summons of the squad to a closed boardroom meeting was a welcome change to their inactive lifestyle that had been thrust upon them. It was also odd, being the first time any single member of the council had met with combat personnel without the rest of the council being present. Buzz's contacts on the outside were saying the rest of the council did not even know of the meeting.

'Please come in, ladies and gentlemen. Have a seat, make yourselves comfortable,' Idolan said, '...and Captain, close the door when your people are in?'

'Will do, Councilman,' TJ said and turned around, counting the squad members. Satisfied everyone was here, he snapped the door shut and found his seat. He knew he had a spot reserved for him at the front and a smiling Daniella waiting for him, he was right.

'Now, before we get too far into things, I just have to be completely sure that you all are who I was told you were. For the record, you nine are the only troops to make it out of the MRS battle, correct?'

'There were a few others that squeaked out,' Ashley said.

'But they were transferred to a convoy escort duty when we got back,' Ken added.

'And there some others that were part of my squadron,' Buzz added, 'I'm anxious to get back to them sir.'

'That won't be for a while, Captain Zedluk,' Idolan said, visibly irritated at learning not all the MRS survivors were in this group. 'At any rate, I have a special mission for some of you.'

'Some of us?' Erik stood up.

'Sit down,' Ken said quietly and pulled the young trooper back to his seat.

'Whoa, whoa, am I hearing you right? You want us to split up?' Paul asked since Erik's question had not been answered.

'That is correct. Some on the Council want the experience of this group on the defence line or with our convoys. I do not agree fully with them, so I believe I have a plan that may save us all. I want to live, ladies and gentlemen, not just prolong dying.'

'I don't follow, sir,' Daniella said shaking her recently cut down hair causing it to shimmer in the dim light of the boardroom.

'She's right; you're not making a bunch of sense right now. And you'll have to explain the secrecy thing too,' TJ said with a quick twirl of his hand.

'Okay, Captain, Lieutenant, I'll try to explain to your satisfaction.' Idolan paused to compose himself, 'I am indeed working outside the authority of the Council but I'd like to explain my motivations if you'll permit me.'

'We have a few minutes,' Drew Webster joked mildly, 'let's have it.'

'Very well,' Idolan was not amused, 'in your reports it was mentioned that Captain Zedluk and Warrant Officer

Nivek made an unauthorized excursion into the Landran starship.'

'Uh-oh,' Buzz muttered and exchanged a glance with Paul.

The councilman stood and strolled to the window and looked out over the cityscape. He wanted a pause in the conversation to let the squad figure out where this was going, if they were able. His return to the front of the group was just as slow and measured. He kept his attention on the floor until it was time to speak.

'Councilman, I…' TJ started.

'As you've likely figured,' Idolan cut in, quite happy with the timing, 'I would like to send a team back to that ship.'

'Whoa! Hey now…' Erik got to say before he too was interrupted.

'Let me tell you why,' the Councilman turned to face the table of troopers, 'that woman you found in the cryo-chamber is probably the only human even partially alive that knows anything about faster-than-light travel. It will also give us a chance for some payback.'

'I'm all for payback but it seems curiosity is getting the better of me. I assume you know little about military operations so I'll only ask the basics. How big is this team you're thinking of sending? And we'll need some heavy support to get in and out,' TJ finally got in.

'The team will be six people only.'

'Six! Fine and our support?' TJ asked.

'No support, Captain. This will be a covert operation. I do not want there to be heavy fighting, just sabotage.'

'No support!' TJ jumped up.

Buzz cut in, 'I'm afraid to ask, but…'

'I would like Captain Zedluk and his best pilot to fly Warrant Officer Nivek, Corporal Krushell, Sergeant Michelson and Warrant Officer Conture into their compound.'

'Me, sir?' Conture asked.

'You are fully trained in the use of explosives, are you not?'

'Yes, sir.'

'Then I have need of your skills on this mission,' Idolan smiled.

'Hold on, sorry sir, but you said we were to fly in?' Buzz asked.

'Exactly, Captain. I need this operation done quickly. So I'll get two Ravens to take you to the site and back.'

'And just what happens to the rest of us?' Ashley asked.

'Yeah, that's what I'd like to know,' Daniella said.

'Well, Lieutenant Klon. I can't have all of the infamous Second Recon disappearing. The rest of you folks will accompany Commander Martel in the evacuation process of Mercury City.'

'Why on…' TJ was interrupted again, but not by the Councilman this time. This break in the conversation came when the door burst open, admitting two armed troopers and Councilwoman Robin Eddley. Her aged face, framed by light brown and silver locks, was etched with anger more than the effect of the years.

'What the hell is going on, Mathew!' she demanded.

'Ahh, Robin. Good afternoon. May I introduce…'

She cut the Councilman off this time, 'I don't care who they are. We know all about you. Your rebel sympathies and actions have finally done you in. As for you people, clear out while I'm still feeling nice.'

The two members of the Eden Council watched silently as the troopers filed out of the room. At the last minute TJ glanced at Councilman Idolan who simply nodded at him. The heavy door almost closed on him when it was slammed shut by the guards.

At TJ's insistence the squad met outside the shining brass doors to the government building where the councillors now fought behind closed boardroom doors. They stood out of earshot of the people passing in and out of the main entrance since their topic of conversation was not fully supported by the government, maybe even the population. Keeping a watch for eavesdroppers, they began to discuss recent events and future tasks.

'That was her being nice?' Erik asked, half-joking.

'What was that about? *Rebel sympathies*,' Ken said.

'I heard there were some upset feelings regarding the way the Council is handling the Bregan and Landran threats,' Ashley said.

'Where'd you hear that?'

'From a guard and that's all you're getting out of me!'

'He probably got more,' Ken muttered, jabbing Paul in the shoulder.

'Regardless of the source, and the circumstances of the attainment,' Ashley blushed but TJ continued, 'We have to assume that Councilman Idolan is a rebel for lack of any other evidence.'

'So what are we going to do?' Ashley asked but stared at the ground.

'It doesn't really matter what his affiliations, Idolan has a good idea. We should go get that lady Buzz and Kain found,' TJ said.

'You heard him, right? No support. And now we're working without his backing there's certainly no chance of further political back-up either,' said Drew.

'We weren't going to get any anyway,' Ken pointed out.

'Right, so what's the plan then?' Ashley asked, finally lifting her head.

'Just like Idolan said. Buzz, Kain, Dolly… sorry, Ken, Conture, Erik and one of Buzz's pilots will go to the ship to get the ice lady. The rest of us will run escort. This is the most covert mission we've had so far. Be careful folks,' TJ said.

The group dispersed and began to prepare for their assigned tasks. Though the idea was Idolan's, this was going to be their mission. For their part, TJ and his group reported to Commander Martel while Buzz took his half directly to the hangars without hesitation. He wanted to leave as soon as possible. Flying out was the best way before someone tried to stop them.

Nine hours after dark, two Ravens slipped out of Port Mars control range toward the southern coast. Rising to a height of two thousand feet, they cleared the cloud cover and most of the haze. By morning the evacuation team bound for Mercury City floated out of the northern pressure gates of Port Mars.

*****

CHAPTER XXXIX
Saturday, 2 June, 2251

Flying at high altitude in a Raven was a surreal experience for those who had not been before. Looking out the window provided the viewer with an image of barely-changing grey and green, more like a dense ground fog than a cloud – giving one the sense nothing was moving. Whisper quiet engines and internal motion compensators added to that sensation.

Relative to the ground below the Raven could have easily been a bullet. The ground speed would have been about one hundred and seventy-five miles per hour as they soared over New Terra. The city was unaware of their passing and would not have been concerned if they had. Their efforts were fully concerned with evacuating to Port Mars, according to reports.

'How long 'til we get to the LZ, Captain?' Erik asked, though his face was still glued to the window.

'Two hours as the Raven flies,' Buzz smiled.

'You mean crow flies, as the… oh, cute,' Conture said.

'You're a little slow there,' Buzz said, making a slow banking turn.

'Well you know us tankers. Lower IQ than you fly boys,' he replied.

'I think he's gonna fit in nicely,' Erik said to the others.

The aircraft descended as it passed the western city then flew at an altitude of the thousand feet until they zipped past the south-western edge of the Raynold's Forest. Fans of old earth roller coasters would have become nauseous if they were watching the Ravens put their energy into diving out of the air and into the trees before leveling off at fifteen feet. Once leveled, the aircraft raced further inside but at a much reduced speed to account for both the trees and the denser atmosphere.

It was midday when the two fighters eased themselves into a shallow pond less than a mile from the western side of the Sky Tree woods. As each ship settled in, the surface of the water rose above the top of the roof. The depth of the emerald water pool rose two feet over its normal resting state.

'Touchdown, everybody out!' Buzz called out.

'Thanks, Jeeves. Take the rest of the day off,' Conture patted Buzz's shoulder.

'Very good, sir.' Buzz smiled as he clicked off the various systems.

'You two better knock that off. Fun time is over,' Erik laughed as he climbed out of the dorsal hatch.

The six troopers made the exit look easy and formed up on the shore of the little lake. The non-airmen had watched as Buzz and his fellow pilot, Air Lieutenant Mike Donovan, set the security systems. This system was a little more than an alarm but rather was intended to enlarge the lake if anyone tampered with the Ravens.

'Alright, folks,' started Buzz by waving everyone closer, 'as you know we are on our own. This is a simple mission – in and out.'

'Fine by me, chief. I don't want to stay any longer than I have to,' Donovan said.

'I second that,' Erik said.

'Okay then, let's go.'

They turned toward the direction of the Landran city and away from Sol letting the sun warm their backs catching the last rays before the shade of the forest swallowed them. Their course was arrow straight for almost a mile before arcing to the north toward to the south wall. Casual observation on their last visit had shown them that that wall was the easiest to breach.

The number of guards had been fewer at that time and the cut line of the trees was closer to the side. It was their best chance.

'I hope we have a little run in with Ann,' Kain said.

'Remember bud, it would be better if we made as little of a display as possible. No side trips,' Dolly said.

'I know, I'm just saying is all. If she catches us it wouldn't necessarily break my heart to put a blade in her.'

'I second that,' Erik said again.

'Why do you keep saying that?' Buzz asked.

'Fine, I'm just a bit of a follower,' he hung his head in mock shame.

Each of the troopers wore a special armour suit from the Port Mars armoury that had black colouring infused into the metal for this type of mission. In addition to the standard equipment of the field suits this armour had advanced motion and imaging sensors. This would allow the troopers to cover the distance to the target far faster and without the same threat of detection. They would also be able to locate enemy patrols before being spotted.

The other piece of equipment they were toting was a collapsible cryo-chamber. Since the technology to repair the woman in the Landran ship required massive equipment, it was the best they continued her cryo-stasis until they had extracted her from the area. The doctors back at Port Mars would have enough time to do the job properly and more than enough security.

Both suns had fallen below the horizon and their light was fading quickly by the time the squad had reached the edge of the clearing around the city. Motion tracking revealed nothing around them from the start of their field trip but that picture was changing this close to the city. The image enhancers showed there were indeed guards, they were just not moving. A dozen of them lined the south wall and watched the darkness. They were not able to determine the colouring of their scale with the darkness and monochrome displays teaming up to show varying degrees of green. Without the colour differential the team could not figure on which of these things was the leader, assuming what they learned the last time was indeed true.

'Listen up, when we get in, head for the green space behind the boarding house. We only get one chance at this. You all have maps in your HUD,' Buzz whispered even though they were on a secured channel.

'Right, gotcha,' Conture said.

'Cool! Okay two groups. Two of you with Kain and the two other with me. Try to stay together.'

'Movement!' Erik called.

'Patrol. Two guards, coming this way. Thirty yards and closing,' Dolly added right behind him.

'If they see us we're screwed!' Erik said.

'You guys go on, move!' Donovan said.

'Move? What are you talking about?' Buzz snapped.

'No time for heroics,' Dolly said, pointing at Mike.

Too late for debate, the young Air Lieutenant burst from his hiding spot and charged the guards. The patrol had no time to react to the black-clad human before the blade erupted and found its target in the nearest of the pair. Mike spun around instantly, ripping the blade out of the Landran and swung at the second.

The other five troopers had no more time to discuss how stupid Donovan's idea was. After a moment of shock at the suddenness of his departure they charged up to the four-foot high wall.

Mike's blade blazed through the air but only managed to rip the guard's rifle in two, blowing it apart. The brilliant white and red blast knocked both of the combatants to the ground, the Landran without his upper limbs. Donovan finished his fall in a roll and seemed otherwise undamaged. Though his fall was a bit rough he popped up and continued his rampage into the woods.

'Good pilot, but a little strange,' Buzz said watching his pilot vanish into the woods.

Cries of alarm sprang up from the city at the sight and sound of the guard's rifle exploding. The enhanced imaging allowed the troopers to track the movements of the guards at the wall. Advancing toward the wall was far less difficult than anticipated. The pale green of the night vision showed the troops when to stop moving and when it was clear as guards ran toward the commotion.

They made it to the wall without detection and paused to regroup. They turned and watched in mild amusement as the green shimmer blade of Mike Donovan danced through the trees a hundred yards off. Intermittently some ruby red lights would race toward the blade but with no visible effect.

'Are all your boys like that, Buzz?' Dolly asked.

'Only the ones that don't get themselves killed,' Buzz replied with a little shake of the head.

'If you run off like that, we're running the other way,' Erik smiled.

'Understood,' Buzz returned the smiled.

'Hey, focus here boys. We ready?' Kain said, ending the conversation.

'Guess so,' Conture said as he got ready to stand up.

Kain rose slowly to have a peek over the low outer wall of the city. He pulled himself up with the hand holding his blade so only his visor was over the wall for a clear scan. At that moment, a passing Landran guard paused in his patrol to look on at the battle within the darkened tress. For what seemed to be a long second Kain and the guard stared at each other in disbelief over the two-foot think wall. The next second Kain's reflexes snapped the blade to life. The stream of excited crystals crossed the gap between the two in an instant and flooded into the guard's skull. The creature dropped without ever making a sound.

Kain switched off the blade even before the body fell and started over the wall, yelling as he went, 'Come on!'

The others cleared the wall in a couple seconds, stumbling over the body of the fallen guard. Instead of expressing shock, they quickly lifted the body and dumped it unceremoniously over the wall. They took the guard's rifle and ran into the city. Their progress was slower than they had planned but understandable since most of the town's guards were rushing to see what Donovan was doing. They managed to snake their way through the maze of houses as separate units but with a common goal. One by one they arrived at the meeting point shortly after planned. Amazingly not one of them was seen.

'Okay guys, since things have changed a bit from the ideal, this is the plan from here. Extra guards have likely been assigned to the ship's entrance so we're going to go through the hull,' Buzz said.

'You sure you're not nuts, sir?' Erik asked.

'Nope.'

'Cutting through may cause too many sparks. They'll see us for sure,' Conture said.

'I've considered that. We're going to dig ourselves a pit before we start cutting to reduce the flashes,' Buzz explained.

'We'll be burning the midnight oil tonight people,' Kain said.

'Let's do it!' Erik started digging.

'Have any coffee this morning, Private?' Dolly smiled. He slapped the back of Erik's helmet and thumbed toward the ship.

They crawled through the last of the green space and into the crater of the ship. With a couple troopers at the top of the crater rim to watch for curious Landran, the other three began to dig deeper along the side of the ship. The hole was only as wide as needed but seemed not much larger than a post hole when the bulk of the armour was factored in. It took a little less than an hour to dig and shore up the seven-foot deep hole. Dolly volunteered to cut the opening and lowered himself into the hole head first. The others then covered him with the collapsed cryo-chamber to block the light from the sparks.

Even though a bit of light from the cutting sparks got through they managed to complete the new orifice in two hours without being set upon by the Landran. Dolly gave a quick squawk on the comm. frequency to signal the completion of the last cut and began to enter the ship. Right behind him the half-squad pulled the cryo-chamber out of the way and started down the hole and into the ship. Once the entire group was inside with the chamber they retraced Kain and Buzz's steps from their trip taken over a month ago.

Their memories were crystal clear on several points of that journey and some were vastly less clear. Progress through the ship went well despite a few episodes of backtracking. Finally they arrived at the damaged elevator shaft leading down to the chamber where the sleeping woman waited for them.

Retracing their movements through the vessel brought back vivid memories of the battles fought in these halls. Buzz smiled brightly as he pointed out the massive dents in the bulkheads from the flash balls they had used on the Landran guards. The smile never faded from his face as he followed Kain into the shaft.

The private room containing the frozen body seemed darker than the two had remembered despite the extra sensors they carried. The darkness that seemed to seep into the men was an inner darkness rather than an alteration of light. The short ranged image enhancers revealed the room was physically the same from when they had left it aside from the door they had opened was now welded shut.

The troopers spread out to do a thorough examination of the room to ensure they were in a secured area. Erik finished his sweep next to the cryo-chamber and paused to take a closer look at their objective. He brushed away the layer of crystals of ice built up on the surface of the glass.

'Whoa! I'm in love, dudes!' he said transfixed by the vision.

'Knock it off, Private. We've...' Dolly started.

'Hush up boys,' Kain said as he reached the end of his security sweep next to the door. He motioned indicating there was noise on the far side of welded portal. Even though the channel was secure to only them it was still best to stay silent.

The group began to work in the green imaging of the HUD as quickly as silence would let them. Periodically they would pause and fall into a deeper realm of silence to draw in any foreign sounds but none came. Two troopers worked on setting up the portable cryo-chamber while two more set about preparing the lady for transfer. Erik was given the task of monitoring her vital signs since he was all but glued to the chamber anyways.

It took a rapid thirty-one minutes to stabilize the portable chamber, a full ten minutes sooner than expected. Erik had planned for the estimated completion time and started the removal process at forty-five minutes after they had started their work. This delay gave the setup crew enough time to work out any bugs in the systems. The extraction crew had to rush their end of the job to keep pace, causing a fair bit more noise than expected or wanted.

Somewhere along the line, Conture removed himself from the chamber swapping process and moved into the corner. He carefully began to fuss over the backpack he had brought with him. It was the pack of explosives the Councilman had wanted him to bring. He put one charge aside and installed a small device resembling a flip-head candy dispenser and he seemed well pleased with his work. Soft sounds of the clean-up of tools slowly filled the room before Buzz's voice whispered into the helmets of the troopers.

'Okay, let's do this thing!'

They reached into the backpacks holding the coolant and removed some canisters of *Absolute Zero* brand freeze spray. Dolly opened the intake valves from the new chamber, this left Buzz and Kain both hands free to empty the contents of each spray can into the waiting mobile chamber. To make the transfer as temperature neutral as possible half the spray was vented to the open room itself. The chilling burst from the fast-acting spray dropped the room temperature to thirty Kelvin. Even the power-assisted armour started to get stiff and moan against the chill. At a signal from Buzz, Erik cracked open the chamber where the objective lay and disconnected her from the instruments, the cold was too deep for the electronic warning beeps to do more than a warbled chirp.

The second the last instrument was shut down the display panel began to flash all sorts of lights. Shortly afterwards an alarm outside the room began its urgent call for attention. Buzz, Dolly and Erik stepped up their efforts instantly while Kain moved to the door. Noises from the other side rose in intensity and seemed to have moved closer. He motioned to the others to hurry up with one hand and readied his blade for a fight with the other. Erik lifted the *sleeping* woman from her resting place and into the temporary chamber and helped Dolly secure the lid and activate the monitors. That much was now done anyways. The frozen metal of the door resisted the guard's efforts to cut through the securing welds but it was still only a matter of time before the fight would be on.

Buzz was already heading up the shaft with Conture right on his boot heels by the time Dolly and Erik hoisted the chamber into the vertical tunnel and began to move upward. Kain waited behind until he was sure the chamber was well on its way up the shaft before he was comfortable enough to turn away from the door and follow his comrades. The door had just started to move when Kain noticed the explosive charge lying by the wall. Realizing what was about to happen made him more than double his pace out of there. His progress up the shaft got him out mere feet behind Erik and the Chamber.

'Okay,' Kain said to Conture as he pushed past him on the way to the exit. He was not referring to anything said but rather giving an all clear signal to the explosives expert. Conture smiled and hit the detonator without even looking back but did pick up his pace.

With a nerve-grating shriek of semi warm metal ripping and the extremely rare sound of frozen metal shattering, the door to the room where the cryo-chamber was supposed to be was thrown open by the guards. Two guards entered the room with rifles at the ready and noticed the chamber was destroyed and its occupant was gone. Confusion could be seen on their faces despite the rigidity of the scales and was replaced in a second by alarm when they heard scraping noises of metal on metal coming from the old lift shaft.

Order ended at that moment when the small device in the corner of the room detonated. The blast was sizable but reduced from its usual brilliance and size by the cold but was still more than enough to reduce everything in the room to atoms and fuse those atoms into the deck plating.

The hallway behind the fleeing humans erupted into a blinding light raging red, yellow and orange from the lift shaft they had been in only seconds before. Shock waves pulsed through every part of the ship and raced up behind them, knocking them to the ground. The group slid to the end of the hall in a haphazard and ungraceful fashion on what was obviously a non-stick floor covering. Even as they slid they could feel the ship's artificial gravity field waver. Subsequent explosions rocked the hull sending violent vibrations down its entire length. Standing proved difficult with the motion but they managed after a moment to collect themselves.

When Buzz finally got his feet under him again he looked around to get his bearings. He noticed the blast had sent them past one of the corners they should have turned at. His figuring put their improvised entrance near the front of the ship; they would have to back track their slide a few yards. Turning to the proper direction showed Buzz that they would have to find a new way out. The various explosions heard and felt had started to collapse that end of the ship. They were going to have to go up to the floor above the main entrance, and that was where he led them.

'What in Earth's name are we doing up here? The exit is one level down according to your diagrams,' Conture said after checking his internal mapping software.

Buzz said nothing but kept moving. He entered the nearest outside stateroom to what he reckoned was midship. A quick study of the interior showed him exactly what he wanted, a porthole. Through it he could see the lights shining in the guard's barracks and on the other side of the glass he saw tall grass waving in the shock waves coming from the ship's demise. He returned to the hall where the others stood debating whether or not he had lost his mind.

'Their emergency crews will be heading in through the main entrance in seconds if they haven't already,' Buzz said as if Conture's question had only now reached him, 'so this is how we're going to get out.'

'That window looks a little small for sleeping beauty,' Dolly said when he looked where Buzz was pointing.

'Conture, use one of your low-yield poppers to open it up,' Kain said while still scanning the hallway they had come up.

'I don't have any low-yields.'

'Ooookay, now what?' Erik asked

'We could knock out the pressure steel-glass and put a flash ball in there. It should be strong enough to widen the hole,' Buzz said.

'Certainly worth a try,' Kain said stepping past them and up to the window.

He carefully looked through the glass to ensure no one on the outside would see what was going to happen. Seeing the Landran were more than occupied with the fires and such he neatly cut the glass out of the frame. The glass dropped to the floor and shattered in a spectacular burst of noise and fragments but with the entire ship blowing up it was unlikely the dragons would have heard.

'Everyone out,' Buzz said as he placed a time-delayed flash ball into the opening.

He barely got out of the room himself before the device went off. The crystal blue energy pulse from the ball had two effects. First was the desired result of widening the orifice to allow an easy exit. The second effect was unexpected to say the least and totally surprising. Apparently Buzz's estimation about the room being mid-ship was correct but being in that location also put it in close proximity to the main structural beams of the vessel. The expanding sphere of energy ripped the seam of the bulkhead and the superstructure attaching the engine pylon. The massive engine, which had survived the rigours of space travel and a crash into a planet, twisted on its remaining support beams then dropped to the ground. The sudden transference of energy from potential to kinetic cracked the ship in half like the Titanic in a line perfectly centred on the porthole.

Seconds of destruction were translated into minutes to human perception followed by an equivalent length of time in shock. The groups stood silently on the new, level portion of the ship and stared at one another in disbelief. Most of the ship's power had come from the engine and was now cut off like a light switch with the sudden relocation of the drive section. Most of the city's power had come from that same source. What few buildings in the city they could see from their vantage point blacked out with a sputtering twinkle of light.

'Yer think can squeeze out the sleeper now?' Buzz asked.

'Might be tight but we can manage,' Conture said as he surveyed the chasm between the two halves of the ship.

'Good thing we didn't use an explosive,' Kain said.

'I think that would have blown up the whole ship,' Erik replied

'Let's go before someone notices us,' Dolly waved at them.

'I'm pretty sure at least one person saw that,' Buzz chuckled.

Laughing to themselves, the group readied the chamber for a short descent. It was equipped with light-duty anti-gravity engines to aid in transport and with their help the drop went smoothly. Kain and Dolly jumped to the ground past the neatly trimmed grass rim of the original crater and got ready to receive the package. Erik then pushed the chamber out to them before he hurriedly jumped down beside them to continue his monitoring of the patient. Buzz and Conture kept a watchful eye during the extraction for any possible witnesses. The chamber's descent was in slow motion due to the engines and was an easy catch for Dolly. He steadied the six-foot long device until Erik got behind to hold the other side for transit. The boys remaining in the ship followed down once it was secured.

'Nice catch, Dolly,' said Erik.

'Watch it kid,' Dolly replied.

'Enough guys. Let's get out of here,' Buzz prompted.

The group manoeuvred the cryo-chamber up a small rise to the backside of the barracks and out of sight of most of the rest of the city. Before they ducked behind the building Conture stopped. He turned and unfastened his pack with one fluid movement then tossed one of his bombs into the open door of the Landran vehicle bay. He had set the device to explode on impact so he did not bother to watch the action. He dove into an alcove the others had found between the barracks and Kraston's office.

As with the adventure in the ship not ten minutes before, the resulting explosion was unexpected. Instead of simple ka-booms that would have shut the building down, wrecked a few vehicles and distracted the guards from their escape, the entire building turned night into day as it blew up. Nearly every Landran still alive went running toward the burning and smoking ruins to try to save anything or anyone left intact. Some came running for other reasons, to hunt down the person responsible for the near total destruction of the city.

'You got some pretty nasty toys,' Erik said to Conture.

'They were a bit stronger than I anticipated,' he replied.

'Hey man, you better set the times and dump the rest. They're a huge liability,' Dolly said.

Conture knelt down and went about setting the timers on all four of the remaining devices. The rest of the group began to move away from the barracks in a hunched over but brisk walk. It only took a moment to arm the bombs and the same length of time for him to catch up to the others at the far end of the barracks. A few yards from the corner of the building two Landran rifle bolts impacted the wall and blew out the window inches above their heads. A third bolt caught Conture in the back of his shoulder and knocked him to the ground.

'Gahhh,' he moaned.

'Hold up!' Buzz shouted to the others.

'Forget it,' Conture waved at them, 'No time. You

have to go now. Get her out of here!'

'We're not leaving you!'

'Yes you are, Captain. My suit is losing power fast. You're not going to make it two feet even if you drag me before they got all of us. Better one than all!'

'We'll come back for you. 'Til then tanker,' he saluted.

'No time is too soon, airhead,' Conture returned the salute.

Buzz waved the rest of the group on and followed a step behind. They melted into the dark and chaos while Phil watched. He rested on the ground for a few minutes and watched as his HUD gradually dimmed and faded to nothingness. Darkness surrounded him briefly before Landran rifle barrels replaced it. Even without his image enhancers he could tell they were not happy with him.

'Hi,' he said.

*****

The day after the convoy left Port Mars was the longest day TJ had ever experienced. The convoy of twenty BRATs traveled all day to get to the shores of Foster Lake. It was the first landmark of any significance they had seen since the Port had faded into the haze. When you were a combat soldier, like TJ and the last several weeks have been filled with various battles and engagements, doing nothing was a special kind of hell.

The crisp blue waters of Foster Lake were an extremely important water source for the peninsula for several reasons. The main reason everyone thinks is that Mercury City has been on this spot since before the lake was here and gives it abundant source of natural water. The other point is that it is the only water source near the Barren Lands and the largest body of water easily accessible for the surrounding agricultural buildings.

Mercury City was actually located five miles past the edge of the desert Barren Lands but the citizens thought of themselves of barren dwellers nonetheless. The old city was originally called New Earth and was founded before the seaside town of New Terra. During cataclysm of the gas giant impact the orbit changes devastated the area around the city and raised the ambient temperature by forty degrees Fahrenheit in an already hot location. The searing heat and the rocky complexion of the surrounding land made the name change justified.

As soon as the transports had come to a stop almost the entire crew jumped ship to stretch. Even in armoured suits, every part of the troopers were tightening and aching up a storm. They were used to walking wherever they had to go. This sitting for the day and a half it took for this last segment was torture. Commander Martel took this opportunity to gather TJ's unit together for a chat. His actions indicated he was upset about something.

'So, gather around folks and tell me what's going on?' he asked.

'Just stretching things out a bit. It was a brutal trip, boss,' said Drew Webster.

'No,' Walter said shortly, barely maintaining his cool. The casual atmosphere died away and everyone focused on him, 'Where is the rest of your unit, Captain?'

The statement shocked TJ. Field Command had assured him the division of his squad was planned and insignificant. Commander Martel's sudden interrogation was something he was not anticipating so he was silent. Grasping TJ's quiet moment Viper spoke first.

'What do you mean?' she asked not quite as innocently as she tried.

'We were told that we were all assigned special duty,' Daniella said.

'I'm afraid that's not going to cut it, Lieutenant.'

'He's right, guys. This is the end of the run on this

one,' TJ said. 'We took it upon ourselves to acquire the woman we found in the Landran ship, sir. I sent a squad down there before we left.'

'I see. Interesting that my own command is sending out operations without my knowledge. By chance did Councilman Idolan have anything to do with that?'

'He did talk to us a few days ago but it was our decision to go. We felt that it was in the best interest of humanity not just a rebel ideal.'

'Explain that to me, Captain,' Martel said, looking more like a true commander than he had in quite a while. 'I must admit that it comes as a big surprise to find out that my own people were working against the Council's wishes and even the rebel's wishes. What do you think you can gain from this woman? She may just be a frozen dead woman.'

'Sir, it's assumed that she would know about faster than light technology. We as a species need that information,' Viper said.

'That may be, or it could be just that, an assumption. However, you may have also just wasted valuable resources and manpower on an assumption! All without going through proper channels or commands,' Walter was angrier than anyone had ever seen him.

'Sir, I'm sure they're fine. They'll probably be back at Port Mars before we are,' TJ said.

'They better be, Captain,' he said, with a touch of malice in his voice.

Walter Martel was normally so calm most people even doubted the Mars winds could rock him. Now, he was fuming. His people were in jeopardy and they were running around out of control. Losing his people to the rebel plots was never part of the big plan. Then again neither was war with two alien species. This should never have happened during his stint of command. He turned and stormed off toward the transports without another word, leaving the group in a stunned silence.

'TJ...' started Daniella.

He raised his hand, 'We may have some trouble getting him to see the benefits to the course of events we've set in action.'

Huge hover-platforms were now taking on the last bits of equipment and supplies from the military base in Mercury City. The true scope of the massive interior space of the BRAT was only amplified when you looked at the amount of cargo the platforms were now holding and kept in mind those same platforms had been stored in the back-end of the transports. The civilian population was evacuated early in the morning on a large portion of the transports brought in. Now the patrol was working into the afternoon and had packed up most of the military base's supplies.

Because of its location near the barrens the population had been kept small in Mercury City by the Eden Council. Even though there were few residents in the city it seemed quite lively only a month before but now with only a couple hundred troopers the place was deserted. A team of twelve troopers had been assigned to act as guards and chose to keep an eye on them from inside the city walls in case there was company and had only recently turned to the use of radar tracking for a sweep of the countryside. Only a mile out of the city the civilians had joined up with a long parade of other Eden Peninsula residents on their journey to Port Mars from points such as Combtown and Crystal City.

The detachment made short work of the base's supplies and were likely ready to go in a few hours. Every couple of hours since they had arrived they were forced to pause to let a convoy of transports go through the city instead of going around. Those transports that were heading in the direction of Port Mars were loaded to the max with crystals while empty ones raced back the other way.

'This is ridiculous!' a dust covered private kicked some tan desert dirt at one of the transports, 'Why in the name of Bane don't these things go around?'

'It's a security thing,' Viper said as she took a break against the wall, 'If the Bregan saw those transports, they'd attack. Here in the city we could defend them a little better.'

'Whatever,' the Private waved his arm in dismissal, 'Get outta here!' he yelled at the last of the latest convoy.

During the late morning TJ had rarely seen Commander Martel and the times he had he appeared to be talking to himself, or arguing to be more accurate. That same behaviour was repeated in the reports he was getting from the various ranks.

'I'm worried about the Commander, TJ,' Viper said.

'How do you mean?' he asked, turning from the woman standing beside him. She was the quartermaster in charge of loading the hover-platforms and BRATs and had been relaying stock levels when Viper had cut in.

'I just saw him nearly attack a private for no reason. At least none that I could see.'

'I'm sure he had his reasons,' he said but knew what she was getting at.

'No he didn't, TJ,' Daniella said, stepping up to the pair after directing a few troopers to a pile of crates that seemed not to be loading themselves into the BRATs, 'I was close enough to hear. The private was just moving a little slow after the last convoy.'

'You sure?' TJ asked. He flipped open his visor for an instant and motioned for her to do the same. A faint hiss escaped as her visor popped up then he leaned in and gave her a kiss on the cheek. The display was over in an flash then their visors snapped shut.

'Yes,' she said around a blooming smile, 'I think you should have a talk with him. He's over on platform four.'

'Okay, thanks, Dani. Take over here. Ash, go tell the Commander to meet me beside Platform Two and make sure he gets there. Four is a bit too busy right now for a private talk,' TJ ordered.

By the time Martell was walking up to the second transport he was visibly pissed off. TJ could see it in his eyes and it made him nervous. Troopers walking past the number two transport were obviously affected by the Commander's aura of displeasure and gave him a noticeably large berth. It was clear those troops had been on the wrong end of Walter's lashing rants regarding inefficiency and laziness at some point earlier. It was up to TJ to use his best diplomatic skills to get through whatever it was the Commander was going through.

'Commander, I'd like to have a word with you,' TJ said and raised his arm in a welcoming gesture.

'Just 'cause you send your little squad tramp to deliver a message doesn't mean I have any time to talk, Captain,' he snapped with unrestrained venom.

'Walk with me, sir,' TJ said calmly but with a subtle force. He turned to a trooper that had been hiding from the Commander's view, 'Sergeant, take over the loading of Two.'

'Wait a minute! How dare you...'

'Walk, Commander,' the subtly was gone from TJ's voice.

TJ dragged his superior officer back, a hundred feet away from the line of troops, before he let Walter get his feet under him. He wanted to be sure no one heard what he was sure was going to happen. The commander was understandably and extremely upset at being dislodged from his post and was ready to tear into TJ. That was until he saw Mercury City's base Commander approaching with Ashley.

'Tell me what's going on, sir,' TJ said.

'I don't know what you mean,' he said.

He made a visible effort to return to his usual demeanor. 'I feel weird. Shut up! Sorry, TJ' He collapsed, resting on the side wall and did not seem to want to move another inch.

'I'm a busy man, Captain,' the base commander said, 'Would you mind telling me what on Mars is so important that you have to send a trooper to drag me out of my base in the middle of all this?'

'I apologize, sir, but it is my belief the Commander Martel is no longer fit for command and I request that you take over this operation.' He indicated the slouching officer beside them.

'That's pretty drastic action, Captain Marso. Commander Martel, how do you feel about this matter?' he asked, turning to the crumpled officer.

'That's absolute crap! You're all out to get me! I'll have your heads for this,' he ranted.

The base commander was obviously not in any need of further proof and waved over two of his troopers that had followed him a few yards behind. Martel continued to fire off on his rant but had turned the direction mostly to himself thankfully. 'Assist Commander Martel to the Med-sled. Have him sedated and get him to Port Mars Medical.'

'Yes, sir!' they saluted before moving to Martel, disarming him on the off chance he became violent and took him away.

'Thank you, Captain,' the base commander said before turning toward the work that needed to be done.

He was either dismissing the situation or getting right down to business, TJ could not decide. With the base commander off to his own tasks, TJ was left to watch as Commander Martel was loaded into the Med-sled for evacuation. The moment was awkward to watch for the troopers from Fort Grey in the area and they found themselves moving to comfort each other. Viper moved to TJ's side and wrapped her arm around him to watch the transport move off then they both returned to where Daniella was still overseeing the fourth transport loading.

'How'd things go?' Daniella asked.

'TJ had to commit Commander Martel,' Viper replied.

'He's not *committed*; he's going to get help. He has problems,' TJ said.

'I'm sorry, TJ. I know that must have been hard,' Daniella said.

'Yeah,' TJ turned his head to avoid showing his emotion.

They had a moment of silence to not only come to terms with what happened to their commanding officer, but also to reflect on when times were better. Those happy moments seemed far away but were only a month in the past. Daniella hugged TJ and pulled Viper in a moment later with a solid clunk of the armour for a group hug then returned to the work of clearing the base. Drew Webster's appearance at a run stopped them before they got too involved.

'Trouble! Let's go,' he waved at them to follow.

The three shared a glance of surprise before their training kicked in and they fell in behind the Blademaster. He led them through the loading zone and flagged down a few more of the troopers from the desert detail. Soon there was a full dozen troopers running through the compound ending their journey outside the base commander's makeshift office.

'Come in, Recon,' said the commander.

'What's the problem, sir?' TJ asked.

'You and your squad have to get an ambush site set up ASAP. The last inbound convoy reported they have unwelcome company.'

'Bregan?' Viper asked.

'Affirmative. We can't let them know where the cargo is going,' he said before turning to address TJ again, 'Captain, meet the convoy outside of town on the east side and make sure none of those things get the chance to report back.'

'Yes, sir. Do we have any intel?'

'Convoy pilot reported seeing at least two dozen.'

'Means there's probably three or four dozen,' Drew said.

'Easy enough,' Viper smiled.

'We're on it, let's get organized,' TJ straightened up to his full height, 'Assemble at the east end of the compound in ten minutes. Full gear. Go!'

Four minutes past D400, TJ's modified recon squad had assembled and moved into an ambush position ahead of the incoming convoy. Armoured troopers busied themselves erecting defenses and camouflage while TJ and Daniella went over the plans of the operation. Viper took charge of the setup of a semi-mobile plasma beam cannon. They kept a radio frequency open to the convoy lead for updates, a crackle over the dead air gave made them aware of the convoy approach.

'screeee… Do not respond to this… eee… we are heading for the co-ordinates giv…. <blazzzzmmmmm> stand by,' the voice sounded tense.

'That was a beam cannon shot,' Viper said.

'Everyone set?' TJ called out.

'Sir!' responded the squad.

'Here we go,' Daniella said getting into position next to TJ.

'Oh, yeah,' Viper said with a too big smile.

Approach from the front side of the camouflaged position revealed nothing more than a small cluster of trees with some moderate undergrowth. The phony trees were placed too close together but nothing too obvious. From a distance the convoy was a blur in the grey haze and red dust kicked up by a slight breeze. The pulsing green from the wings of the Bregan was only slightly more visible.

'Stay ready,' TJ said as the convoy passed a quarter mile range, 'Steady.'

The Bregan were obviously not making much progress in stopping the convoy. A group of the gargoyles raced ahead of the transports carrying a large piece of equipment and landed only a few yards from Viper's concealed position. The group only numbered six Bregan but was more than enough to get their equipment set up and it was looking a lot like a missile launcher. Viper glanced at TJ, neither one moving even slightly. TJ nodded inside his helmet.

The missile launcher had begun to register a lock-on on the lead BRAT when Viper burst from the fake trees and bowled over the group of Bregan. Her blade ripped through the air and neatly cleaved the missile launcher in half. She winked playfully at the gargoyle, who was obviously the gunner, before she brought her blade sweeping through its chest.

TJ did not want to alert the other Bregan to their position and held off on ordering the cannon to fire. Instead he waved half of the troopers to engage the other five beasts. The element of surprise was so successful that the rest of the group of hostiles was taken down without much more difficulty than the first one. The path was cleared for the convoy to pass before the first BRAT slid past. The Bregan continued to harass the BRATs and seemed only slightly scattered that their missile had not destroyed the lead transport.

The nose of the first BRAT had barely entered the cluster of trees when TJ's squad burst from cover, knocking down the phoney trees as they did. The cleared horizon allowed the beam cannon crew a clear shot of the Bregan and it lit up the sky. Brilliant blue flashes illuminated every rock for a quarter mile like a lightning storm and with each flash another Bregan fell. The blades of the troopers cut into the Bregan ranks as well but the creatures were fast to react. The gargoyles used every defence they had to reverse the direction of the fight from wing flashes to arm scythes to physical attacks. They stabilized the fight to two to one odds in favour of the Bregan but lost the convoy.

These creatures wore no armour and carried no blades whether to maximize their speed or because they had simply burned out the components. Blade met scythe time and again, showering the area in light that made a disco ball look like a dim flicker. The Bregan had clearly identified the threat of the beam cannon and quickly incapacitated the heavy weapons specialists but did not have the time to kill them off. TJ, Daniella and a young Corporal advanced on the ones attacking the specialist despite the Bregan having back up only a couple yards behind the three.

TJ blocked a slash with his forearm deflector then spun around to bring his non-blade arm elbow into the back of his opponent's head. The blow knocked the creature unconscious, which meant it could not move away when TJ quickly stuffed a time-delayed flash ball into a nook under the creature's wing. Two nearby Bregan did see this stunt, jumping into the air to avoid what was coming. The three humans within the coming blast radius found themselves facing the last three of the Bregan that had not been taken down the specialists. The creatures were stunned by the pointed assault and took only a half moment to study the new development. After the half moment though, the flash ball went off.

The expanding sphere threw the unconscious gargoyle into the air like a rocket though without the finesse of one. The timing worked out perfectly for the organic missile, sending it crashing into one of the airborne creatures with a bone-crushing thump. The backside of the sphere impacted with the advancing reinforcements, sending them sprawling. With the body of the fallen Bregan behind them they knew they were in for a ride when the front side of the wave hit the three humans and sent them bowling into the ground forces. Troopers were spaced several feet apart and had extended their blades in anticipation. As they tumbled their blades helped turn them into an industrial sized blender.

The Bregan's numbers had dropped in an instant from two - one in favour to two - one against. Only six creatures remained and they pressed the fight like they still had superiority. The second airborne Bregan dove at the line of humans still standing but its trip was cut short by a blast from a specialist that had struggled back into a firing position. One of the grounded Bregan jumped the distance to the master sergeant and cut deep into his armour. TJ and the corporal rose to their feet and readied for a fight. Daniella did not stand with them.

'Dani, get up!' TJ yelled to her.

'TJ,' she said softly.

He was worried the blast from the ball had damaged her power supply so he bent and rolled her over to open her visor so she could breathe. He held his blade at the ready and shot glances at the advancing Bregan while he rolled her over and glanced at Daniella's armour and the two slashes near her right shoulder. The Bregan she had been thrown into had defended itself quite well. One slash cut into the armour near the neck but did little more than cosmetic damage. The second was lower and had cut into the armour, deep enough to draw a lot of blood.

'Grab Sgt. Conners over there, Corporal!' TJ ordered.

Two troopers not engaged began to drag their wounded comrades away even with the battle advancing toward them. The advancing Bregan were intercepted by a blur of shimmer blade energy held by a berserk Blademaster charging the battle line. After the first creature was cut down two more troopers joined the counter assault. Three whirling blades were too much all of a sudden so the rest retreated into the air to avoid the blazing crystals. The distraction allowed the troopers to move the wounded to safety.

More Bregan joined those in the air, and with the confidence of numbers they dove at the scrimmage line. Now numbering only nine members the fight erupted with a deafening screech. The fight had been a rolling one for the last few minutes and none of the combatants realized exactly their position until the cannon from the Mercury City base creased the sky. The explosion of the first Bregan sent visible ripples through the air and shattered the confidence of the remaining creatures.

The troopers made no effort to chase the retreating gargoyles but rather let their fatigue finally set in. A couple were assigned to keep an eye on them from a distance but not to pursue. The major portion of the team instantly turned their attention to the wounded. Daniella and Sergeant Connors were the main focus of the medical team. The main focus of Viper and Drew were now the two injured Bregan left behind.

*****

CHAPTER XL
Late Saturday, 2 June, 2251

As Dolly and Erik shuffled along with the sleeper, Kain and Buzz kept scanning the surroundings for signs of pursuit. The group now consisted of four troopers but their mission was still succeeding. They scuttled along the vine covered buildings, never standing more than four feet tall, and darted from cover to cover. Kain had taken point and was proceeding along the path of least resistance. Buzz was the sweep in the lineup to ensure everyone got to cover before prying eyes fell upon them. Buzz turned his head occasionally to see if Conture had managed to catch up but there was nothing behind them. Several minutes after they had left their comrade behind a large explosion ripped through where the barracks would have been and lit the darkened city for almost ten seconds. Hope of their man rejoining the ranks faded with the light from the blast cloud.

'Damn,' Buzz mumbled.

'Was that…' Erik started to ask.

'Conture's toys,' Dolly finished.

'Seems like there aren't too many Landran about,' Kain said as he looked around a corner, seeming to ignore the events behind him.

'Last time we were here this place was packed,' Erik said, 'I doubt the commotion at the ship would empty the city that fast and so thoroughly,' he continued as he stepped around the corner with the rest.

'Maybe there are still a lot of them up at Fort Saturn,' Buzz said.

'Would seem logical,' Dolly said.

The absence of inhabitants seemed to make the city

come alive with running shadows and sounds of pursuit. They managed to creep along the walls of businesses and houses at a good pace despite seeing trouble in every darkened leaf flutter. They made it to the northwest gate of the city without incident and surprisingly on time, according to their schedule. They stopped at the end of a street and found that despite the commotion and light show in the centre of the city the sentinels maintained their posts. Oddly, the guards were not even interested in the events toward city center but rather were intently scanning the darkness of the forest beyond the walls. The distraction allowed Kain to duck behind cover after he had boldly stepped around the last corner.

'Now what?' Erik asked, 'This sleeper won't keep much longer.'

'We could rush them,' Kain said, 'They aren't paying any attention this way.'

'But we all aren't as good at bolt deflection as you are,' Dolly said.

'Or we could just wait 'til the cows come home,' Buzz said.

'Okay, have it your way,' Kain said.

Kain checked his equipment even to the point of flashing on his blade on and quickly shutting it off. Everyone stared in silent awe, for deep down they knew what was about to happen. He was satisfied his equipment worked as intended, stood and strolled from his hiding spot toward the guards. The other three tried to stop him from his causal approach but could only watch as he walked up to a group of Landran. They did not even see him coming, feeling the real show was in the forest somewhere. Lightning moves from Kain swung a brutal attack at the first guard. The blade lit halfway through the swing and ripped through the back of the Landran and his comrade then dug into the third dragon beside them.

The three lizard-like creatures fell as one, without

making a sound. A fourth guard heard the thumping of the others and turned. It attacked Kain apparently without formulating any battle plan. Another nearby Landran became aware of the engagement and charged to join the fight letting out a hiss that was loud but did not seem to echo. Kain easily deflected away the incoming rifle fire and advanced on the fourth guard. The fifth guard skidded to a halt to get better aim on Kain. The creature was so focused it did not see Buzz flanking him.

Buzz professionally threw a flash ball in an over-hand style to a point ten feet in front of the fifth guard. The guard did get a couple shots off while the ball was in transit and was looking quite pleased with itself. The ball hit a little off target and impacted the wall a couple feet away and suddenly there was no more guard. It was not blown to pieces, since that was not the nature of the flash ball but the blast wave did throw it hard enough against an adjacent building that it went through the wall.

Kain had just dealt a fatal blow to the number four guard when the first shot clipped him in the rib shield. The shot spun him around and off to the side, which luckily meant the second shot sailed wide. He used the wall to catch himself and steadied himself while he checked the damage read out.

'Man, I really want to be a Blademaster,' Erik said, strolling up with the other two.

'When you get older boy,' Kain smiled.

'Shall we go?' Dolly asked.

They ran as fast as carrying the cryo-chamber would allow in a northwest direction from the city with the intent to circle more to the west later and make it into the trees before they encountered trouble. Even before they had entered the trees, green energy bolts began to rip through the foliage. Scans of the immediate area did not show any Landran despite the deadly rain. With no visible pursuit, they continued into the trees before they rested and checked their gear.

'Those must have been automated defenses,' Kain said.

'Idiocy,' Buzz said after a moment of silence then pointed into the trees.

The other three troopers slowly followed Buzz's gesture, though they were a bit confused by the change in attitude, and gazed into trees. Ahead of them and a little to the right came the thundering figure of Air Lieutenant Donovan at full charge. Behind him were six irate-looking Landran. The pursuing guards spotted Buzz right away and shortly after saw the rest of the extraction team and gave up the chase before they were engaged.

'Lieutenant!' Buzz called.

'I think you won your adventure,' said Ken.

Donovan slid to a halt on the undergrowth of the forest when he heard Buzz. Once he had stopped, he shot a glance behind him then to the sides. Having determined his running mates had left he stood tall then bounced over to his CO.

'Hi, guys!' he smiled, 'is that her?'

'Yeah,' Erik replied, 'you been running all this time?'

'You bet! I did stop a few times but for the most part running.'

'You feeling okay, Mike?' Buzz asked.

'Sure, but we better get going. I'm getting a bit tired.'

An alarm flashed in Buzz's helmet, drawing his attention away from his subordinate. The indicator showed there was trouble at the Ravens. He turned to the group to tell them what was happening when the sky lit up for the third time this evening. The dazzling light lasted for ten seconds before slowly fading to the turbulent darkness of this evening.

'Guess we can't fly out of the forest now,' Buzz said.

'Tell me that wasn't our ride!' Erik pleaded.

'Okay,' Buzz changed the subject, 'Now, how 'bout we start walking.'

'Aw, man!' Erik whined and punched the air.

They only managed to walk for two hours before they had to come to a stop. The evening's action was enough to take away most of their energy. Lieutenant Donovan was further down the path of fatigue than the others and he was given the first rest shift for his marathon through the trees. The break in travel also gave their suits of armour a chance to recharge since the recharge rate was slower than consumption if used at full output.

Buzz took the first watch while the others tried to get some much-needed sleep. The troopers did not bother lighting a fire or setting up some powered lights to better keep their location hidden from any Landran that might be following. The sentry did not require the use of external light sources since the basic night vision had enough range to spot anything they would bump in the night within the trees.

Their time spent digging into the side of the starship and activities inside messed up the troopers' internal clocks and the fatigue from those same actions resulted in them forgoing a check on the suit's time keeping system. As such, the night melted away into the dawn much sooner than they had thought it would and revealed to them that they were at the edge of the Sky Trees. The newborn light of the day also showed them something they had not expected. Two large and slow moving vehicles were drifting not more than four hundred yards ahead of the camp.

'Oh, no way!' gasped Erik.

'Those wouldn't be the same tanks we set loose after MRS, would it?' Dolly asked as he stood up from his sleep spot on the far side of the cryo-chamber.

'The timing is about right,' Buzz was, the thought of not walking anymore excited him.

'We'll give 'em a look. Anyone remember the lock codes for those tanks?' asked Kain.

'You really think that the very same hover tanks we set loose weeks ago are these beasts here?' Dolly put a hand on the Blademaster's shoulder.

'It couldn't hurt to try,' he said, 'Besides, they couldn't be anything else. So again, anyone remember the codes? I know I don't.'

'I guess I do,' Dolly said.

'So do I,' said Buzz, 'We'd better get it right 'cause those things will end us if we don't.'

'So go already,' Donovan said from the spot in the grass where he still lay.

The two former Second Recon *Reconers* ran off toward the crawling hover tanks, while the others remained in the shelter of the trees with the cryo-chamber. It took less than a minute to cross the shallow decline spanning the distance to the tanks. When they got to less than ten yards from the sides the massive turrets swung around and drew a bead on the soldiers. The men hit the dirt hard, not as much as a trained manoeuvre but one borne of surprise. They realized it was an auto-defense measure when the barrels did not erupt with death. That and the red confirmation code request flashing on their visors.

Buzz opted to enter the codes from where they were laying rather than risk provoking the battle machines further. As soon as the tanks recognized the incoming codes the turrets swung to their resting position and the vehicles stopped in a synchronized slide. Dolly walked to the rear tank then waved at the troopers buried in the trees while Buzz jumped aboard the lead vehicle and began to access the finer systems.

By the time the others had traversed the field Buzz and Dolly had managed to get the tanks open and had familiarized themselves with the basic controls. The internal space was perfectly suited to hold three people in full armour each. This left them with only one problem to solve – a six by three by three problem to be exact.

'It's not going to go inside,' said Buzz.

'And they made him Captain?' Kain asked Donovan.

'Best of the bunch.' Donovan joked, 'Anyways, we could tow it.'

'There's a person in there, pal,' Erik snapped.

'Easy, buddy. You'll have to excuse the private, he's grown a little attached to our objective,' Kain soothed.

'How's about we strap it to the back of the turret of number Two. We won't be able to swivel but it's the most secure place for it. Certainly can't tie it down on the front,' said Dolly.

'Good thinking, Dolly,' smiled Donovan.

Buzz stepped off the tank he had been sitting on and positioned himself between them in an effort to keep Dolly from killing his favourite pilot. He quickly ordered both Dolly and Erik to secure the sleeper unit to the second tank. Next, he directed Kain and Donovan into the turrets and began showing them the necessary instruments to operate the tank's main guns. After a few minutes of familiarization, they hopped down to the ground to go over the details of the trip to come.

'Obviously, we have to go straight to Port Mars. That course will take us first to New Terra. They'll have medical facilities there,' Erik said as if this could actually go without saying.

'Going direct to Port Mars is a better route. There is no reason to stop over before we get there. Besides, they've probably evacuated New Terra already,' Donovan said.

'Actually, I think Erik is right. The sleeper is running out of time,' Buzz said.

'Again I go back to the evacuation thing.'

'They'll at least have cryogenic supplies left over. At the very least I think we'd be able to catch someone anyway.'

'Let's just do it already. I think we're being watched,' Kain said.

'Good idea,' Dolly said as he turned to the trees.

'Great, Kain, Ken and Erik will take the number two and Don will ride with me,' Buzz said and left with a twirl of his hand.

'Yes, sir,' they replied.

*****

CHAPTER XLI
Monday, 3 June, 2251

The journey out of Landran territory was relatively dull compared to the rescue they had just undertaken. Dull except for an ambush by a small band of Landran during the first day of the estimated four-day trip. The dragons were obviously not expecting the lumbering pair of tanks but that did not stop them from firing a few shots. The fight was over after the first shot from the tank's gun.

They had spent the first night at the base of the plateau supporting the Sky Trees forest they just left. The Raynold's Forest started only a mile and a half beyond that to the north. In the morning the forest was visible through the brightening haze as a dull dark line under the greenish hue lit by Bane and Sol in the morning.

Erik spent the night switching his watchful glare from the surrounding field and the cryo-chamber instead of sleeping. Despite the urging from Buzz he had stayed there for half the night. The other half he was still, after he had passed out. He was still out when the others began to pack up the tanks for the second day of travel. His companions had a great time at his expense for staying up all night with a mysterious woman. Erik bore it well but it still made for a long day.

The joking stopped once they came into view of the southern coastal city. The protective dome shone in double-barreled sunlight. The sight of a full sized city was breathtaking but even more stunning was the view of the southern gates. They stood wide open, letting the cleansed air of the interior mix with the heavy air outside, clearly not a planned circumstance. No movement could be seen anywhere near the gates or deeper into the city for that matter.

'Ghost town,' Donovan muttered.

'Go easy. There is probably a reason for this scene. Maybe there are people still left inside. Could be a doctor in there even,' Erik said.

'Doubt it, bud,' Dolly said.

'Yeah, the Council ordered a total evac.' Kain added, 'Not even military here.'

'But she can't make it to Port Mars. The temperature is already rising in the sleeper.'

'We'll see if they left some *freeze* behind,' Buzz said as he scanned the city wall, 'and maybe some food.'

'Yeah, they probably left some of both,' Dolly said to assuage Erik.

The two tanks drifted through the doors and the visible mixing of the air into one of the eeriest places any of them had ever seen. An empty city is a frightening vision even to a hardened combat trooper. Everywhere they looked was another spot where people should have been. Shadows danced away from the lights in a dizzying blur from behind one building to the next. Noises with seemingly no source echoed off those same buildings. While noises from the group seemed to blast back in an effort to bring silence but to no avail.

'What was that?' Erik spun in position.

'What? Listen kid, don't go snaky on us,' Dolly said.

'I heard a metal clang too. Things don't clang without help.'

'Hold up, I've got movement. Thirty degrees to the right,' Mike said from inside the tank.

The two massive hover tanks slid to a halt on a bridge in the middle of the city. The river running through the city of New Terra had spanned a full third of the peninsula and was still clear flowing, all the way from the Comb plateau to the sea. The water reflections danced across the buildings and the environmental dome making it difficult to get a visual on the signal.

Buzz used the movement tracker to find the bearing then spun the turret to face it. The troopers were in full battle mode, ready to blast Bregan or Landran. Those not gunning jumped down and snapped their blades into existence filling the abandoned city with a steadier glow.

They knew they were behind the Landran front line and readied themselves to fight a patrol or possibly even a Bregan ambush. For all their prep and training they were shocked by what was approaching the bridge. Half a dozen ragged looking humans emerged from around the side of the central control building. As the people neared Buzz could see they were civilians and their gear was almost entirely improvised. Based on their reactions the troopers could tell the civvies were not expecting to see the combat group.

Buzz and his group quickly lowered their stance and deactivated their blades; both groups had a bit of recovery to do. The civilians were still so stunned at the sight of the tanks pointing their guns at them Dolly was able to walk up to them before they made their first move. Buzz popped his head out of the tank to address the newcomers since the tools they carried were not much of a threat. As he scanned the group he noted something was not quite right with them.

Buzz started by calling out orders to the squad to gather up the civilians and securing the tanks from combat conditions. Out of nowhere, the group of residents began chanting and advancing on the tanks. The sounds of the chants echoed off the surrounding buildings, mixing with other echoes into more of a methodical buzz of noise. Though he could not understand the chanting Buzz guessed it was something like an all clear signal as he quickly saw more civilians begin to emerge from the surrounding structures and filling the windows to stare at them.

'Get out, Militia!' yelled a man coming through the gathering crowd. People moved out of his way giving

Buzz the notion he was in charge.

'What are you people doing here?' Buzz asked the leader.

'This is our city now,' he responded.

'We run this city. The council has no power here!' another man screamed.

'Sir, I think there will be trouble if we push them,' Donovan said through the secured comm. channel in their suits.

'Noted,' Buzz nodded his head.

'Get out!' the leader shouted again and was joined by the rest of the crowd.

The group of angry residents now surrounding the troopers surged toward, them waving their clubs. Their weapons posed no threat to the armoured soldiers but reflexively they lit their blades and readied themselves. Kain faced the northern edge of the bridge while Erik and Mike covered the rear of their formation. Though Kain's lone figure did not seem as imposing as the two in the back, the mob at that end stopped their advance and the chanting as fast as they did for the other two.

The blades were not lowered until the crowd had backed off several feet to what was deemed a safe distance. The silence remained long after the glowing weapons were turned off and the troopers relaxed. Buzz figured this was a good opportunity to try to persuade the mob to disperse.

'Please listen, we're not here to force you out even though I do think it's a good idea. We just want to pass through.'

'He's lying. He came to take our homes!'

'No! Listen, you can stay here for all we care. We just need to get some medical supplies. Soon as that's done we're on our way to Port Mars.'

'Still think you're lying, soldier boy!' a lady in the crowd called out.

'Hand to Sol, I'm telling the truth. Will you help us?'

'Well how 'bout that?' the leader mocked, 'soldiers asking civilians for help.'

'Where we come from, that's not such a rare event,' Kain said.

'And where would you be from then,' the woman asked.

'The majority of us are part of the Second Recon squad out of Fort Grey,' Buzz was hoping that that name would carry some weight with the crowd and he was right. The mob visibly reacted to the name by lowering their weapons and murmuring amongst themselves.

'You're Second Recon?' asked the leader.

'Yes, sir. I was the XO 'til recently, Captain Bill Zedluk' Buzz said.

'Captain? As the XO?' the leader raised an eyebrow.

'I was recently promoted.'

'So then you would be Buzz.'

'At your service,' Buzz bowed from the top of the tank.

The crowd laughed at the gesture and could be seen relaxing their stance except for the crowd facing off against Kain. They had come to the conclusion that the lone trooper in front of them must be the blade specialist they had heard about. The thought that they had almost rushed him made them back up a few steps further away.

'You would be Sgt. Paul Nivek,' a nervous man in the front row asked, 'the Blademaster?'

'Yes, sir,' he too bowed, the man then passed out.

Everyone laughed at the man's reaction but still managed to go to his aid. The leader of the crowd calmly walked up to the lead tank as Buzz finally hopped down. They shook hands as would old friends beside the grey keystone of the bridge and apologized to each other for their actions and reactions.

'So what was it you needed from the medi-centre, Captain?' the leader of the mob asked. He had identified himself as David Randall, once the excitement had died off.

'Call me Buzz, please. What we were after was some cryo-freeze for a chamber we have on the back of number two tank.'

'I'm afraid there are not that many supplies left and I'm pretty sure that stuff is gone,' David waved over the woman that had been one of the more vocal mobsters. 'This is Dr. Shirley Masters, our only medical practitioner.'

'Good afternoon, Doctor,' Buzz smiled.

'Captain,' she replied while covering for her embarrassment by overcompensating with an exaggerated air of authority, 'How may I help you?'

'Buzz needs some cryo-freeze for his sleeper,' David spoke up first and indicated the chamber on the back of the tank.

'Why are you transporting an active cryo-chamber, Captain,' she questioned around David.

'To make a long story somewhat shorter, we have a critically injured person in there and she has to get to Port Mars for surgery.'

'Maybe I can help her,' she said and brushed past him to move toward the sleeper. She looked over the readouts and became agitated almost instantly, 'Oh, shit! Midbeal, get me two of those canisters of cryo-freeze right now!' A young man in the crowd raced off with another fellow to a nearby building that was apparently the medi-centre. They came close to knocking a few members of the crowd over in their rush. Buzz and the other troopers barely suppressed smiles as they watched the two guys stumble their way into the structure.

'Does that mean you can help her?' Ken asked.

'How long has she been in cryo-sleep?' she asked no one in particular.

'I'm guessing thirty or forty years,' Erik said.

'Wha… then why hasn't she been reconstructed since?' she now focused on Erik.

'Like I said, long story,' Buzz smiled again and moved between the two, 'David, I was wondering if we could spend the night in one of your hotels. We have been traveling a long time and the rocks aren't near as soft as you'd think.'

'By all means. Your people still have a full day's travel to get to Port Mars.'

That night the remaining civilians in the city crammed into one of the finest hotels in the city. They gathered most of the supplies left behind and had a grand dinner in honour of the troops from Fort Grey and even though Donovan was from Port Mars he was welcomed with as much enthusiasm as were the others. Stories were swapped until the wee hours of the morning until they could hear no more including the tale of Lieutenant Ladore. Both sides needed to clear up the story she had told about the militia kicking people out of their homes. The troopers thanked their hosts throughout the night for this taste of peace.

Once the festivities had died off the soldiers finally got some sleep and it was one of the best sleeps these troopers had had in more than a month and their efforts of the last few days made sleep come easy. The hotel was one of the four star types with a plush blue carpet in the halls transitioning to a light tan in the bedrooms. The beds had no equal in their minds. Queen sized mattresses allowed them to spread out to the ideal positions. Everyone slept so well it was almost criminal, except Erik, who slept fitfully.

*****

CHAPTER XLII
Monday, June 3, 2251

The forest rustled uneasily in the dim light of day. The ground still seemed to vibrate from the drama of the night before last. Buildings lay in ruin, vegetation smoldered and starship parts remained where they had landed after the engines had exploded and the militia explosives had left a new crater. Nothing in the Landran city was at ease, least of all the sole human resident.

'You scaly bastard!' the Blademaster cursed.

'Please remain calm, Miss Huston,' Kraston said without really talking to her.

'If you had listened to me from the start instead of playing your little games this never would have happened. So rather than licking our wounds and crying under this busted up ship we'd be well off this rock by now,' Ann was almost shouting.

'Everything is under control. Their attack damaged nothing of dire consequence to our goals. The plan is proceeding just as it had been worked out from the start.'

'How can you even think that let alone say it? Our only source of knowledge regarding faster-than-light travel was just taken out from under your forked tongue, even though I warned you they would try it. Not to mention your previous folly when you killed all the surgeons in Fort Saturn. They could have rebuilt her and we could have talked to her.'

'Sit down, Miss Huston,' his scales shimmered as he shouted.

She sat in a huff and glared at the Marshal. She obviously had more to say but had wisely opted for a quieter form of protest. She used her searing glaze to try to get her side of the argument across. Whether Kraston understood the glare or not, it bounced off his scales like so much rain. He turned from the woman to face the shattered wall of his office and thought of the situation he was in for a moment.

'How is our guest?' he asked out of the blue.

'Fine, I guess, still out cold,' she replied, too shocked by this new direction of the conversation to get fully into her rude gear.

'Excellent,' Kraston looked to her in her funk, 'I suppose you'll continue to harass me until I either kill you or tell you what's going to happen.'

'Darn right, so spill it,' she hoped she had chosen the same option he had.

Kraston laughed, 'How like you humans; automatically assuming that I am going to let you live.'

'If you were going to kill me, you would have done it by now,' she smiled in victory.

'I suppose you're right on that point. In that case, you should accompany me so I can explain the full extent of the operation.'

The Landran Marshal walked past her to get to the door and she noted, despite his impressive size, he was very graceful. Even if she had had her armour on he would have stood taller and longer than she. His scales never stopped shimmering even when he stopped moving.

They left the wrecked building and walked onto the browned patch of soil that made up the parade ground. The area normally reserved for troop reviews and the like was now overflowing with Landran running by, carrying crates and components of all sizes. Some were rushing to the more damaged buildings but not to repair the wreckage but to loot what they could before dashing off around the corner. Kraston seemed unaffected by the apparent looting and led her round the far side of the barracks or what was left of it. He drew her attention from the view of one trashed building to the next and commenting how the next barracks would be bigger.

The explosive charge Donovan had detonated had flattened half of the building Kraston was pointing to, which made it hard for Ann to visualize a new structure sparkling in the sunlight. For a moment she thought he meant the hardened command centre next to it, which was only missing a section or two. A major bulk of the glorious advancements in the reconstruction seemed to be focused at filling in the gaping hole between the buildings judging by the sheer number of Landran shoveling away.

As their path made its way through the centre of town Ann noticed they were angling toward the massively damaged vehicle bay where the reconstruction effort consisted of clearing debris but not actually replacing it with new framing. Kraston then paused in their trip and focused on the Blademaster.

'As you can see here, we're just going to be tidying this area up.'

'This place isn't a vehicle bay,' Ann said absently.

'You assume that because of what evidence?' he asked.

'The structural reinforcements are not like the barracks but more like the hardened command centre we just left.'

'You have a good eye, Miss Huston,' a smile crept to his face, 'This building that Captain Marso misidentified as a vehicle bay has a far more important purpose. If we can keep the upper portion from collapsing, our plans will not be affected. Indeed, if you look…'

'So when are you going to tell me the big secret?' Ann said while still looking at the wreckage.

Kraston was irritated at his story being interrupted and frowned down at the little human woman. He hesitated to consider his response but quickly decided the truth's time had come. 'Very well, come with me to the far corner,' he pointed south.

The walk to the corner took longer than one would think due to all the debris but his graceful movements did not seem affected. Their arrival failed to impress Ann to any degree and she was set to tell Kraston he was full of shit when he pulled her to a stop. He nodded to a nearby guard and stepped into what was obviously a designated position. A second later they dropped into the bowels of the planet, leaving the destruction far above them.

The trip was made in silence after the floor met up with a glass enclosure for the journey down. The view beyond the walls showed Ann the true secret of the Dragon City. Several dozen feet below the surface there came the vision of a massive cavern. Huge steel girders kept the walls and vaulted ceiling in place. The red of a natural Mars was predominant in the scraped out walls. Since this part of Mars had been constructed using surface rock the entire cavern was red instead of a more granite colouration that should have been present. The roof itself bore no resemblance to the rock but instead screamed like a hatchway.

Huge machines occupied many points along the walls and floor of the cavern with intent of their design only guessed while in the middle was a true centrepiece of clear purpose. A massive vessel rested there, a starship, looming over everything. It was larger by far than the disabled vessel on the surface. Ann was unsure if the hull had the same tint as the rocks around it or if the colour was merely a reflection on a mirror-like surface.

'Wow!' was all Ann could say as she stepped off the lift.

'I take it by your comment that you are finally impressed,' Kraston smiled.

'Very. So you used that crate up there as a distraction.'

'Correct. We were expecting an attack even without your warnings and we wanted them to destroy that *crate*, as you called it.'

'But they still got the girl…' she started the next thought.

'Yes and no.' Ann looked confused while Kraston continued, 'We let them take her as a part of a plan, to give them some hope if you will. We delayed them long enough to exhaust their cryo-freeze supply before they could get back to Port Mars.' Kraston smiled again.

'But New Terra is halfway to Port Mars. They could have got some more stuff there.'

'Again, yes and no. Yes they would have made it in time and no, because by the time they arrive, the city would have been abandoned for several hours.'

'So they'll look incompetent, having lost their prize on the way home.'

'You are clever, human,' Kraston put his arm around her shoulder and continued the tour.

'So what about the FTL drive? That woman was the only one among us that knew about it.'

'Yes, you mentioned before. That's comforting to hear,' he said, 'but when her ship crashed into ours, we were in the middle of an FTL repair. So you see, we have the technology and they don't.'

'We win,' she laughed.

'We, win,' Kraston only smirked.

*****

CHAPTER XLIII
Tuesday, 4 June, 2251

In the morning a small group of civilians, including David and Dr. Masters, escorted the convoy of tanks and troopers to the north gate of the city. Like the south gate, this one stood ajar which allowed the outside atmosphere to flow freely through the city and mix in an almost liquid display. The militia wore their armour once again and the civvies had returned to their respirators to compensate for the change in air.

'Thanks for your hospitality, Mr. Randall,' Kain said

'You are welcome, sir,' he replied but was not entirely at ease.

'I wish you'd reconsider relocating to Port Mars. The Landran are not that far away and are likely to march straight through this place to get to the last human settlement,' Buzz pleaded with him.

'The city has been abandoned and cleared out, Buzz. There is nothing left here for them.'

'Okay,' he raised his hands, 'Just promise this, if they do show up, you overload the reactor and run as if Bane had come for you directly.'

'Sure, Buzz, sure,' David smiled.

'Good luck to you all,' Shirley said, 'With your patrol and your chamber.'

They saluted their new friends and mounted the tanks again. The last leg of their journey was on and they wanted it to be done as fast as possible. The ground between New Terra and Port Mars was mostly flat with a few patches of trees and shrubbery, nothing the hover tanks could not handle though. The usual green of the growth in this area seemed to have dimmed since they had last seen it but it was mostly in their perception only. The world had closed in on them with the Bregan on one side and the Landran on the other, there was little room left for the beauty of nature.

The journey back to Port Mars from New Terra was a relatively relaxing one. They had collected more than enough cryo-freeze and food from the ruined city for their trip. Speaking militarily they were the best-equipped group of five troopers on the planet. Despite that, Buzz was still unable to relax and the others could see it.

'Dude, what's up?' asked Erik, 'You've been checking our six every five minutes since we left.'

'That much? Maybe I'm just trying to keep pace with Kain,' he quipped back.

'Hmm?' Kain spun to face forward again, 'Nope, I'm one for eight.'

'We're way ahead of any Landran patrol,' Donovan said.

'I'm not watching for Landran, Lieutenant,' Buzz said.

'They're looking for signs that those New Terrans are following,' Ken said from the inside of the second tank.

'Aww what do you know, Dolly? You've been in there for the last six hours,' Donovan called with a teasing tone.

'Shut it, boy.'

'Whoa, easy fellas. Ken is right. I'm convinced that New Terra will be attacked and those folks will have to leave,' said Buzz

'I'm looking for Landran,' Kain said and returned to his watch.

'I suppose it doesn't matter now anyway. We're here,' Erik said.

They turned to see the impressive structure that was Port Mars emerge from the mist. Unlike the other major population centres on the Eden Peninsula, which were several rings of walls under a basically common environmental dome, Port Mars was several different environment domes linked together. From the distance, they could make out many creatures moving between the domes like tiny black ants between anthills. Each of the troopers knew those tiny dots were some of the best Blademasters of all mankind.

Between the domes were the same common, massive turrets the other cities had, the difference was the close range at which these ones operated made them doubly lethal. Arcs of fire allowed full coverage of the dome surface and surrounding area.

'Signal our clearance codes, Ken,' Buzz ordered though still distracted.

'On it.'

'Clearance confirmed, welcome home. Follow the course uploaded to your flight systems. Do not deviate,' said the gate control.

'Roger control. Proceeding on course,' Ken replied.

As the hover tanks drifted along the designated path, the troopers riding on top looked around to see if they could determine what made the security so tight. Their breath was stolen by the new landscaping outside the city. Bunkers dotted the fields with troopers manning large weapons of lethal potential. The view to the far edges of the domes was obscured by not only the haze in the air but also the deadly field of hover mines resting a full three feet above the ground. A squad of heavy weapon specialists with enough firepower to pulverize their tanks in a second guarded the doors.

But the most amazing sight was the huge vehicle standing directly in front of the doors. It was easily twice the size of the tanks on which they rode and had no beam cannon. Instead, it had a sixty-tube missile launcher.

When the tanks were right in front of the missile launcher it fired the hover jets to rise above the convoy. Once past the massive door stopped its ascent and went down to resume its watch over the southern approach.

'Wow!' Erik stared at vehicle.

'Looks like we're ready this time,' Kain said.

'Ready for what? The Apocalypse?' Donovan asked.

'You a God fearing man?' Ken asked.

'No, but it's the only thing that might warrant that kind of firepower.'

'I think survival of the species warrants it too,' Buzz said.

They parked their tanks next to the medical building and sent a quick radio message to bring a medical rescue team rushing out in a matter of seconds. Erik kept his vigil with the sleeper as they took her to the reconstruction chamber while the rest of the troops went in search of TJ and the others.

TJ's evac-convoy arrived at the other end of Port Mars at the same time but they were given a special medical clearance because of their wounded. This got them through the gates far quicker than Buzz's team. Whereas Buzz's group had no trouble getting through the heavily crowded streets, TJ's BRAT could only lumber along at the flow of the traffic. People tended to not want to stand in front of a hover tank.

Once the BRAT entered the medical dome the crowds ahead of it seemed to disappear except for the foursome of armoured troopers on their way out. TJ happened to look up from the navigation console as they passed them. He recognized the badges on the suits and saw that the vehicle codes identifying the trooper to them.

'That was Ken!' Ashley said from the pilot seat.

'Yeah, but keep going to the centre. We have wounded to take care of first,' TJ said before making his way to the rear compartment.

The BRAT slid to a halt at the main doors and was settled on the ground no more than a few seconds before the response team came out. TJ and Drew released the rear hatch and began to remove Daniella and Trevor Connors. Once they were in the hands of the medical team and TJ was forced to leave Daniella's side, the walking members of his team could turn their attention to other matters.

'Drew, could you go in and see how Commander Martel is doing?' TJ asked.

'No problem, chief.'

TJ turned his full attention to the troopers approaching from the gates of the medical dome. Ashley finished her lock-down procedures and stepped out in time to greet her friends as well.

'Hi,' she said to Ken. There was a hint of relief and a touch of something else in her voice.

'Hi,' he smiled.

'Welcome back, boys,' TJ said, 'How'd things go out there?'

'Went perfectly, Captain. We got the sle...,' Donovan started.

'... the *package*, with some effort,' Buzz finished.

'You seem to be short some couriers.'

'Erik is inside. He seems to have grown attached to the package. We also lost Conture in the pickup,' Buzz said, 'How'd you do?'

'We got attacked just before we left the evacuation zone. Lost some good people and Daniella got hit pretty bad,' Ashley said.

'Sorry, man,' Ken put his hand on TJ's shoulder.

'She'll be fine,' he shook his head, 'I can't worry about her right now. I am worried about Commander Martel though.'

Buzz was shocked, 'He got hit too?'

'Nah, he just went loopy for some reason,' Ashley said.

'Commander Martel seemed to have had a nervous breakdown. He's inside undergoing treatment,' TJ spun the official story.

'Whatever. He's nuts all the same,' she continued the train of thought.

'So, is he going to be okay?' Ken asked.

TJ looked to the medical centre as Drew emerged and gave a quick wave and said, 'They're expecting a full recovery but it will take a little while.'

'Drew, buddy, so good to see ya,' Paul smiled.

'Just about didn't get that chance,' he said as he shook Paul's hand.

'Oh good, you're all here,' Councilman Idolan said, stepping around the parked vehicles and opened his arms wide, 'I was getting worried.'

The councilman was approaching from the direction of the gate leading to the rest of the city. He and his entourage were decked out as if they were welcoming a visiting dignitary. Walking a few steps behind him was Councilwoman Eddley. Though she was not as animated as Idolan, she still managed to pay keen attention to the conversation.

'I figured you two would still be at each other's throats,' TJ said.

'We've worked out our differences, but enough about civic affairs. Please tell us of your adventure, Captain Marso. We are eager to hear if the objectives were accomplished.'

'You know already or else you would have waited for the report to be processed through the proper channels.'

'Humour us, Captain,' Eddley said.

'Fine. As requested, we've evacuated Mercury City with only a moderate level of resistance at…,' TJ started.

'We know about the evacuation. We need to know more about the other mission,' Idolan interrupted.

'Successful on all objectives, Councilman,' he said.

'Well done! She is inside then?'

'Yes, sir,' TJ said, but raised his hand to stop them from entering.

The two Blademasters took the cue from TJ and took up position beside him, a formidable wall. The others then stepped behind the captain to block the door further.

'She's under guard, sir, and I don't think that she'll want to be interrogated first thing after a coma of more than eighty years. We don't want to have our hard work ruined so quickly. We'll watch her and bring her to you when she's ready.'

'What do you people think you're doing?' Eddley asked.

'She may not survive the reanimation but if she does, she's going to need a few days to adjust to this new world she's in,' he repeated himself.

'You can't...' she started up again.

'Calm yourself, Robin. It appears that the good Captain has made up his mind,' Idolan said as if it was really no concern of his.

'But he...' she sputtered.

'Let's just go and come back tomorrow.'

The two members of the council turned and led their entourage away without another word. TJ's own people started in with the questions once they were out of earshot.

'You know I'll support you whenever you need, but would you mind telling me what in Bane's name do you think you're doing?' Paul asked.

'You're more of a nut job than Buzz,' Donovan added.

'Maybe you should be sitting next to Walter,' Drew chimed in.

'Whoa, whoa! Let the idiot speak,' Ashley said.

'The idiot thanks you, I think. Look, I don't trust the

council anymore, especially those two. Idolan is a self-professing rebel and now it looks like he's in charge. I don't think that handing over this lady is a good idea,' TJ said in his own defence.

'Makes some sense, but to openly defy the council? That's not too smart, chief,' Ken said.

'So now that that's done, what's the plan?' Buzz asked.

'Paul, I want you to set up a watch rotation for the lady's room. Except for Erik and myself, I want everyone involved.'

'Yes, sir.'

'I'm going to see if we can't scare up some help. Just in case.'

*****

CHAPTER XLIV
Wednesday, 5 June, 2251

The marvels of modern human medicine could cure any ailment or injury afflicting the human race at one point in history or another but on this day the profession failed in its first attempt to reconstruct the sleeper's occupant. Something in the nature of the injuries made the body reject most of the replacement parts before they were even completed. The doctors were able to stabilize her condition after hours of adding and removing segments of her lower body until they found a balance between rebuilt and alive.

Finally with the new parts of the body stable, the doctors were able to repair her existing physiology. Only then, when they knew she could survive being thawed, did they begin to drain the cryo-freeze from her systems and warm the operating theatre. Medical aides began removing the doctors' environmental suits while they monitored the sleeper's progress toward a warm and awake state. The doctors welcomed the removal of the suits, except for the surgical lead, who chose to remain in the suit.

'Heart rate?' asked Dr. Imatrelli, the chief cryo-surgeon.

'Nominal deviation from normal parameters.'

'Yes, but what is it?'

'Uh, sorry doctor. It's at twenty-four beats per minute and rising.'

'Continue watching her until her temperature reaches fifty degrees Fahrenheit, then increase heat and raise internal heat to full level,' she reminded the staff even though they had done similar procedures over the last few weeks for injured soldiers, 'I'll be outside.'

She stepped out of the operating theatre and into a

crowd of waiting troopers, all eager to hear the results of the surgery. She smiled to their querying faces but dodged their questions and made a dash for the drink machine. Despite wearing the environment suit during the operation working in the near-zero temperature will eventually frost your bones.

'No answers until I get some coffee,' she said to Erik, 'Hot coffee, two teaspoons of sugar,' she said to the machine.

She savoured the heat from the drink as it radiated through her chest. Each sip warmed her as if she was the one newly awakened from cryo-sleep. Her suit continued to warm her extremities but the only relief she was consciously aware of was from the drink.

'Now, you had some questions?' she asked after she had gulped more than half the less than modest sized cup of coffee.

'How is she?' Erik blurted out.

'Who is she?' Paul asked in a less hurried fashion.

'Can we see her?' Erik asked before the words faded from Paul's lips.

'Whoa, hang on now. One at a time, I'm not that warm yet,' she waved her hands as if she could actually fend off the queries. 'First, she's going to be fine. She had severe injuries but we were able to patch them up.'

'Do we know who she is yet?' Paul asked again.

'I've sent a DNA sample to Records but I haven't heard back.'

'When can we see her?' Erik repeated.

'Not for a while. We weren't able to completely rebuild her body so we'll have to keep her quarantined until we get a few more procedures done.'

'Which parts?' his grilling line of questioning continued.

'Look! I can understand you are concerned but I really am too tired to answer any more questions. The important thing is that she'll live and probably come around in the next few days,' Dr. Imatrelli said, the weariness creeping into her voice.

'Thank you doctor,' Ashley said as she shoved Erik back into a nearby seat, 'We appreciate what you were able to tell us.'

Dr. Imatrelli turned from the group and walked toward the residence structure, she would be up to her room on the third floor in no time. She was not as tired as she had led them to believe but those military armour suits made her nervous. Those troopers were bad enough with their helmets off, but the fully armoured troopers in her lobby made her furious.

When the patient was admitted they had referred to the trooper who had stayed with her when they had brought her in as *Ken* but the tag on his armour said *Dolly*. Obviously there was a story there, which she would not mind hearing someday, without the armour. It was one of the many oddities, of the military type, she would never understand. He was standing further down the hall from the group of troopers she had left a moment earlier. She noticed him watching her before the elevator door opened to take her up. He had bowed his head slightly then returned to his vigil at the entrance of the hospital.

She stepped into the elevator but kept an eye on that suit of armour as long as the doors would let her. The lift rose to the third floor quickly and released her into the hall with equal efficiency. The turn toward her room offered her a view of a man in a dark suit waiting next to her door. He straightened as she approached but did not block her way or say anything to her.

'What do you want?' Imatrelli asked as she released the card lock on her door.

'We have matters to discuss, Doctor,' the man said.

'Like I told your friends in the waiting room, I don't know who she is.'

'They aren't my friends. I'm merely enquiring for my employer,' he said and followed her into the room despite her efforts to prevent it.

'I'll know in an hour or so, and then your boss will be the first to know. I have a nurse with her now and she'll get the information before the people from Idolan's group does.'

'Then we'll wait with you,' Eddley said from the corner of the room.

The first day of operations, tests and medical personnel hovering over her drained her more than the fifty years in cryo-sleep had. No one would answer her questions aside from what year it was which was more than enough to deal with on its own. Instead, the two men asked her so many things regarding her faster-than-light tests that her head was spinning. Why would they need to know from her rather than going to the program director?

She did not like these men for many reasons, one of which was the fact they kept forcing Corporal Krushell out of the room when the inquisition was about to start. She did like Erik. He was a sweet guy and he seemed to care a lot about her despite her deformities.

The upper portion of her body and the lower part from mid-thigh up was as she remembered it and the surgeries had left no scars, but the rest of her legs were now mechanical. For now, she could not see herself as anything except a cyborg but Erik saw past the false limbs and she adored him for that.

The door slipped open to admit the two men for the day's questioning. 'You know the drill, Corporal,' the bigger of the two said.

Because Erik was not on guard duty he was not in his battle armour but his sense of duty remained. He stood and puffed up defiantly, 'I think she's answered enough of your questions. You're done here.'

'I don't think you know what your resistance could cost you, Mr. Krushell,' said the smaller one.

'I believe he has reason not to worry about your threats, gentlemen,' Stacey said from her bed and pointed to the door behind the men.

The bigger one turned, expecting to mention to the orderly he assumed was there that his interference would cost him his job. He froze in place at the sight blocking the door. Although the door stood open, little light penetrated the room from the hall because of the suit of power-armour standing there. The ID tag on the left side of the chest simply read KAIN.

The big guy tapped the smaller fellow and urged him that now would be a good time to leave. These guys were internal muscle, which was to say they rarely left the city, but they had heard of the Second Recon's Blademaster nonetheless. They hastily slipped past the armoured trooper and ran down the hall and exited the medical centre

'Thanks, Paul,' laughed Erik.

'Paul! He's still asleep from the last watch. I just borrowed his armour,' smiled Ashley from behind the suit.

'Ash, how did...' Erik smiled wider.

She raised the small remote in her hand and hit a small button near the top. The six and a half foot tall power armour suit raised a couple of inches off the floor before she pushed it into the room. She gave Erik a quick hug and smiled at the *cyborg*.

'Ashley Sanders,' she said and extended her hand without hesitation.

'Stacey, Adderby,' she took Ashley's hand, 'and thank you. I was getting tired of those two.'

'Glad to help. I actually came to see you after I heard that the doctors say you're good to go.'

'Yeah, I'm still a little unsteady on these things though.'

'Not to worry. You're going to travel in style!' Ashley snapped her fingers.

Within a matter of a few seconds Ken came wheeling into the room in a hospital wheelchair. He hopped out and whirled around to the back with a theatrical flair. Stacey let out a giggle of joy at the sight of this big man bouncing around like a kid.

'Your chariot awaits, mademoiselle. I even kept the seat warm,' he said with a bow and a sweep of his arm.

'Why thank you my good sir,' she smiled.

'Ash, chief says we have to leave now. The heat's been turned up to high,' Ken said behind his smile.

'What do you mean?' asked Erik as he steadied Stacey for her transfer to the chair.

'Radar's picked up some signals inbound and we have no hardware left out there. Since that only leaves bad things in great numbers out there the odds makers aren't laying good numbers for us. The council has ordered all civilians and space flight personnel to evacuate.'

'Space flight personnel?' Ashley raised an eyebrow.

'I think that means me,' Stacey said.

'So I guess we go.' Erik said then slipped behind the chair ready to push. They began to head for the door at a brisk pace when he stopped and nodded at the suit, 'Oh, and Ash, Paul may need this.'

'Good thinking,' she replied.

TJ met them outside the main entrance with a large group of armoured troopers. They had with them four extra suits and a rather irate looking unarmoured Blademaster.

'Let's go folks, danger lurks at every turn,' TJ said motioning with an armoured glove.

'I'll take that off your hands,' Kain said to Ashley.

'Sorry Paul, but...' Ashley started.

'Viper, suit up. We leave in fifteen,' TJ snapped.

Erik had finished securing Stacey into a suit before a blast from a portable cannon dismantled the wheelchair. Blades lit up an instant later and the troopers jumped into a protective stance around the pair of them.

'What the hell is going on?' Erik shouted.

'We got word that a faction within the council sees your friend there as a threat to the survival of the human race and blames her for both the Bregan and Landran invasions.' TJ said, 'So we figured we'd leave before they got here. Looks like we're cutting things a bit too close. Let's move to the departure station.'

The group moved off, leery of every shadow in the late day suns. Occasionally, a shot would fly at them, only to be turned away by one of the four Blademasters. Once through the gate and into the city proper they expected a full on assault to come at them.

Erik and Ashley stayed with Stacey who was having a bit of trouble adapting to the use of the power armour. The suit would carry her but still needed some input from her weakened legs. The blasts from the cannons were throwing her off. There was nothing like that kind of weaponry or armour when she came from.

City guard troops charged the field-combat veterans at the gate into the city as though tactics little better than those of a mob would stop them. They engaged while brandishing their blades wildly in front of them looking like kids playing with sticks. They got one point of combat correct and had a steady barrage of cannon fire descend at the meeting point of the two groups.

The dual-mode attack was primarily aimed at the Blademasters and resulted in mixed results. The timing was off on one angle of attack, which led to some of the beams striking an attacker rather than one of TJ's group. A second barrage caught one of the Blademasters off guard and threw him to the ground. The corresponding attack on Drew was neatly turned aside as he charged into the mob. All things considered, things were not too bad with the guards working off thirty-three percent success.

The failed results of a combined attack of mob and cannons must have crushed the hopes of the assailants long before combat started. With every bit of combative aggression being turned away, it would have looked much like they were fighting a deity. A beam shot meant to distract or kill Kain was instead deflected off his forearm shield and into one of the charging guards. The shot did manage to knock him slightly to the right, which was nicely out of the way of a lancing strike by a second mob member who he then slashed across the back, effectively paralysing him.

The path cleared by the Blademasters allowed the group to pick up the pace and run toward what they hoped would be safety. They had only lost one trooper in the initial fight and Drew had run off somewhere. Fighting maintained its intense pace with blades snapping off each other and bits of metal raining to the ground as they were shaved off the armoured suits of both the troopers and the guards.

On occasion, where the two groups would pause in the fighting, TJ could make out Drew a ways off. He was running through the city with half a dozen or more armoured guards either running ahead of him in fear or chasing him. The scene would have been comical if there had not been more than thirty armed men and women surrounding his own group. That was not counting the snipers hidden in the city.

Ahead of them was the gate to the docks but the fighting was escalating as fast as the light was fading in the harbour. TJ's backup plan would have to be implemented now, before things got much worse. He gave the signal to the squad to switch tactics and readied himself. He paused and counted to four in order to throw the guards off the rhythm. As soon as he finished he and five others dropped flash balls into the crowd.

Those that saw the balls falling to the ground tried to get out of the way but were fenced in by the rest of the mob. The non-lethal bombs went off perfectly and tossed the entire mob to every corner of the square. The blast pattern was three balls on each side so as to have the blast waves counteract each other and not knock the squad down. It did put a lot of pressure on the trooper's armour.

A beam intended for Stacey was also pushed off course by the blast waves and passed overhead. The shot did find a home in a flying guard, halting her murderous rampage before she hit the ground. Now that the fighting had reached a forced lull, TJ's group made a break for the door. Their enhanced running speed kept them ahead of the shots from poorly or hastily trained gunners.

Warning messages in TJ's heads-up-display from the crushing effect of the flash balls almost prevented him from seeing Drew spring from a side passage and dive through the dock gates. TJ's squad was still at a run and descended close behind the full-charge trooper and crashed into a guard in full pursuit mode.

Blades struck blades; armour crashed with armour and in some cases blades hit armour in the massive collision involving fifteen troopers and guards. The force of the impact left armoured men and women strewn across the gateway, mostly on the inside portion. Drew managed to close and lock the gate before a fit of laughter overcame him.

Only four of the pursuers were able to get to their feet out of the half dozen that had been flung to the ground but they were quickly surrounded by eight of the escort squad. Erik chose to stay with Stacey since she was still shaky in her suit, but improving.

'You enjoyed that, Mr. Webster?' TJ asked from the group surrounding the four prisoners.

'Oh, very much, sir,' he laughed.

'Ken, Ashley, please disarm these fine folk and remove their primary power cells,' TJ ordered, 'Erik, is she okay?'

'She's fine,' Stacey replied.

'Guess she's fine, sir,' Erik said.

'Don't mean to snap but us civil engineers aren't used to being lynched.'

'I understand,' TJ smiled.

'Um, boss? Where're Lt. Klon and Commander Martel?' Ken asked.

'Corporal Skye and I removed them last night. They're waiting for us at Dock Six. Let's get moving and head over there people and leave these four to try to let their friends in.' TJ said and pointed down the almost abandoned wharf.

*****

CHAPTER XLV
Wednesday, 5 June, 2251

Councillor Robin Eddley paced in her pastel coloured office and angrily waited for her commander to report in. He was overdue and that was never a good sign. She had sent her loyalist forces to detain Idolan's rebels. Those militia troopers had signed their own arrest warrant when they had taken the sleeper from the medical centre and that Commander from the southern fort out from under her as well. At least that is what her commander had reported almost an hour ago.

Idolan not only took her patients but also ninety percent of the city's population. She could not believe she had been conned into trusting him, even for a short while. When he had told her there was a good chance of a Bregan attack she had foolishly thought he meant to strengthen the city not run away. She had confidence in the power of the city and its walls and knew the people would return once the threat was eradicated. That rebel and his followers were trying to leave the city and the planet behind but she had every confidence in her military units.

The rebels would be stopped before they got too far, that much she knew. With any luck her commander would also arrive with Idolan and that Captain of his in tow. That thought made her smile as she paused to look out her window at her almost abandoned city. She could imagine it full of people again, the noise, the atmosphere. She sighed.

A chime at the door derailed her train of thought for the moment. She stood for a minute to recall if she was expecting anyone. She remembered her commander was on an important mission and opened the door by a remote on her desk and welcomed the soldier.

'Councillor, they've eluded capture. We did manage to capture one and kill another, however,' he reported.

'So, let me see if I understand you clearly,' she started as she returned to her desk and sat in the oversized chair, 'You failed your primary objective to retrieve Star Officer Adderby and you think your petty accomplishments will glide over this obvious shortcoming?'

'No, ma'am. I'd just like to point out that we have no need of that woman or her friends.'

'Oh? Well this would be news indeed,' she sat back and smiled. 'Please explain.'

'My men have acquired enough information to recreate the FTL Drive she had been using. My people have successfully copied the data and I believe we could escape on our own, if we had to.'

'Well now, that is good news. Let them run then,' she said, 'Now tell me of the Bregan situation.'

'Yes, well. Scans are showing they've slowed their approach and are beginning to surround the city. We have enough people to man the emplacements plus four squads. The remaining civilian population has taken temporary control of the power facilities,' he said and pointed out the locations on a wall map to the right of Eddley's desk.

'We'll be fine then, by the sounds of it,' Robin said, 'Keep an eye on the Bregan and the cowards and let me know of any changes.'

'Yes, ma'am!' he saluted then marched out.

'You think you've won Matt Idolan? I'll see you cower before my new Council once we've taken care of these animals. You and the rest of your cowards will pay for this embarrassment,' she muttered to an empty room.

Edderly turned away from the door with a smile on her lips for her impending double victory and returned to the window looking over the city. Her mind's eye recapturing the images of a city in the near future sheltering tens of thousands of citizens, excited to be under her watchful eye. She basked in their love for her.

'Maybe, I won't need the Council either. I will rule alone, forever!' she raised her arms to absorb the cheers of her subjects.

The commander stepped out of the Council building and into a waiting GCR. He was starting to get nervous about what he and his men were getting into. This militia that just stormed out of here were good fighters, no doubt about that, and *they* had shown real fear of fighting those Bregan creatures. There may be something to their stories, he thought to himself.

'Sir?' asked the officer next to him.

'Nothing, Captain. They're only militia, not regular soldiers,' he regrouped after having realized he had said that last part out loud.

'Yes, sir,' acknowledged the Captain, though he still had no idea what his superior was talking about.

After a moment of silence to finish his brooding, the commander switched gears. 'What is the status of our friends and guests?'

'The cowards left our radar range while you were away and the Bregan have now completely surrounded the city. Estimates of their numbers are more than one hundred thousand.'

'One hundred... thousand!' the commander was stunned.

'Yes, sir.'

'Driver, get us to the north gate now! Captain, have the launch team prepare the escape vehicle. We're not going to sit around here and get our asses sliced off.'

'What about the Council?'

'They're all screwed in the head. Seems like Idolan and those people were smarter than we were led to believe. Signal the field troops to retreat to the city as soon as we stop, and get those Blademasters off the dome!'

'Sir, I think you're over-reacting. They're just animals,' said the captain.

'Captain, do as I order or I'll have you guarding those loons back there by yourself.'

The GCR slid to a halt in front of the gate but that was not fast enough. The commander was out before it even reached walking speed. He stumbled then regained his footing. He marched directly to the leader of the squad guarding the gate.

'Lieutenant, we're leaving. Prepare to receive our troops from the perimeter,' he shouted as he approached.

'Yes, sir!'

Relief was visible in the faces of the soldiers and officers around them. As orders started to fly, troops worked with renewed energy to make ready for the escape. Those at the gate moved far faster to remove the blockade than when they put it up.

Ten minutes after ordering the final evacuation the captain returned from the communication bunker. He was visibly nervous about something but hesitated in talking about it with the commander.

'Well, Captain, what is it?'

'Sir, the order has been sent for the field troops to fall back but we have a problem. The sergeant in charge over there felt that a mass communiqué was more efficient that secured signaling,' the captain said in a low voice.

'Good thinking. What's the problem then?' the commander asked, still not totally into the conversation.

'Well, you see, in order to send mass communications, she had to use a broadband channel. You remember what those Fort Grey people said about open channels and the Bregan don't you, sir?'

'Yeah, they're... oh, no.'

'Yes, the Bregan are now advancing rapidly. They're homing in on that signal. They'll be here in the next hour for sure.'

'Evac, now!' shouted the commander before racing to the guards house communication console.

Still lost in her vision of a perfect world under her rule, a world of peace and prosperity, she almost did not hear the intercom chime. Edderly walked back to her desk and casually hit the *receive* button. She was convinced that it would be former councillors wanting his or her job back or perhaps a citizen group calling to give her another award for her excellent work on behave of the planet at large.

'Yes?' she answered.

'Councillor, this is Commander Ramirez. We have a problem.'

'Whatever it is, I'm sure you can handle it,' she said, still hanging on to her daydream, bubble world.

'That's true in most instances; however, we are more than a little outnumbered by the hundred thousand Bregan that are now charging the city. I've ordered everyone to head to the launch bay for evacuation. I suggest you do the same.'

Pop! – The bubble burst.

'You can't do that, Commander! I'm in charge and only I can give the evacuation orders.' she whined.

'Fine! While you decide, we're leaving.' He hung up.

'Well, well, that's just great. Now I'm going to have to set that man straight myself. Yes, that's what I'll do,' she smiled at herself.

She left her office without stopping for even her jacket and flagged down her office security. He gathered up three others and followed the Councillor out the building. They hopped into the Council GCR and raced off toward the launch bay. She was eager to rip into that *traitor* Ramirez. So, instead of worrying about the impending assault, she spent the ten-minute trip trying to decide who she would get to replace the commander.

'Get those civilians strapped in!' shouted Ramirez to a private who was doing just that.

'Sir, all military personnel and heavy equipment are in position around the launch bay,' Captain McNeil said.

'Good, we'll start loading them by squad in the next few minutes. First we need to load up the supplies into the orbital rockets.'

The soldiers worked flawlessly to load the three space vehicles. Their military proficiency was echoed in their labour to ready themselves for transport. The two cargo rockets were loaded in fifteen minutes from start to finish, and certified for launch minutes afterwards. The thirty-year-old Terran rockets were ready for flight again.

'Okay, Squads four-zero and two-seven, load up now,' called Ramirez.

The remaining squads repositioned quickly as those two groups left formation but not fast enough to stop a jet black GCR tearing through the secured perimeter. It made good time straight for the commander and his staff. He recognized the vehicle before the shouts rose up and prepared himself for the worst. He called the captain over to tell him to assume directing the evacuation. He stepped off the platform as the GCR came to a rest a few yards away.

'Good evening, Councillor Eddley. Glad you could make it. We've saved a seat for you in the lead cabin of the transport,' he managed a smile.

'Stow it, Commander! I'm here to relieve you of command on charges of insubordination, so your little act is a wasted effort,' she sneered.

'Yes, ma'am. You're the boss,' he bowed.

'Good, now where is…'

A blast shook the city and put a halt to all activity in the launch bay. A second blast knocked everyone out of the split second, frozen state and into a frenzy to finish loading the rockets.

'Commander,' a panicked lieutenant called out.

'He's not a commander anymore!' Edderly said.

'Commander,' he ignored her, 'the Bregan have entered the mine field and have already breached the south gate.'

Ramirez calmly turned to the Councillor with a quizzical look. She was so shocked by the news she was totally silent, the first time in months. The commander savoured the feeling for a moment then turned to his command.

'Guards, take the Councillor to the transport. Lieutenant, please show the rest of them to their seats. Captain, take two more squads to the transport and prep for lift off. The rest of us will hold them off while the ship warms up. We'll try to join you when you're ready.'

'Yes, sir!' they saluted.

'I hope this will be quick either way,' he sighed before closing his visor and running to reorganize the front-line.

*****

Made in the USA
Middletown, DE
21 December 2015